FORGET ME NOT

A NOTE

The Never Forget series is written in British English and contains British spelling and grammar. This may appear incorrect to some readers when compared to US English books.

NEVER
FORGET HIM

PROLOGUE

"Once upon a time there was a handsome soldier. He was strong and brave, and whisked the princess off her feet.

"The soldier was a hero, fighting all the bad guys and giving people their lives back.

"He was more than that, though. He wasn't just a brave soldier, he was thoughtful and caring, funny, and a little bit of an idiot." I smile to myself as memories start playing out in my mind of his slightly wonky smile when he was winding me up, and the infectious sound of his laugh.

"One day, I'm going to be just like Daddy. I'm going to be big and brave and rescue people," Denny says sleepily.

I stay where I am, sat on the edge of his bed, and watch as he loses the fight against sleep. Denny looks just like him. Most days I find it comforting, but there are times, like right now, after he's made me recite his nightly story, that it's painful. The memories of him threaten to rip me apart.

I gently sweep his hair from his forehead once I know he's fast asleep. "You already do that, baby boy. You rescue me every day," I whisper as I take one last look at his gorgeous, peaceful face.

CHAPTER ONE

"Erin, come on, at least look a little excited about this. It's your twentieth birthday, for fuck's sake," Frankie, my best friend, complains when I sit on her bed, looking less than enthusiastic about our night out.

"I'm good, Kiki. I am looking forward to it," I lie. "It's just I'm—"

"Worried about your mum." Her words come out softer, showing she does understand. They still make me feel guilty, maybe I'm being a little too self-involved.

"I'm sorry. I'm going to forget all that and we're going to have an amazing night," I announce, summoning up as much excitement as I can muster.

Frankie is the ultimate party girl. She loves nothing more than spending all weekend either getting ready to go out, or being out and getting very drunk. That whole scene isn't really me; I much prefer to spend my Saturday night at home, in my den, working, but I don't have a chance in hell of getting away without going tonight, seeing as it's my birthday.

"Here, get this down your neck. It'll help chill you the fuck out," she says, thrusting a glass of vodka Red Bull at me.

"Haven't you got anything else?"

"Nope, suck it up. We're gonna get ourselves nice and drunk before heading out. Seeing as we're two weeks away from our next loan payments coming in, I'm fucking skint. We don't all have a cushy job like you," she says before necking her drink in one go. I, on the other hand, sip at the vile liquid before putting it down behind me. If I never taste vodka Red Bull again I'd be happy. "Although," she adds, with a wiggle of her eyebrows, "a little birdie told me there're some hot soldiers in town tonight. Maybe they'll buy us some drinks."

I can't help but groan at her mention of soldiers. Frankie makes no secret of her desire to bed a hot army guy. She has some obsession with being the one to make a soldier's leave the best he's ever had, to let him use her to blow off steam before sending him packing to wherever it is he's based with some amazing memories and no intention of ever seeing him again.

"Oh, don't give me that, E. You know you'd want it if you had the chance."

I don't respond other than to lift my eyebrow at her. She knows exactly what I'd say, anyway. My dad was in the army and I watched what it did to Mum every time he left to go on tour. I vividly remember the day she answered the door and collapsed to the ground wailing before the men on the other side had even spoken. From as early as I can remember, I've said I'd never touch a man in the army. Dad broke my mum—totally shattered her. I never want to experience anything like that. Ever.

"Anyway, what do you think?" Frankie asks as she holds a small piece of silver glitzy fabric in front of her.

"I think it looks about the right size to be a dishcloth, Kiki."

"I don't know why I bother," she complains, throwing the dress on the bed.

Frankie and I are complete opposites. She's tall, I'm short. She's blonde, I'm some boring shade of brown—to say brunette would probably make it sound too good. She's outgoing and adventurous, and I'm shy and reserved. Our choice of clothing is also at different ends of the scale. Frankie follows fashion and must be seen wearing what the celebs are. I, on the other hand, love the 1950s look, so when I'm not in a pair of jeans and a t-shirt you can find me in something like the high-waist pencil skirt, white shirt, thick red belt with matching court shoes I'm about to change into. It's not exactly a look most of our fellow students rock on a night out, but it's what I love, so I go with it. I wouldn't be seen dead in the tiny scraps of fabric Frankie steps out of her flat in.

"Who told you that, anyway?"

"Lisa rang me this afternoon from a bar in town. Apparently, they came in all boisterous and sexy and offered to buy her and Tara a drink. Once they found out their plans for the night, they excused themselves to ring me. I can't fucking wait, E. Soldiers! Actual soldiers!"

"Yay," I say, feigning excitement.

Frankie throws her lip gloss at me. "If you're not excited for yourself then at least be excited for me," she says, before stripping off her robe and reaching for her dress.

"Ready?" she asks excitedly as she finishes off the drink I abandoned some time ago.

I take one last look at myself in the mirror and run my hand down the fabric of my skirt. My hair is pulled back into a sleek ponytail with my fringe swept to the side and pinned behind my ear. My eyes are lined perfectly and my lips are fire engine red thanks to Frankie's skills—I could never achieve this look on my own. I may be good with my hands but it doesn't seem to translate to putting make-up on.

"I guess," I mutter as I grab my bag.

Frankie ignores my less than enthusiastic response and takes my hand to pull me through her flat to the awaiting taxi. She can barely sit still during the short ride to the city centre, and I hate to admit it, but her excitement is a little infectious. This may not be my kind of thing, but seeing my best friend this happy does make me feel better about everything.

"We're here," Frankie exclaims, throwing money onto the passenger seat and practically bouncing from the taxi.

I thank the driver and get out in a slightly more composed manner. I wasn't paying much attention to where we were going, but I groan when I see which club we've just pulled up outside.

"Smoke? Really?"

"Yes. This is where Lisa and Tara said the soldiers were heading."

I'm not a fan of nightclubs in general, but I have a particular hatred of Smoke and Frankie knows it, which is probably why she didn't tell me.

"We're meant to be out celebrating *my* birthday. Shouldn't I have the final say?" I ask, refusing to move from the curb.

"Yeah, I guess you're right," Frankie says, thinking about more than her sexy soldiers for a second. "Where do you want to go?"

I desperately want to say home, but I know that isn't going to go down well. I also don't know if it's actually the truth. The place I love being isn't the same now I'm watching Mum fight this losing battle with her business. I think where I want to be is anywhere but here. I don't want to be stood outside this club I hate, and for the first time ever, I don't want to be in Bristol. I need to get away from it all, from the stress and the pressure. Being in uni should be pressure enough, but that's not even half of it. Even my love of jewellery making has been tainted by it.

Frankie stands in front of me. I can see how torn she now is about tonight. She's a good friend, and I know that if I were to say I didn't want to go in there, she wouldn't. As much as she wants those soldiers, I know she'd choose me over them. I'm just not sure I can do it to her.

"It's fine, let's go."

"Really?" she asks, all hopeful.

"Really. But if one sleazeball tries touching me up on the dance floor again, I'm leaving right after kicking him in the bollocks."

"Fair enough. Just let me know which one it was and I'll kick him too."

I reach forward and grab her hand, and then together, we walk toward the end of the queue.

"It's fucking freezing," Frankie complains after a couple of minutes waiting in line.

I look over at her in the flimsy bit of fabric she calls a dress and raise my eyebrow.

"Oh shush," she sulks.

"ID please," the bouncer demands when we eventually get to the front.

I can't lie, even I'm cold now it's taken us so damn long to get here. Frankie had a text from Tara ages ago to let us know they were inside, but there was no sign of any soldiers yet. That news didn't help Frankie's quickly depleting excitement.

"Thank fuck for that," she grumbles when we begin walking up the stairs. "I swear my tits were about three minutes from freezing the fuck off."

"Let's go and get a drink," I suggest, hoping some more alcohol will put the spring back in her step. For my own sake, I really hope these soldiers are real and actually turn up. I don't think I'm ever going to hear the end of her disappointment otherwise.

"Oh there they are," Frankie points to the other end of the bar when we get through the crowd.

We do the usual shouted greeting that always has to happen when in a club; we all nod and smile at each other like we have a clue what the other is talking about, but in reality, the music is so bloody loud I can barely hear my own thoughts, let alone someone talking to me.

When Lisa begins pulling something from her bag, I immediately want to run, but instead I'm forced to smile and look happy about the fact they've got me a happy birthday sash and flashing badge.

Brilliant. Now I really will attract unwanted attention. It's like they don't know me at all, or more so that they do and they're all finding this hilarious.

Tara hands me a drink and I stupidly take a sip assuming it's my usual Malibu and Coke. Huge mistake. "What the fuck is that?" I shout as I try to scrape the taste off my tongue with my teeth.

"Jägerbomb," Frankie announces proudly as she knocks hers back.

"That's disgusting, Kiki." And to think I was under the impression that vodka Red Bull was the worst mix of drinks in the world.

"Here," Lisa says, handing me another glass after I shove my previous excuse for a drink at Frankie. I sniff it this time, just in case, but I know I'm safe because I can smell coconut.

"Thank you," I say, before quickly taking a swig to hopefully remove the lingering aftertaste of the Jägerbomb.

The three of them stand and shout at each other for a few minutes. Every now and then, Tara and Lisa look around, I guess hoping to spot their soldiers. I can see Frankie's excitement waning as the minutes go by. I told her not to get her hopes up.

When the latest Pitbull song starts pounding through the speakers, Frankie perks up, grabs mine and Lisa's hands, and pulls us to the dance floor. We end up in the middle of the crowd, exactly where I don't want to be, just as the smoke fills the dance floor, blocking my vision of what people are doing around me.

I stand and dance a little but I'm still relatively sober compared to my friends so I don't quite get into the flow of it like them. When the smoke begins to lift, all three of them are bumping and grinding away without a care in the world. As I stand and watch, I realise I'm jealous. They are all able to put everything to one side and just enjoy themselves. I need that; I need to forget everything for just a few hours and chill out, but no matter what I do I can feel it all weighing down on my shoulders. Mum's business isn't really my problem, but I'm not the kind of person who can just let her deal with it. She's been my rock my entire life, and now I feel like it's time for me to return the favour.

I'm smiling at my friends' antics when I feel the need to look over to the bar. I don't know what it is but it's like something's calling me. When I look over, there's a guy staring right at me. Thinking I must be wrong, I look over my shoulder expecting to see someone looking back at him, but everyone's too engrossed in their dancing.

When I glance back, he's still looking my way. I'm just about to turn when one of his friends puts his hand on his shoulder and distracts him.

I continue watching them for a few seconds before I hear Lisa. "Oh my God, they're here," she squeals, making Frankie immediately stop dancing and look around.

"Where?"

"Over there, by the bar. That group of lads."

"The hot ones?"

"Yes. Let's go."

I stand back and allow Frankie and Lisa to force their way through the crowd toward the bar. Tara and I follow behind, neither of us sharing their excitement. Tara has a serious long-term boyfriend and only comes out to spend time with us, unlike Frankie and Lisa, whose only reason for coming is to pull.

I watch from a few feet away as Lisa walks directly up to the guy who was just staring in my direction. I'm not going to say staring at *me*, because that can't possibly be the case, unless he's also amused by the girl wearing the bright pink sash and flashing badge. Frankie latches herself onto his friend and leans into his side shamelessly.

Tara and I continue to stand slightly out of the way and just watch as Frankie and Lisa make drunken fools out of themselves.

The four of them stand together talking, or shouting, for a few minutes before I see Frankie look up and point our way. It's the first time the guy has glanced up since they approached, and when he does, his eyes widen slightly as he looks at me before they drop and run down the length of my body. Tara moves when Frankie gestures for her but I'm frozen to the spot as the guy continues taking me all in. Usually, I hate being ogled by men but there's something about this one that doesn't want to make me kick him in the balls for looking at me the way he is.

Frankie scares the shit out of me when I feel her slide her arm through mine and tug me toward the group.

"What the hell is up with you? I know you're not interested in a soldier, but they won't bite," she says, coming to a stop when we're directly in front of him.

"I-I... I know," I stutter when I look up to find him still staring at me. Lisa's practically dry humping his leg but he doesn't seem to be noticing it.

"Bax," one of the guys shouts. "Hey, Bax," he repeats, until the guy looking at me rips his eyes away.

"What?" he snaps.

"Here," his mate says, handing him a small glass full of golden liquid.

He nods his chin at him before bringing his gaze back to me, continuing to hold my eyes as he slowly tips the glass up to his lips and drinks it down in one. My eyes break from his as he swallows, distracted by the movement of the muscles in his neck. I continue downward, taking in his grey striped shirt, stretched over his shoulders and chest, before dropping down to his black, almost skinny, jeans. I'm not interested for two reasons:

1. he's a soldier, and
2. I have enough drama in my life right now,

but even *I* can admit this guy's hot.

Telling myself those things is all good and well, but I don't think my body believes a single word of it. My pulse is racing and my palms are sweating from just looking at this guy. When my eyes connect with his again it's like everything around me fades away and it's just me and him.

———

"OH MY GOD!" Frankie squeals as the four of us walk into the toilets a while later. "Dean's so fucking hot. I mean, have you seen those arms? What I wouldn't give to see him in action, all army man," she says as she fans herself in front of the mirror.

I leave her to it and make use of the toilet. I smile to myself the whole time when she doesn't even stop for a breath talking about him. Lisa is much less enthusiastic because, after getting the cold shoulder from Bax, she moved onto another of his friends, who also doesn't seem all that interested.

An hour or so later, I leave everyone dancing in favour of getting a glass of water. Frankie and Lisa managed to convince Bax, Dean and their friends to join us all on the dance floor. It's clear Dean is loving all the attention from Frankie, and Lisa has at last found herself a friend who is interested. Tara and I have kept to ourselves and danced with each other, but that doesn't mean I've lost Bax's interest. He still seems way too intrigued for my liking. I could feel his gaze while we were dancing and every time I looked up those dark eyes were on me.

"Thanks, E, I needed that," Frankie says, taking the glass of cold water from my hands and downing it in one. "Bax totally has the hots for you. You should go for it."

"I'm good, thanks."

"Oh, come on. You need someone to pop that cherry. I think it's got his name written all over it. Plus, not every woman can say she had her cherry popped by an incredibly sexy soldier; I bet he's well good with his hands."

"Enough," I snap. I really don't need her shouting the details of my love life—or lack thereof—out to all the strangers I'm stood at the bar with.

"A night with him will chill you right out." At that moment, Dean appears from out of nowhere and runs his hands down Frankie's sides. She spins in his arms and they both disappear into the crowd together. I shake my head and turn back to the bar to order another glass of water.

CHAPTER TWO

I continue standing at the bar, watching everyone for quite a long time. I don't see the girls or any of Bax's friends—not that I'd recognise most of them—but this is fairly standard procedure. Eventually, I'll get myself in a taxi and head home, leaving them to party the night away.

I'm just getting myself ready to go when I feel something. I look over my shoulder and find Bax right behind me.

"Oh hey," I shout over the music. His eyes are intense as he stares into mine. Feeling awkward I smile at him and I'm just about to excuse myself when he speaks.

"Your friends just left," he says, leaning into my ear. His warm breath caresses my neck and makes me shiver, even though it's swelteringly hot in here.

"Oh, I'll just get a taxi." I turn to leave but stop when I feel his hand wrap around my wrist. I look back to see his eyes once again boring into mine. I'm not sure whether I should feel intimidated by his intensity, but I don't, not one bit.

"No," he states before stepping up to my side, placing his arm around my waist and pushing me toward the exit. I feel his thumb gently stroking my skin and it ignites butterflies in my stomach, but not the type I'd expect to feel whilst being touched by some random guy in a club. I'm not scared, and I don't want to cause him physical harm; I actually kind of like it.

He directs us to the coat check and hands over a ticket.

"You don't have one?" he asks when I don't make a move.

I shake my head and we wait in silence for the girl to return.

When she hands his jacket over, he drapes it over his arm, and with his hand on the small of my back, he gently moves me toward the exit. His touch burns and sends tingles racing around my body.

I don't feel the cold like I did waiting to get in. I try to push aside the thought that it's because he's touching me, but I'm not very successful.

"Here," he says, placing his leather jacket over my shoulders.

"No, it's fine, you have it," I try to argue, but now he's removed his hand, I'm freezing.

"You need it more than me, Skittles."

Skittles? I don't get the chance to ask, because his fingers thread through mine and he encourages me to start walking away from the club.

We walk in silence, past the closed shops and dodging other drunk partygoers who are trying to make their way home.

"Where are we going?" I ask eventually, not concerned in the slightest that I'm currently walking through the city in the middle of the night with a man I've just met.

"Everywhere. Nowhere," he answers cryptically, before falling silent again.

I can't really argue with him, because although what he's just said makes no sense, I kind of understand it and it feels pretty perfect. I continue to hold onto his hand and walk alongside him silently through the city.

I've never really spent much time out here at this time of night, but for a place that's usually chaotic, it's strangely calming with the orange glow from the street lights ahead and the twinkling stars above.

Nothing is said between us for the longest time, and it's weird, because it's the most content I think I've felt in a long time.

Bax eventually breaks the silence. "There's a takeout curry house. Do you fancy anything?"

I'm not really hungry, but the thought of eating something warm gets the better of me.

"Sure." He changes direction and pulls me across the road.

We both order a chicken curry and chips along with two cans of Coke before heading back out into the night.

"Come on," he says, and I follow along, our hands once again intertwined.

We come to a stop when we get to the harbour side. He walks down a couple of the steps that descend to the water before tugging on my hand to encourage me to sit with him.

"Here," he says, handing my food over once he's unwrapped it.

"Thank you. Are you sure you're not cold?"

"I'm fine, Skittles."

"Why are you calling me that?"

"Because it suits you."

"Why?" I ask, but he just shrugs his shoulders. After a couple of seconds of silence, I decide he's not going to elaborate. "You know my name's Erin, right?"

"Of course. Can I ask you something?"

"Sure." I'm a little surprised by his question because he's hardly said anything to me since I met him.

"Why did you come with me? I'm a stranger you just met in a club. You don't even know my name."

"It's Bax," I say, trying to prove I do know something about him. "And... I don't know. It just felt right."

"Hmmm," he hums before throwing a chip covered in curry sauce into his mouth. "You should be careful who you decide to spend time with in the middle of the night, Skittles. They could be dangerous."

"Are you?"

"Very."

For some reason, his warning doesn't scare me off in the slightest. He might be the quiet, brooding type, but I'm not sure he falls into the *dangerous* category.

Once we've finished eating, we continue looking out to the dark water before us. There's no noise out here, and we're the only sign of life. I have no idea what time it is, but to be honest, I really don't care.

"I used to come down here in the middle of the night when I was a kid. I'd sneak out of my house and spend hours looking out over the water," he says quietly. I'm not sure whether he wants me to respond or not, so I decide to stay silent and listen. "It was the only peace and quiet I could get unless I was under a car in the garage. I used to sit here for hours."

Bax falls silent. I guess his memories are taking him far away, so I allow him to do his thing as my thoughts drift once again to Mum and her gift shop.

"Erin?" he asks abruptly, and I turn to look at him.

"Yeah."

"I haven't wished you a happy birthday," he says, staring deep into my eyes.

Before I know what's happening, I feel his cold palm against my cheek and he leans in toward me. My eyes instinctively close seconds before I feel his warm, soft lips against mine. He holds still for the longest time with our lips pressed together, but he doesn't push any further. When he eventually pulls back, I can't help feeling a little disappointed.

"I'm sorry. I should get you home," he says, quickly taking his hand away and leaving me cold without his touch.

"No," falls from my mouth, shocking the hell out of me.

His head snaps to the side to look at me. He doesn't need to ask; I can see the question all over his face.

"Can we stay here a little longer?"

"Yeah, if you want."

"So, are you on leave or something?" I ask after a few more seconds of comfortable silence have passed between us.

"Yeah, two weeks," he says, but he doesn't sound very excited about it.

"Would you rather be at work?"

"Quite honestly, yes."

"Why are you here then? Surely you could have gone somewhere other than Bristol?"

"It's my home, I guess. I didn't really think about it. Everyone goes home to their families when they're on leave. Plus, my mate lives down south, and wanted a night out here before travelling on, so here I am."

"Don't you have family?" I blurt out, and then instantly regret such an intrusive question.

"My mum's here."

"Well, she must be excited about seeing you."

"I doubt it. I think I might just grab my car and take off."

"And go where?"

"Everywhere. Nowhere," he says, just like he did earlier.

"Sounds amazing," I admit, revisiting my thoughts from a few hours ago.

Bax's movement as he turns to look at me catches my eye, so I do the same. As he stares at me, I can see a small smile tugging at his lips, and just like every time he's looked at me this evening, his eyes twinkle in excitement.

"What?" I ask sceptically.

"Come with me."

"I'm sorry, what?"

"Come with me," he repeats.

"Where?"

"Everywhere, nowhere, wherever we want to go."

"Are you crazy? I don't even know you."

"You knew me well enough to walk off alone with me in the middle of Bristol, so I can't be that scary. You're a student, right? So you're free the next two weeks. We could just disappear."

My heart's pounding in my chest the more he speaks. I shouldn't be getting so excited about the prospect of running away with this stranger, but suddenly, it's all I can think about.

"What if I have work?" I ask, trying to play it cool.

"Do you?"

"Nothing I couldn't do on the move," I answer honestly. Yes, I've got an assignment to write, and I've always got more jewellery to design or make, but there's no reason I have to be here to do that.

"So is that a yes?"

"This is insane," I admit with a laugh, but he doesn't say anything. He just continues staring at me intensely, waiting for an answer. I quickly run through every reason in my head why I shouldn't be doing this. Weirdly, any concerns about him being a mass murderer don't even feature on my list. "YES!" I blurt out.

"Yes?"

"YES," I scream into the night.

Suddenly I'm on my feet, my body pressed against his hard muscles as his lips find mine again. They feel the same as last time, only they don't stay still. I feel them part before his tongue gently sweeps across my lower lip. My mouth opens without any instruction from my brain, and in seconds, our tongues are tangling together. He steps forward and my bum hits the wall behind me, stopping my movement, but it doesn't stop Bax because he presses further into me. His hands run from my face, over my shoulders, and skim the sides of my breasts before they come to a stop on my waist.

By the time he pulls back, I can feel his hardness pressing into my stomach. The thought of causing that kind of reaction has butterflies exploding in my belly.

Our foreheads rest together while he catches his breath. His eyes don't stray from mine. "Your eyes are purple," he whispers.

"Violet."

"Stunning."

I can't help looking away as embarrassment washes through me. No one compliments me like that, and I don't know how to take it.

"Hey," he says, gently forcing my head back with his fingers on my cheek. "You're going to have to learn to accept compliments if we're spending the next two weeks together, because I have a feeling I'm going to be paying you a lot."

I feel heat rush up my neck to my cheeks.

"Fuck, you look so sexy when you blush."

I desperately want to pull my eyes away from his, but his stare is too intense.

"Are you sure about this?" he asks as he steps back away from me.

"I think so."

"No, Skittles, I need to know you're doing this because you want to. Do you want to get away from this place?"

"Yes."

"Are you sure you want to do this with me? You've no idea who I am or what I'm capable of."

"Yes," I answer, a little more forcefully than before. It might sound crazy, but I know he's not capable of hurting me—not physically, anyway. I may have only just met him, but I already feel as if I've known him my entire life.

"Okay then, let's go."

"Right now?" I ask in a panic.

"Well, no, not right now. I was thinking we should get some sleep first. You can get some stuff together in the morning, I can get my car, and then we can go."

"Everywhere and nowhere," I state.

"Exactly. Come on then, Skittles, let's go find us a bed for a few hours."

I take his outstretched hand and together, we head off into the night.

It's not long until we're stood in the reception of a 24/7 hotel getting *that* look off the middle-aged receptionist. She thinks we're just checking in for a late night hook-up. The thought makes me panic and it only gets worse when Bax hands his credit card over to pay for the room.

I look away from the desk and allow him to take my hand to pull me in the direction of our room once he's finished.

"Bax, I—" I manage to say when he puts the card in the little machine to unlock the door.

"I got a twin room," he says, obviously seeing where my thoughts were going.

"O-okay," I stutter, following him in.

When I look up, true to his word, there are two single beds. I look around the room and try not to let my thoughts show on my face. I don't want to seem ungrateful.

"No wonder it was so fucking cheap," Bax says from behind me.

I let out a sigh of relief that he sees it too. The place looks like it last saw a decorator in the eighties. The walls and ceiling are definitely yellower than they're meant to be, and the few bits of furniture in here look like they're about to fall apart.

"I guess it'll be okay for a few hours," I say, slipping my shoes off and wiggling my toes as I sit on the corner of one of the beds. It creaks loudly, making us both laugh.

"I've stayed in some bad places, but this is up there," Bax says as he empties his pockets on the bedside table.

I watch as he undoes a couple of his shirt buttons before he reaches back and begins pulling it over his head. I'm fairly sure it all happens at normal speed, but I could swear time slows down as he reveals the most incredible body to me. His skin is a stunning golden colour, like he's recently been in the sun, and it flawlessly covers perfectly sculpted pecs and abs.

I know I'm staring, but I can't help it. It's like my eyes are glued to him.

"Fuck, Skittles," Bax complains when he catches me ogling him.

"Shit, I'm so sorry," I say in a panic as I spin on the bed so I'm facing away from him. My face heats and I drop it into my hands in an attempt to hide my embarrassment. I shut my eyes, but it's like the image of him shirtless is burned onto the inside of my eyelids.

I noticeably flinch when his hands land on my shoulders. "It's okay, look as much as you want; just know that I can't be held responsible for my actions when you do."

I try to swallow but my mouth is suddenly drier than a fucking desert, so I end up nodding instead.

"Hey, stop hiding from me," he says, pulling my hands away from my face and turning my head so I have to look at him. He runs his fingertips over my cheeks and his eyes look over every inch of my face. His mouth opens like he wants to say something, but he must change his mind because instead, he drops his hand and steps away from me.

"Here," he says, holding out his shirt. He must sense my reluctance because he drops it into my lap before saying, "Well you don't want to sleep in that, do you?" as he gestures at my outfit.

"No, not really," I mutter as I gather up the fabric and head toward the bathroom. I look over my shoulder before entering to see Bax with his back to me, undoing his jeans. He's just about to drop them when he must feel my stare, because he glances over at me. My breath catches at the look on his face. His eyes are smouldering.

"Keep it up and you won't be getting any sleep," he warns.

His words spur me into action and I quickly step into the bathroom and lock myself in.

I rest back against the door and try to get my head together. How the hell did this night end with me in a shitty hotel room with a soldier? I wonder briefly what happened to Frankie, Lisa and Tara. The only reason Frankie and Lisa ever disappear on a night out is because they've pulled, so I can only imagine they're both currently warming a soldier's bed. I'm happy for Frankie in a weird way; she's getting to live out her fantasy, I just hope she doesn't end up getting hurt. She likes to make out she's all about easy sex and whatever, but I know her, and I know deep down she wants more than that, even if she won't admit it.

I eventually make use of the bathroom before stripping off my clothes and pulling Bax's shirt over my head. It's huge and almost comes down to my knees, but I'm grateful because it does a good job of covering me up. I do my best with the complimentary soap and water to remove what's left of tonight's make-up, and comb my hair through with my fingers before plaiting it over my shoulder. I pull my thick-rimmed glasses from the bottom of my clutch and slide them on after disposing of my contact lenses.

I'm just reaching for the doorknob when I get a sudden bolt of nerves as I think about who's on the other side of the door. How do I trust him so much when I've only just met him? There's no way I should be this comfortable about spending a night in a hotel room with a man I hardly know. I shake the thought away because there's something telling me this is exactly what I should be doing, that for some reason I was meant to meet Bax tonight. I roll my shoulders and let out a breath before pulling the door open and stepping out.

He was obviously waiting for me, because he starts talking before I round the corner.

"So where did you want to... holy—" he stops mid-sentence when I appear. His chin drops and his eyes race around me like they don't know where to look first. I want to be all confident like Frankie would be in this exact situation, but unfortunately, that's not who I am, so instead of standing here proudly, I fold my arms over my chest and look down at the ground.

"Oh no you don't," he says. I expect to find him out of bed when I look up, so I'm surprised to see him still sat there with the covers over his waist. "Never be embarrassed by looking that incredible."

Heat races up my neck and I feel my face flush red. I manage to break from his gaze and rush to get into bed. The way he's looking at me right now scares and excites me in equal measures.

I lie myself down on my side and pull the covers up to my neck before looking over at him. He's still sat exactly as he was, and staring where I was stood.

"Are you okay?" I ask after a few minutes when he still hasn't moved or said anything.

"I'm not sure," he answers honestly.

"I... uh... can go," I offer, thinking he doesn't want me here.

"Trust me, Skittles, that's the last thing I want right now."

"Okay then," I whisper because the emotion in his voice just then knocked me for six.

"Goodnight, Skittles."

"Goodnight, Bax."

CHAPTER THREE

I wake to the weirdest sound. I lie there for a few seconds, firstly trying to remember where the hell I am, and then secondly to work out what it is that's woken me. As soon as I open my eyes, it's obvious. Bax is at the foot of our beds doing sit-ups, and the noise is his exhale every time he does a crunch. I grab my glasses silently and shift myself so I have a better view. I watch with delight as he continues. His muscles flex in the most delicious way. I lose count after fifty, but eventually he turns over and starts doing push-ups. I almost groan at the sight of his firm arse clad in only his white boxer briefs. Every woman should get to wake up to this every morning.

I stay still and watch every single push-up, taking note of the straining muscles in his thick arms each time he drops to the floor. The longer I watch him, the more my sleepy body wakes up. My heart is pounding, and I'm dying to fling the covers off me, but that means telling him I'm awake and watching, so I lie here suffering. It's totally worth it.

After an insane number of push-ups, he jumps to his feet. He's got his back to me but the second he raises his eyes to the mirror in front of him, they stare directly into mine. I see them widen slightly in surprise before they darken. We're both frozen, staring at each other for a few minutes. I'm not sure if that means he's pissed off that I was watching him.

Eventually, he turns. I'm desperate to run my eyes over his body again but the intensity in his keeps mine held hostage. In seconds, he's inches from my face, hovering above me.

"You need to be careful what you wish for, Skittles," he warns, his voice deeper than it was last night.

"I-I... I didn't," I stutter.

"I told myself I wouldn't do anything until you were begging for it, but you're making it really fucking hard to keep that promise."

I swallow, but my suddenly dry mouth makes it a challenge. Does he mean...?

My thoughts are cut off when his lips brush mine. It's a kiss like the first one we shared last night. There's no movement, but it feels like there's a promise in it.

His lips are gone as quickly as they appeared, and when my eyes focus, he's walking away from me. I only get a quick glimpse of his arse before he disappears around the corner and into the bathroom.

I stay where I am, listening to the sound of running water and imagining how his body would look wet and glistening.

When he emerges I get a shot of exactly what that's like because he's still wet with only a towel wrapped around his waist.

"I thought you would've gone back to sleep," he says when he sees me still awake.

"It's fine, I don't sleep much," I admit. I've always been a bit of an insomniac but since things with Mum and the shop have been getting worse, so has my sleeping.

"We've only had two hours," he says, sitting on the edge of his bed.

Okay, I do usually manage a little more than that. "You shouldn't have woken me up with all that huffing and puffing then," I say with a smile.

"I can assure you, I was not huffing or puffing."

"Okay then, army man, whatever you say."

Bax narrows his eyes at my piss taking but he doesn't say anything about it. "I was going to find some coffee. Would you like one?"

"There's stuff over there," I say, pointing to the little kettle.

"Knock yourself out, but I want real coffee."

"Real coffee would be good, now you mention it."

I watch in amazement as Bax stands, turns his back to me, and drops the towel. I cough to cover my groan but from the movement I see in his shoulders, I don't think I do a very good job. Once his jeans are on, he turns back toward me.

"I'm gonna need my shirt."

"Uh... hang on," I say, diving under the covers.

I squirm around and manage to get his shirt off before I poke my head out, followed by my arm, and hand it over. My other hand keeps the covers pulled up to my neck, although it doesn't seem to matter because the way Bax is staring at the duvet, you'd think it was see through.

"Thank you," he mutters before pulling it over his head. "Motherfucker."

"What?"

"It smells like you."

"Sorry," I whisper, feeling embarrassed.

"Don't be. It just means I'm even less likely to be able to get the image of you wearing it out of my head."

"Oh."

"I'll make sure I'm gone for twenty minutes to give you time to get dressed and shit."

"Get dressed and shit?" I repeat with a smile.

"Yeah, well, I don't know what girly shit you might need to do," he admits.

"Okay, well... thank you."

Seconds later, he's gone and I'm left alone in this dingy hotel room, questioning my sanity once again. I try to put my thoughts to one side as I rush into the bathroom to shower and dress before he gets back.

"SKITTLES, ARE YOU DECENT?" Bax shouts through the crack in the door exactly twenty minutes later.

"Yes," I answer with a laugh.

"Fuck's sake," he grumbles, making me laugh even more. "Here, I made an educated guess," he says, handing me a Costa cup and McDonald's bag. The smell makes my stomach grumble.

"McDonald's coffee not good enough for you either?" I ask with amusement, looking at what's in my hands.

"No," he says after taking a sip.

"Aren't they at opposite ends of the high street?"

"And?"

I don't really have an argument so smiling to myself I pop the top off the cup to allow it to cool down. I'm not overly fussy when it comes to coffee but when I see what I think is a cappuccino, I can't help but smile. "Perfect," I say, and Bax's face lights up. My heart flutters slightly at the sight and I desperately want to tell it not to be so stupid.

I take a tenuous sip and when it's even hotter than I was expecting, I put it down and grab the bag. "Yum," I say, opening up the muffin, "just what I needed."

We both polish off our breakfast in record time before falling back into a comfortable silence.

"So what's the plan?" I ask eventually, my curiosity getting the better of me.

"You're still up for it?" Bax asks, incredulously.

"Of course. I wouldn't have said yes if I didn't mean it."

I get another smile off him and it affects me no less than last time. What is it about this guy?

"Is it okay with you if we don't have a plan? My life is one strict routine; I'd quite like to go with the flow for once."

"Of course. So when are we going?"

"I thought once we're sorted here, we'd go, get our stuff, and head off."

"I thought you didn't have any plans?"

"Once we're in my car and driving out of Bristol, I have none," he says with a laugh. He looks away from me but not before I see a serious look fall over his face. "This is just a two-week thing, no exchanging numbers or anything. Are you sure you're okay with that?"

My heart sinks a little at the thought of whatever this is having a time limit, but I'm aware that it's what I signed up for when I agreed to this last night. "Yeah, that's fine with me," I answer, although a little reluctantly.

It's still crazy early when our taxi pulls up outside Bax's mum's home. It's not quite what I was expecting after spending the night with him. In my head, I had the image of a standard three-bed semi with a cute little garden, but in reality, his mum lives in a flat in a seriously run-down area of town.

"Thanks, mate," Bax says, paying the driver. I hop from the taxi and he follows behind me. "This way. My car's in the garage." He places his hand on the small of my back and pushes me toward a set of dilapidated looking garages. It's obvious which one his car is in because there's only one with a working door. The rest are all hanging off at odd angles or missing completely.

When he pulls the door up, my eyes almost bug out of my head. "You're a boy racer?" I ask in shock as I run my eyes over his immaculate white Peugeot.

"I can assure you I'm not. We won't be cruising with a banging bass or hanging out in any McDonald's car parks."

"Riiiight." I can't help laughing at the look on his face.

"I love cars, especially classic ones."

"I'm not sure a nineties Peugeot 106 is a classic, Bax."

"Maybe not, but she's a beauty. I've totally rebuilt her from the wheels up. You won't find a better 106 out there. Anyway, get in, get comfortable, and I'll be back in a few."

"You're leaving me here?"

"Yeah, I'll only be a minute or two. My stuff's packed already from getting back yesterday."

I agree, but only because I can tell by his stance that I don't have a chance in hell of going with him. He's decided that I'm staying here and that's what's going to happen. I realise I'm getting my first look at Bax the soldier, and it's hot.

I've never been in a car quite like this before. I drop my clutch on my lap and look around. The red and black interior is a stark contrast to the perfect white paintwork on the outside. I've no idea when Bax last drove this, but it's sparkling clean. The black dashboard almost shines in the morning sun, and the red leather bucket seats look brand new. I continue looking around and come to the conclusion that Bax is a bit of a neat freak. There's nothing in the door pockets—not even an old packet of chewing gum—and the glove box is definitely different to any I've ever seen before as it only contains one very neatly folded cloth.

I'm distracted from his perfect car by some movement in front of his building. I look over, thinking I'm going to be able to ogle him as he walks this way. Only, when I look up, it isn't him on the doorstep. Instead, there's a woman. She's got to be in her fifties at least. Her hair is a mess and sticking up in all directions, and her make-up is so heavy I can see it all smeared down her face from here, but the thing that makes her stand out the most is what she's wearing—or *isn't* wearing. The lace nightie covers nothing, and I *mean* nothing. The much younger man she's with hands her something before turning and walking away. I quickly look down, not wanting to be caught watching them.

I grab my phone as a distraction and send a text to Frankie to ask how her night was. I don't expect an answer for hours yet. If I get any contact from her before two o'clock this afternoon, I'll be amazed.

"Hey, you haven't run," Bax says as he drops down next to me after throwing a bag into the back seat.

"I'm not sure I'd want to around here." I regret my words instantly when I remember this is where he lives.

"Wise move. This place is a shithole." His obvious dislike of it makes me feel a little better. "I didn't grow up here. We used to have a lovely house in a nice neighbourhood, but when Dad left, it all went to shit."

"I'm sorry."

"It's fine. I joined the army the second I could, and left Mum to ruin her own life." As the words leave his mouth, I can't help but wonder if the woman I just saw was her.

It turns out we can't go anywhere until Peggy the Peugeot—yes, the car has a name—has a thorough once over, so our first destination is to an ancient looking garage on the edge of town.

"Are you sure this place is still in business?" The old tin building looks like it's about to fall down. I'm not sure it's somewhere I'd want my pride and joy to be.

"Yeah, it's open."

I see he's right the second he pulls the car to a stop, because a door opens and an elderly man steps out with a huge smile on his face.

"Bax! I wasn't expecting to see you. What a lovely surprise on this sunny Sunday." The man's joy couldn't be any clearer.

Bax jumps from the car and I watch as the two hug it out. I've no idea who this guy is, but they're clearly close.

They're just pulling apart when I reach them. "Erin, this is Arthur, my grandad's best mate. Arthur, this is Erin, she's..."

"A friend," I finish to help him out, although calling us friends might be pushing it slightly.

"Well, it's nice to meet you, Erin. Bax here needs a good friend," he says, elbowing Bax in the arm and winking at both of us. I try to play it cool but I can feel heat rushing to my cheeks at his insinuation. "Let's go and get some coffees, young lady. If I know Bax, you're in for a long few hours."

It turns out he wasn't lying. I spend a couple of hours chatting to Arthur in his little makeshift kitchen before venturing out to sit at a bench in the sun. The benefit of being out here is that I get to watch Bax bent over the bonnet of his car, and let me tell you, he has one fine arse.

I hear nothing back from Frankie so I can only presume she's had a good night. If she'd gone off with someone who wasn't Bax's friend, I might be concerned, but something tells me she's okay.

"I promise I'm nearly done," Bax shouts over as he wipes his hands on a rag.

"Take your time." His eyes light up and I can only assume that's because I'm not rushing him and his darling Peggy.

I look back down at the paper I asked Arthur for and smile. It's been quite a while since I've been able to just sketch for the fun of it. That's what all this used to be—fun. I'd design and make jewellery because I loved it, but now I feel like I'm under pressure to deliver because it could be what keeps Mum's gift shop open. We both do well from my jewellery sales so I keep pushing for more. Unfortunately, that also means pushing my creativity out the window, and recently, I've found my designs getting more and more generic and boring. I used to thrive on being unique and different, and sadly the generic designs are the ones that sell and make money.

Once I run out of inspiration from my surroundings, I start to work on something totally different. It's not the easiest thing in the world because he keeps moving, but I do my best.

"Fucking hell, Skittles, that's incredible," I hear over my shoulder, bringing me back to reality. I'd totally lost myself in what I was doing.

I drag my eyes away from the tiny section I was working on and look at my sketch as a whole. It's not too bad, I guess. I shrug my shoulders at Bax before looking up at him. What was a smooth shaven face when I first met him yesterday is now covered in a layer of stubble, and he has smears of oil on his cheeks and forehead. It's really pretty sexy.

"What?" he asks when I sit there staring at him.

"Nothing."

"No, go on, you're clearly thinking something."

"It's nothing. Are you finished?"

He leans forward a little more until our noses are almost touching. "Tell me what you're thinking," he whispers.

I look away from his eyes before muttering that he looks hot.

"What was that? I couldn't quite hear you," he says, grabbing my cheek gently so he can turn me back to look at him.

I try to move away from his stare but he holds me in place. "Fine," I huff. "You look hot, okay?" I force his hand off me and stand up, gathering the paper in front of me as I go.

"Now, was that so hard to admit, Skittles?" I can hear the humour in his voice and it makes me want to kick him.

"Shut up," I mutter. "Can we go now?"

"Yes, let me just say goodbye to Arthur."

When we arrive at my house, thankfully there's no sign of Mum. It's not that I don't want her to meet Bax; it's more that she'll try to talk me out of this. She'd probably be right, because disappearing off with a guy I've just met is a little nuts, and very out of character for me, but right now I don't care about any of that. I just want to get away. What we do find is the bottle of vodka and sleeping pills she's left behind on the dining table. The sight reminds me of everything I'm trying to push to the back of my mind, and a massive ball of guilt has me on the verge of turning Bax down on his offer to disappear.

One look at him stood in the doorway behind me and I know I'm doing the right thing. He glances at the items on the dining table, then gives me a sad smile. If my assumptions are right about that woman being his mum, I'm guessing he kinda knows how I feel right now.

I point Bax in the direction of the shower and strip out of last night's clothes in favour of something more suitable for a road trip before I start gathering my stuff together. I pull my suitcase down from the top of the wardrobe and bang the dust off. It's been quite a while since it's seen some holiday action.

I fill it with clothes before pulling open my pyjama drawer.

"Fuck," I mutter to myself when I see the only sets left are the silk lacy ones Frankie bought me for Christmas last year that I'd hidden at the bottom. I glance over my shoulder at my washing basket to see it overflowing. "Fuck."

I hear the water shut off and I know I'm running out of time. I really want to get out of here as soon as possible.

I grab the pyjamas and throw them in my suitcase. *We'll get separate rooms, it'll be fine,* I think as I pull my savings card from my desk. I'll pay for my own room. It'll be safer that way.

"Hey, you ready?" Bax asks when he pokes his head into my room as I'm zipping up my suitcase.

"I think so."

"Let's hit the road then."

"WHERE ARE WE GOING?" I ask when we've been driving for twenty minutes. After spending all day at Arthur's garage getting Peggy ready for her road trip, the sun is already setting.

"I found this in my room." Bax reaches behind my seat before dropping a bottle full of two pence coins in my lap. "I thought we could have some fun with those," he says, pulling away when the lights change.

"Oh my God, are you serious?" I know I'm acting like an excited child but I don't care. My dad used to take me to the pier in Weston-Super-Mare when I was little. It's one of my best memories with him.

"I've been collecting them for years. Now seems like as good a time as any to spend them. I need food first, though." Arthur made us a sandwich earlier but it's definitely starting to wear off.

Bax parks the car on the side of the road in front of a row of B&Bs. "Let's find somewhere to sleep for the night, then dinner."

I follow him into the first B&B to be told it's full, then the next, and the next. At this rate, we're going to be sleeping in his car. It's a nice car, but it's not good enough to be our bed for the night.

Thankfully, the fourth B&B has a room left. I lose the argument about paying for it and Bax hands his card over after trampling any point I tried to make about why I should foot the bill this time.

"Up the stairs, right at the end of the corridor, then it's the door on the left," the lady behind the counter says, pointing us in the right direction. "I would take you but I'm here on my own and trying to make dinner for some guests."

BAX OPENS the door and gestures for me to enter. I take two steps into the room before I stop. Bax isn't paying attention and crashes into the back of me, his arms coming around my waist to hold me up.

"Shit, sorry. What's the... oh," he says when he sees what I'm looking at—a giant four-poster bed. "We can try somewhere else," he offers.

"We might not find anywhere else." We drove past loads of 'No Vacancy' signs and I don't fancy spending the night trawling the streets hoping to find something. This place is nice and clean, unlike where we spent last night, and although it's only one bed, it looks pretty comfortable.

"I'll sleep on the floor."

"You don't have to do that."

"Anything to make you happy." I swoon a little at his words.

After dumping our stuff, we head out to find a restaurant for dinner. There's a bar and grill not far down the street, and we grab the last empty table.

"So what do you do in the army?"

"Recovery mechanic."

"You fix vehicles?"

"Not really. We recover them when they've broken down or got into trouble."

"Oh, I thought with your car and everything you'd be working on them."

"I wanted excitement and my job definitely gives me that. The mechanics are usually at camp fixing vehicles whereas I'm out in the thick of it rescuing our men. I love it." I can see in his eyes how much he enjoys his job, even if the thought of him being somewhere dangerous makes my stomach flip.

"What about you?"

"I'm doing business and marketing at uni."

"I thought with what you were doing earlier you'd have said art or something."

"No," I answer sadly, making his eyebrows raise in question. "My mum has a gift shop, it hasn't been doing so well since the recession so I went with business in the hope of helping bring it back to life."

"You don't sound like you enjoy it."

"It's okay. I just want to help. The shop's getting the better of her at the moment, it was her dream and she refuses to let go of it. If she carries on the way she is I'm convinced she'll put herself in an early grave."

"You can't do everything for her, Skittles. You've got your own life to lead and she shouldn't be holding you back from that," he says. It's not the first time I've heard similar words. Frankie's always going on at me.

"I'm not doing it because she tells me to," I snap.

"I know, but it seems to me that because you're nice and caring, she doesn't need to tell you. Hell, I doubt she even needs to ask—she already knows you're going to do it." I hate that he can see right through me. I didn't realise I was quite so transparent. He can tell there's something off, because he reaches across the table and grabs my hand. "It's not a bad thing, Skittles. You just need to make sure people don't take the piss, and I can't help but think your mum is, but probably without knowing it. Did you want to do a business degree?"

"Of course."

"Honestly, if you had your pick of anything, you'd have stayed in Bristol and done business?"

I stare into his eyes for a bit as I roll the real answer to the question around in my head. "No."

"I didn't think so. You're too talented to be doing business."

"You've seen one drawing."

"All I needed to see."

We're silent as we eat. His observations about my life choices hit a little close to home and have shaken me slightly. I always dreamed of moving away from Bristol and doing something where I could be creative every day. Unfortunately, I never even got the chance to look at possible courses because I got sidelined into business. Bax is right; Mum never told me to do anything, but things were hinted, and as he says, I'm too nice and I went along with it all because it felt like the right thing to do. It leaves me with the question I try to keep pushing to the back of my mind. What am I going to do when Mum's shop inevitably goes under? I'm left with a degree in a field I'm not interested in, and no qualifications in the field I want to go into.

"Erin?"

"Huh?" I look up to see Bax smiling at me and a bored looking waitress stood next to him with her hand on her hip.

"Would you like pudding?"

"Oh sorry, no I'm fine, thank you." I smile politely but she still huffs as she walks off. "Sorry," I say again.

"Are you okay?" Bax's eyebrows are drawn together in concern.

"Yeah. It's just what you said about my life."

"I didn't mean to upset you."

"I know you didn't, but you've nailed it. Everything you said is true, and it makes me wonder where it leaves me." It also freaks me out that he has my life pegged when he's only known me for a day, but I don't voice that.

"You'll be fine, Skittles. I think you're stronger than you give yourself credit for."

"You don't even know me."

"I don't think that's true. One look at you in the club last night and I knew everything I needed to know."

I open my mouth to respond but nothing comes out. How can he say that? I'm a stranger to him.

"Come on, let's go have some fun. There's plenty of time to deal with the serious stuff."

I can't argue with that, so after paying the bill, we head off toward the pier. It's so modern compared to the memories I have with Dad. I kind of like it though, because it makes me feel like I'm making new ones with Bax and not overwriting the old ones I'm so fond of.

"How long do you think this lot will last?" Bax asks with a laugh as we stand just inside the arcade.

"Two hours, tops."

"Let's see."

We don't get to find how long the two pennies would've lasted because we end up getting kicked out when they close for the night. We walk back down the pier hand in hand with wide smiles on our faces. I feel light for the first time in a long time.

"Walk on the beach?"

"Sounds perfect." And it is. The sun has set and there are a million stars twinkling above us. Amazingly the tide's in and the only sound is the waves crashing onto the sand.

We walk with our hands intertwined for a long time before Bax stops. He takes me closer to the water and we sit on the last bit of dry sand.

"Do you ever worry you're not going to come out of some of the situations you get put in?" I ask.

"Of course. I've been in the middle of some very hostile situations, but that's what I signed up for. It's also what gets my blood pumping. I feel alive in the middle of it all, and like I'm really making a difference."

"My dad was in the army," I admit. "He died in service when I was little."

"I'm sorry."

I give him a small smile and shrug my shoulders. What's done is done. "I've always told myself I'd never fall for a soldier. Mum fell apart after he died. It's an image I've never been able to rid from my head." When I look up, Bax has a shit-eating grin on his face.

"What?" I run through what I just said in my head and then panic. "Oh no, no, no," I say adamantly, shaking my head.

"We'll see about that. Now tell me, Skittles, when was the last time you did something wild?"

"Uh..." I think he already knows the answer is probably never.

I watch as he rises to his feet before pulling his hoodie over his head. "Come on, get up."

"Why?" I ask sceptically. I have only one idea as to what he could be planning on doing, and I'm fairly adamant I'm not up for it.

"We're going for a late night swim," he says.

"You can. I'll watch from here."

"Don't be so boring," he says as he toes off his shoes and drops his jeans.

He throws his discarded clothes up the beach a little before running full speed into the sea. He doesn't even flinch, and I know for a fact it must be fucking freezing. He splashes water everywhere and makes a right show of himself. Thankfully, it's dark and there's no one around to witness his antics.

"Come on," he encourages. "It's lovely."

"Nope."

"Strip and get your cute little arse in here, or I'll come and get you myself and you'll end up in here fully clothed."

We stare at each other for a full minute having a silent argument, him trying to convince me to join him and me standing firm with my refusal. It's not until he starts moving toward me that I cave, because as much as I really don't want to join him, surely being able to get out to dry clothes is preferable.

"Fuck's sake," I scream at him as I start unzipping my jacket.

"That's more like it! Strip for me, Skittles."

My face flushes red. It's only Bax who can see me but I think his eyes on my almost naked body are going to be worse than a stranger's.

The second my jeans hit the sand, I run into the sea, not wanting his eyes on me for too long.

"Holy fucking shit, Bax, it's fucking freezing," I squeal as the cold assaults my body.

"Keep moving, you'll soon warm up."

"I can't believe you convinced me to do this." I try to slap his shoulder but he's too quick and my wrist ends up trapped by his fingers. He gives my arm a quick tug and in a second I'm pressed up against his almost bare body. A shudder runs through me when I feel his heat against me.

"You need to let your hair down more. You're young, remember that."

"You're not," I say, pointing out the fact that he's clearly older than me for the first time.

"Hardly." His eyes flash as he lifts me up so my belly button is in line with his nose.

"Bax, no," I squeal in a panic. "Please no, Bax, please," I beg. I may be okay with water but I have a huge fear of my head going under.

"Okay, okay," he says softly as he lowers me slightly.

When I look down, he's gazing up at me but he looks lost in his own thoughts.

"It's Jay."

"What is?"

"Me. My name's Jay. Well, Jayden really. Bax is what the boys call me. My surname's Baxter," he says.

"Why are you telling me this now?"

He loosens his arms and I slowly start to slide down his chest. It's not until our eyes are level that he answers my question.

"You're not one of the boys."

"Who am I then?" I'm too lost in his eyes twinkling in the moonlight to put much thought into what I'm asking.

"Definitely *not* one of the boys." As he says it, his hands slide down my back and grab on to my arse. He pulls me tighter to him and I feel something press into my stomach.

I clear my throat, the sudden tension taking me by surprise. "No, I'm not."

"No, you're not," he repeats before running his nose against mine.

As I stare into his eyes, with our lips millimetres apart, all I can think is how badly I want him to kiss me again. The memory of our kiss by the harbour yesterday isn't enough.

He stops moving and we stand stock still in the water with him holding me tightly, my feet a few inches from the seabed. He looks deep into my eyes and that saying about someone being able to see into your soul suddenly doesn't seem so stupid.

It feels like an eternity but eventually he leans forward and presses his lips against mine. I moan the second I feel their heat and he must sense my approval because he opens his mouth and runs the tip of his tongue along my bottom lip. I don't waste any time in responding.

What started out as something soft and gentle soon turns into something much, much more. I lift my legs so they wrap around his waist, and my hands alternate between running over his short hair to gripping onto his shoulders. It's not until I feel the vibrations of his groan that I realise I'm moving my hips. Oh shit.

I pull back and immediately avert my gaze from him.

"What's wrong?" he asks, slightly breathlessly.

I try to let go of him but he holds me too tightly to be successful. "Erin?"

I look up at the moon as I try to pull together what to say to him. "It's just... I haven't... uh... I don't..."

"Hey," he says as he nudges my cheek with his nose. He clearly doesn't want to let go of me in case I run. Reluctantly, I turn to him. The look on his face takes my breath away. His eyes are dark and hungry but he has this sexy smirk playing on his lips. "It's okay," he reassures. "I'm sorry, I shouldn't have pushed you. We can take this at your speed. This," he says, flexing his hips, making me gasp at the sensation, "isn't what this is about."

The look on his face is so sincere I have no reason to doubt him. "Thank you," I whisper. I lean forward slightly when I realise how badly I want to resume our kiss, but instead of doing the same, like I expect him to, Bax, or Jay, pulls back.

"Maybe we should get out."

"Oh."

"Trust me, Skittles, it's not because I want to, it's because I have to. We stay like this and I can't promise I won't do something I shouldn't." To prove his point, he flexes his hips again, pressing his hardness into me.

"Okay," I mutter as I unwrap myself from him and begin heading toward the shore.

It's not until I'm out of the water that I realise how cold I am. Jay had successfully distracted me but now my teeth are chattering, and try as I might, I can't get my skinny jeans up my damp, sandy legs. Jay doesn't seem to have the same issue; when I look up, he's almost fully dressed.

"Here," he says, handing me his hoodie.

I pull it on and just like his shirt last night, it almost comes down to my knees. "Thank you."

"Our B&B isn't far."

Once we've got our shoes on, we make our way back for two hot showers. Being the gentleman he is, Jay tells me to go first and I'm too cold and sandy to argue, so I grab what I need and head into the bathroom. I intend on being as fast as possible but once the powerful jets of water hit me, that goes out the window.

I spend longer than necessary putting moisturiser on my face and faffing with my hair, even though it will always dry exactly the same —straight as a die and falling just past my shoulders.

I give myself a once over in the mirror. My cheeks are still rosy red from the chill of the sea, and my eyes are still alight with the feelings Jay brought to life when he kissed me. I look down at the silky cami and short set I'm wearing. I feel completely exposed with my breasts only just covered and what feels like the bottom of my arse hanging out. If it's possible, I feel more naked than I did in just my underwear on the beach earlier, even though there's more fabric.

I take a breath and square my shoulders as I grab the doorknob. *I am confident,* I say to myself as I pull the door open. *I'm a grown woman with a body I shouldn't be ashamed to show off.*

The second I step into the doorway, he looks up. His eyes pin me to the spot and I stand there as he looks over every inch of me. I might be barely covered in floral silk but the way he's staring at me right now, you'd think I was naked. My heart pounds as his eyes burn into skin, leaving tingles in their wake.

When they come to a stop, staring at my tits, I manage to remember how to speak. "Your turn." I don't even recognise the sound of my own voice.

I move to sit myself on the edge of the bed, and eventually he gets up and disappears into the bathroom. He doesn't say anything—not that he needs to, because his eyes say it all, and I'd be lying if I said it didn't freak me out. It's not often I think this, but I wish I could be more like Frankie right now and be able to embrace what's happening between us, to put all my insecurities and fears to one side and enjoy everything Jay's offering, because I want it—of course I do. The feeling of his hands on me is incredible, but I'm scared to take it further.

He doesn't spend as long in the bathroom as me, and when he emerges, he's just wearing a clean and dry pair of boxers. I've got myself into bed and pulled the covers up to my neck in a pathetic attempt to hide from him. It doesn't stop him running his eyes down my body. He knows exactly what it looks like, how it feels, even with the duvet covering me.

As he starts to walk around the bed, I roll over. I don't mean to shut him out but I've got so much going on in my head that I need the space. What I really don't need is him pulling me to him and kissing me like he did in the sea again. That will only mess my head up more. I shouldn't be feeling the way I am about him. I shouldn't like him this much already when I've only known him for a day. Plus, he's not just a guy, he's a soldier—exactly what I said I never wanted. I'm not sure I'm strong enough to deal with an army relationship and all the stress that comes with it.

I've no idea how much time ticks by as I lie there thinking, but I know he's not asleep behind me. I can tell by his breathing. A huge part of me wants to turn around, to make the most of the situation we've found ourselves in, but another part is screaming at me that this is only going to end one way, and that's with me left behind with a broken heart. I may have only known Jayden Baxter for a day, but I already know he's going to change my life. I'm just not sure I'm ready for it.

CHAPTER FOUR

Once we've had breakfast the next morning, we decide to hang around instead of getting in the car and heading off to our next unknown destination. We spend the day wandering through town whilst Jay picks up a few things he didn't have in his case. We stop and have a coffee whilst watching some street entertainers, and then another one a few hours later watching an old couple fighting with their fish and chips and a swarm of seagulls.

We shy away from any kind of serious conversation about our jobs or our futures, and it amazes me how quickly I allow myself to forget about the stress of home and just enjoy this time doing pretty much nothing with him.

We spend the rest of the afternoon walking hand in hand along the beach, talking, watching families building sand castles, flying kites, and those who are brave enough to venture into the sea. I have first-hand experience of how cold that is, and no intention of testing it out again.

WHEN THE SUN starts to drop, we decide we've probably walked far enough and start heading back. I've no idea how many miles we've covered, and I don't really care.

Once we get back into town, we opt for crossing over the road and walking past all the bars and cafés as we debate where we're going to have dinner. We eventually decide on a little Italian on one of the backstreets. It's quaint, the owner is someone you'd likely see on a comedy sketch show. He keeps us entertained for hours before we head back to our room and spend the night chilling out. Jay flicks through the channels whilst I sit with my sketchpad, coming up with some beach-themed jewellery based on our day. His eyes flick over to my designs every few minutes and when he looks up at me I see him asking the same questions I do of myself regularly. Why am I doing a business degree? What am I going to do next if—or more so *when*—Mum's shop goes under? I don't answer his unspoken questions because I have no answers. I wish I did.

When we eventually get into bed, I can't help but have a smile on my face. I've had the most incredibly relaxing day and the fact that I've been able to switch off has everything to do with the man lying beside me.

"Jay," I whisper, a few minutes after turning the light off.

"Yeah?"

"Do you have to be so far away?"

Not a second later, I feel his body heat against my back, before his arm wraps around my stomach and he pulls me to him.

I have the best night's sleep I've had in years.

"HEY, SLEEPYHEAD," Jay says when the sound of the room door shutting wakes me up.

It takes me a few seconds to register what's going on, but I soon figure out that he must have been for a run. His fitted t-shirt shows off his sculpted chest and a pair of slim shorts hug his thighs. It's quite a sight to wake up to.

"What time is it?"

"Almost ten. I asked June if we could have a late breakfast before hitting the road. She's keeping it warm for when we're ready."

"Almost ten?" I ask in shock. I don't think I've slept in this late before, ever. I sit bolt upright in bed and look to the clock at the other side of the room.

"Fucking hell," Jay breathes, making me look back over at him. Only, he's not looking at me—well, not my face, anyway.

I look down to see my nipple is just about to pop out from behind my cami. "Shit." I shift around and quickly cover myself up.

"You ruin all my fun," he says with a laugh, but then disappears into the bathroom for a shower. A wave of anxiety rushes through me as I think about how I'm acting. It's clear he wants more from me but I'm running scared. Will he eventually get fed up of playing this cat and mouse game? He said our time wasn't about *that*, and he's happy to take my lead, but is that really true?

I try to put my thoughts to one side as I get dressed and go down for breakfast. I know it won't make the situation any better, but at least I can ignore it for now.

"WHERE DO YOU FANCY GOING NEXT?" Jay asks once we've polished off our fry up.

"I thought we weren't making plans?"

"No, but I'd like to have an idea of what direction I'm driving in. Would you like to carry on down south or...?"

"I'd prefer to go up, if that's okay with you. I'd love to see the scenery of the Lake District and Scotland. I've only seen it on the telly and it looks incredible."

"It's stunning."

"You've been?" I'm not sure why I'm surprised, because he's probably been to most places, but I'm a little disappointed it's not something we can discover together.

"I've had a few exercises up there. No holidays, though," he says, making me feel a little better.

"So you don't mind then?"

"Of course not. Anywhere you want to go, we'll go."

"Australia?"

"That might be pushing it. Maybe next time," he answers with a laugh. My heart does a little dance at the sight of his joy. I love seeing him smile and hearing his laugh. I feel pathetic even thinking it, but I think it's my new favourite thing. "Ready?"

"Ready."

We grab our stuff, say goodbye, and get ourselves into Peggy for the journey up north.

"I'm so excited," I mutter, more to myself than Jay when he pulls onto the motorway.

"You're too cute, Skittles."

"Are you going to tell me why you call me that?"

"I already did. It suits you."

"That's not a reason."

———

IT'S late afternoon and we're just over halfway to our destination when my phone starts ringing. Our very loose plan is to get as far into the Lake District as we can, and find a B&B before the sun sets.

"Well, it's good to know you're not dead," I comment as a greeting to my best friend when I put the phone to my ear.

"I could say the same thing. I've just been to your house; your mum said you left a note saying you'd be gone for two weeks. Where the fuck are you?"

"Uh... I'm not entirely sure, other than on the motorway heading toward the Lake District."

"The fucking Lake District? It's all mountains, lakes, and sheep; why the fuck are you going there?"

When I said before that Frankie and I are complete opposites in every way, this is what I meant. She can't imagine a holiday that doesn't involve getting wasted in a club full of sweaty, drunk people. I want to see places and experience other cultures and their history rather than getting drunk off my arse and not remembering most of the holiday.

To save myself further scrutiny I change the subject. "Have you had a good weekend?"

"OH MY GOD! Erin, you have no idea how incredible Dean is." She squeals so loudly I have to pull the phone away from my ear. Jay looks over and raises his eyebrows in question. I shake my head at him and roll my eyes.

"So it was all you wanted it to be?"

"And some. Seriously, E, I thought he was going to kill me with all the orgasms. I can barely fucking walk."

"TMI, Kiki. TMI."

"I don't care. I'm telling you everything. I've been waiting my whole life for this and I want to relive it with you."

"Great."

"No need to sound so excited about it," she chastises. "So anyway, after we left the club…"

She talks for almost thirty minutes as she tells me the ins and out —literally—of her weekend with Dean.

"So, are you seeing him again?"

"Yes, he's on leave for another week, I think he said. To be fair, we haven't done much talking, but he's taking me out tonight. He's left to do some crap, thank fuck, I can finally take a shit now he's gone! Now stop changing the subject, and tell me why the fuck you're going to the Lake District."

"I'm going with Jay."

"Who the fuck is Jay?"

I let out a breath before explaining who he is.

"Wait... that seriously hot guy from the club? Dean's mate, Bax?"

I don't need to look up to know Jay's smiling beside me, I can feel his amusement. "Yes, that one," I confirm.

"WOOHOO! Way to go, Erin. I bet he fucks like a fucking stallion as well."

"Uh..."

"Oh my God, please tell me you had a go on that."

"I... uh..."

"ERIN!" she screams. "For the love of all womankind, you need to tap that. Fucking hell, what's wrong with you?"

"Nothing's wrong with me, thank you, Frankie." I want to say something like, *what we have is more than just a quick roll in the sheets like you've had with Dean*, but I'm suddenly very aware that Jay's listening to every word I say, as well as how those words would make this sound very serious and meaningful. I'm not ready to think about that kind of thing, let alone say it out loud.

"I'm sorry, but seriously, girl. You've got what, a week or so with him? Make the fucking most of it. You'll be a long time cold and lonely when he's gone back to wherever it is he came from. You may as well have some amazing memories to keep you company. Remember, you never regret something you've done, only the things you didn't do," she says, trying to sound wise all of a sudden.

"Thanks for the pep talk."

"What are best friends for if it isn't to tell you to fuck that hot as shit guy sat right next to you?"

I sit in silence for a few minutes, running the conversation around in my head. Is she right? Am I going to regret holding out like this? I soon distract myself when I think back to what I wanted to say about this being more than just sex, because it is. It scares the shit out of me to admit it to myself, but I feel like this is the start of something. Something serious. I don't want to just jump straight into bed with him. I don't want to rush whatever this is between us just because we've got a limited amount of time together. There's no reason we can't take this one step at a time.

I finally arrive at the depressing part of all of this as I think about him going back to wherever it is he's based, and not seeing him for God knows how long.

"So who exactly was that?"

"Frankie, the blonde girl in the silver dress Saturday night."

"I'm not sure I'd describe that as a dress, but yeah, I know the one."

"She's had this fantasy about having a fling with a soldier, showing him a good time and then sending him off to war. You know, like in the old black and white films. She just took great delight in telling me all about her weekend with Dean."

Jay's response is to start laughing. It's not the reaction I was expecting.

"What's so funny?"

"You just told me she has a soldier fantasy and then backed it up by saying she spent the weekend with Dean."

"Right, and..."

"Dean's not in the army. He's a mechanic for Arthur," he says through his laughter.

My mouth drops open in shock.

"Fair play to him, though, he's clearly had a fantastic weekend pretending to be a soldier."

"Wanker," I mutter.

"What? Don't you think it's kind of funny?"

"Yes and no. Frankie's ecstatic about her fantasy coming true and he's lied to her. What's he going to do next week when she's expecting him to put his uniform on and head back to work?"

"No clue. Knowing Dean, he probably hasn't thought that far ahead."

I'm not sure if I'm pissed off that Jay's mate has outright lied to Frankie, or if I'm amused by the whole thing like he is. Frankie is going to be gutted.

"So..." Jay asks. "Know anyone else with that fantasy?"

"Not that I know of. I don't think soldiers are all that hot, really."

"Ouch," he says, putting his hand over his heart, making me laugh. "That's a real shame because I know a soldier who's got some moves."

"They also tend to be a little big-headed."

"It's not my head you need to worry about the size of," he deadpans.

"Oh please. I'll believe that when I see it. What the fuck are you doing?" I squeal when he makes a show of taking his hands off the wheel in favour of his waistband.

"I'm joking," he says with a laugh as he takes control of the car again. "I've had no complaints though, just so you know."

"I'll keep that in mind."

***

"DO you have any idea where we are?" We went past the sign for the Lake District over an hour ago but soon found ourselves in the middle of nowhere with no phone or GPS signal. We haven't seen a house or any kind of life form other than sheep for miles.

"Not exactly."

"By that you mean no, right?"

"We'll come across something eventually."

"You really think we're going to find a B&B out here?"

"No. Maybe a town, though. There's got to be one at some point."

We continue driving through the gorgeous countryside as we watch the sun set over the mountains ahead. I get the feeling we're going to be spending the night in Jay's car. I was all for not planning this trip, but I'm now feeling a little stupid for not at least aiming for a B&B, or a town where we might find one.

"Look, there are lights over there," Jay says as we drop down a hill. It's been dark out for hours now, we're both starving, and I'm desperate for the toilet. I don't have the luxury of being able to relieve myself on the side of the road like Jay did a few miles back.

"Oh please, God, let it be somewhere to stop."

Jay laughs but continues driving toward the lights. For a building that looks to be fairly close, it takes a hell of a long time to get to with the winding roads. By the time we pull up to the somewhat derelict old farmhouse, I start to have second thoughts about stopping here.

"It's got a B&B sign," Jay points out sceptically.

"Hmm." Said sign was missing most of its letters and hanging at an angle. If it's an indication for how unloved this B&B is, I'm not sure it's where we should be staying. It already looks like it could be the setting for a murder mystery programme.

"How badly do you need the toilet exactly?"

"Badly, but I'm still questioning this decision." Maybe peeing in a bush wouldn't be so bad.

"Come on. I'm sure it's owned by some lovely old couple who just struggle with maintenance."

I try to go with his way of thinking but I can't seem to get the idea out of my head that we could quite easily be killed here and no one would ever find us. I think I watch too many unsolved murder documentaries.

My desperate situation means that when he pulls the car to a stop and goes to get out, I rush to do the same.

We're just about to give up after standing at the front door for a few minutes with no response when there's some noise from inside. The door gets opened slowly to reveal the most hillbilly man I've ever seen in real life. His hair is long and greasy, his teeth are either black or missing entirely, and he's wearing the stereotypical checked shirt and threadbare jeans. He's not that old, so Jay's assumption of this place belonging to an old couple wasn't right. I'm fairly sure my idea about being murdered here could be closer to reality, because this guy has a look in his eye I really don't like.

"Hi, sorry, we're a little lost and need a bed for the night."

"And a toilet," I add.

"Oh... uh... yeah, sure." I swear I see an evil little smile appear on his lips. "Come in, toilet's down there on the right."

I give Jay a concerned look but he nods for me to go ahead. I really want to refuse but it's getting pretty painful now, so with an unsure smile at him, I head off.

It's a sight to behold. The toilet and basin are avocado green, the tiles are an aqua blue colour and covered in a layer of mould, and I can hardly see the taps for the limescale. Thankfully, I've got some anti-bacterial gel in my bag so I forego the hand washing facilities in favour of that.

When I find Jay, he's stood at a rickety old reception desk with a room key in his hand. My stomach turns over at the sight. I really don't want to stay here; it gives me the willies.

"It'll be okay," Jay says, obviously reading the look on my face.

We grab the bags from the car before venturing to our room; after seeing that toilet, I dread what it might be like.

I stand behind Jay as he puts the key in the lock and pushes the door. Nothing happens so he gives it a quick shove with his shoulder and after a loud creak, it opens. He doesn't give anything away as he walks in ahead of me, but even still, I hold my breath.

When Jay stands aside, I get my first look. I could already see the bare floor but the walls are almost the same. There are just a few bits of wallpaper here and there. When I look into the room, there is a double bed in the middle with a naked mattress, and a single chest of drawers in the corner. That's it.

"Uh..." I go to announce my refusal to stay here when there's movement behind me.

"I'm sorry it's not much. Here's some clean bedding though, and a new duvet and pillows," Hillbilly says, handing everything over along with a couple of soggy looking sandwiches.

"It's fine. We just need a bed."

"Well, the bathroom is down the hall. You're my only guests and Mother and I use the one upstairs, so it's all yours."

Jay thanks him again, because words elude me.

"This is very domesticated," Jay comments when we're halfway through making the bed together.

"None of this is what I was expecting to be doing this week."

"Me neither," he says sadly.

"What were you planning on doing before we ran off together?"

"No idea. Probably would have spent it either in bed or at the pub with Dean. I know you saw my mum the day we left, so you understand why I wasn't happy about being there."

"Why come back? Why not book a holiday or something?"

"Same reason you didn't go off to uni like you wanted, I guess. Some kind of fucked up loyalty to my mother. She was an incredible mum. When I think back to my childhood, there isn't anything I would change. I had what I thought was the perfect family. My parents were still together, and as far as I knew, they were happy."

"What happened?"

"Dad suddenly announced he'd met someone else. He packed his bags that same day and we haven't seen or heard from him since. Mum fell apart. She started with alcohol, then came the drugs, and now... well, you saw the state of her. Every time I come back I expect to find her dead."

"I'm so sorry."

Jay shrugs it off and continues making the bed, clearly putting his memories behind him again.

"What's wrong? You look like you want to say something."

"It's not that, it's just... I really want a shower."

"Sooo... go have one."

"That guy really freaks me out."

"Well, don't invite him to join you then," he says with a laugh, clearly not understanding my issue.

"That wasn't what I meant, you idiot. I just don't want to go alone," I admit.

"You want me to shower with you?" I see a smile twitch at his lips and his eyes darken a few shades.

"Not *with* me, just be in the room."

"You want me to sit in the room whilst you're naked in the shower?"

"Yeah." Hearing him say it aloud makes me realise how pathetic I'm being about this, but I don't care.

"What if it's got a glass door?"

"You'll have to keep your eyes shut."

"You're shitting me."

"If I wanted you to see me naked, I'd have invited you to join me in the first place."

"What if *I* want to see *you* naked?"

"Jay," I huff. "Will you please just come with me?"

"Of course."

"Thank you."

I gather my stuff and we go to check out the bathroom. Much to Jay's disappointment, there isn't a glass shower door, just a mostly mouldy orange curtain which really sets off the blue bathroom suite.

I have to give him credit because he turns around when I ask him to, and I'm pretty confident he doesn't peek, either.

He spends the whole time I'm showering complaining about how torturous the whole experience is for him. It amuses me greatly.

When we're walking back toward our bedroom, I'm reminded of why I wanted Jay with me, because loitering outside our room is the hillbilly.

"Is everything okay?" Jay asks when we get closer.

"Oh... uh... yeah. I was just checking on you guys." The way he says it and the look in his eyes creep me out. He then notices me stood behind Jay, and his eyes drop to my bare legs. I made Jay give me his hoodie so I didn't have to walk out in just my cami and shorts in case this exact thing happened. I hear a weird growl-like noise come from the back of Jay's throat before the guy backs off down the hallway.

"You locked the door, right?"

"Yeah, but he owns the place, so I'm sure he could get in if he wanted to." Jay's answer doesn't put my overactive imagination to rest at all. "You're right, he's creepy," he admits for the first time.

Jay lets us into our room and hands me the key so I can lock it myself. I think he's beginning to understand how uncomfortable I am.

I turn back around after pulling the key out to find Jay stood right in front of me. He's looking at me with hunger in his eyes and a small smirk playing on his lips.

"What?"

"You've no idea, do you?"

"Uh…"

Instead of explaining, he reaches back and pulls his t-shirt over his head, throwing it onto the bed behind him.

"What are you doing?"

"Distracting you."

My mouth opens in shock.

"You tell me when to stop, and I will."

I nod at him to show I understand, but I can't form words because my heart's hammering so damn hard my brain's gone fuzzy, and I have a whooshing sound in my ears.

It's like time stands still as I wait for him to do something, but the second he touches me, someone presses fast forward.

He steps toward me and his lips go to my neck. They dance over my skin as he peppers kisses from my ear to my collarbone. I lean my head to the side to give him the access he needs.

My heart continues to hammer, and tingles fire around my body, but they all meet between my legs. I've never felt anything like it but I already know I don't want it to stop.

Jay moves his head back at the same time I feel him start to lower the zip on his hoodie. He stares into my eyes for a few seconds before he drops it and stares at my chest like it's not still covered by my cami.

"You've no idea how hot you are, do you?" I bite down on my bottom lip. I have no idea how to respond to a question like that. "Fuck." He lifts his thumb to my mouth and pulls my lip from my teeth. "Mine," he mutters before he crashes our lips together.

He kisses me with an intensity I've never experienced before. His tongue licks and caresses while his teeth nip and tease. His hands slip inside his hoodie and rest against my waist. I can feel his fingers twitching to move and explore, and in a moment of madness, I grab his wrists and encourage them to do just that.

Slowly, he slides his hands up my ribs before he grabs on to my breasts. A moan I wasn't expecting falls from my mouth as he squeezes. "Oh my God," I breathe against his lips. I feel him smile, obviously pleased by my response.

He kneads my breasts for a few more seconds whilst he continues to kiss me. Then, his hands lift off before I feel him pinch my nipples. I suck in a sharp breath as what I can only describe as a bolt of lightning strikes between my legs.

"You look so hot, coming apart. If my hands make you like this, I can only imagine what else I could achieve," he mumbles into my neck.

"Please," falls from my mouth. I think it shocks him as well because he suddenly pulls back from me and looks into my eyes.

I stare back at him, silently pleading for more.

"You sure?"

I can only nod my reply. What he's done to my body has turned my brain to mush.

"Okay then," Jay says before lifting me so I'm pinned against the door by his hips. He grabs my thighs and wraps them around his waist, making his hardness press into the exact spot that's pulsing with need. The pressure against my sensitive flesh makes my head fall back. "Has anyone ever made you come before?"

I keep my eyes shut and shake my head.

"Good. I'd want to kill any fucker who'd already had the chance to touch you. You're mine, and I'm going to make sure you know it. You'll be feeling the after-effects for days," he promises.

His continued hip movement ensures I'm unable to respond with more than a moan.

His lips continue exploring the skin of my neck before he ventures down over my collarbone and along the edge of my cami.

"Are you particularly attached to this?" he asks as he tugs at the strap.

At this exact moment, I'd tell him I'm not attached to my legs if it meant he'd continue what he's doing.

"I'll take that as a no," he says when I don't respond.

Seconds later, I hear a rip before cold air surrounds my boobs. My head lifts from the door and my eyes spring open. When he comes into focus, he's staring right at my bare chest. After a couple of seconds, his eyes lift to mine. They're dark and hungry, and I'm sure there's a warning in them. My mouth waters for him as I take in his pained face.

"You're so fucking beautiful and your tits are fucking perfect."

He leans forward and I feel the incredible heat of his mouth as he sucks on one of my nipples. The feeling of his tongue running slowly around my sensitive peak has me trying to close my legs, but the only thing I achieve is to press him harder into me.

"You taste like heaven," he says, licking across my skin to my other nipple.

I'm panting and moaning as he continues to torture me. My whole body's tingling and the tension inside me is beginning to get unbearable. I have no idea what it is I need him to do, but it doesn't stop me begging for it.

"You want more?" he grates out, his voice deep and gravelly.

"Yes, yes," I repeat.

All of a sudden, I'm moving. I'm pulled away from the door before being lowered to the bed seconds later.

"Tell me you want me to make you come," Jay demands.

Embarrassment flows through me and I have the sudden need to cover myself up. Jay must sense it because he straddles my hips and pins my wrists together above my head in one of his hands. The other slowly teases the skin of my breasts. I can't help myself and I shamelessly arch my back as I try to get more of his touch.

"That's what I want—you begging for it. Begging for me to tip you over the edge," he says as he stares down into my eyes. "Now, tell me what you want, Erin."

I can't find the words he wants me to say. This is all new to me and I can't help fearing I'm going to say it wrong or sound stupid.

"Tell me to make you come, or I'll stop. I need to know it's what you want." To drive his point home, he pinches one of my nipples and I feel heat flood my core as it continues to pound uncomfortably.

"Make me come," I whisper, so quietly I barely hear it myself.

"Louder," he demands.

"Make me come."

"What was that?"

"Make me come."

"Scream it." I don't know what it is, but the way he's looking at me leaves no room for argument, so I immediately find myself following orders.

"MAKE ME COME," I scream, and in seconds, he's off me. I feel his hand skim the skin of my lower stomach before it disappears into my knickers.

Embarrassment heats my cheeks momentarily as I think about what he's doing, but the second I feel him touch me, all thoughts leave my head.

"Fuck," I breathe as I once again try to close my legs.

"Nope." Jay pins one of them down against the bed with his as he stares down at me.

"You're going to come on my fingers."

I nod; I have no doubt what he's saying is true.

His fingers circle my clit and just as the tension in me builds up to breaking point, he moves and starts to tease my entrance.

"Please tell me I'm the first to be here."

I nod.

"Tell me."

"You're the—" I let out a sudden intake of breath as I feel him press inside, halting my words. "Shit." I don't know whether I like it or hate it in those first few seconds. It doesn't take me long to make up my mind.

"Erin?" His eyes come back to mine from watching where his hand had disappeared.

"You're the first," I confirm. My voice quivers as I say it.

"Fucking hell."

"What?" I ask in a panic, thinking I've done something wrong.

"You're fucking perfect."

Jay leans forward and sucks one of my nipples into his mouth again as his fingers start to slide in and out of me faster. I feel his thumb graze my clit and all my muscles tense.

"You feel that?"

"Uh-huh," I confirm.

"Fuck, you'll feel amazing on my cock," he mutters. Everything gets tighter as I think about what he just said, how it might feel, how he'd look on top of me. "That's it. Let go."

"Oh my God," I squeal as something inside me explodes.

When I come back to myself, Jay is sat next to me, running his eyes over my skin. What the fuck did I just do? I've no idea who that was a few minutes ago, but I'm sure it wasn't me. I grab onto the sides of his hoodie that I'm still wearing and wrap it over my boobs.

His eyes find mine and I see panic in them as we stare at each other. Part of me wants to tell him that shouldn't have happened, but a bigger part knows I'd be lying.

In the end, I go with offering a favour in return, even though I have no idea what to do.

"Do you want me to...?" I ask, gesturing to the obvious bulge in his chinos.

"What? No," he says, sounding horrified by the suggestion. "Shit, no I didn't mean it like that," he quickly adds when he sees the look on my face. "If you touch me, Erin, then there won't be any stopping until I've owned you."

My mouth snaps shut and a gentle throb starts up again down below.

"Fuck." He gets up from the bed and paces back and forth a couple of times. "I need a shower. Are you going to be okay?"

With everything that's just happened, I've completely forgotten where we are and why I was so freaked out earlier. I guess he came through with his promise of distracting me.

"Yeah, just lock the door behind you."

"Okay."

I watch in silence as he rummages through his bag for what he needs. He's just about to step toward the door when he turns to me.

"Here, wear this." He throws me the shirt I slept in on our first night. "I won't be long."

The second I hear the door lock, I strip out of my ruined cami and shorts and pull his shirt over my head. His smell engulfs me and I immediately wish I'd told him not to leave me. I sit myself on the edge of the bed and look around at the almost bare room. This whole thing with Jay is utterly crazy, but I can't imagine being with anyone else right now. From the second I met him, everything just felt right. I knew I needed to get away, but I wasn't aware there was something—or someone—missing from my life. I'm starting to realise Jay is filling a gaping hole. If you'd have asked me about a boyfriend a few days ago, I'd have said I didn't have time, and although that's still true, after only a couple of days I'm realising that I would make whatever time Jay needed because he's somehow managed to creep his way in, and it scares me to admit that I don't see him finding his way out very fast.

"Hey, are you okay?" Jay asks when he steps back into the room a while later to find me in bed with my laptop.

"Yeah, I wasn't murdered by the creep whilst you were gone."

"So I see," he replies with a laugh. "That wasn't what I meant, though."

My cheeks heat a little. "I'm good."

"What're you doing?"

"Trying to work on a uni assignment. I'll stop now you're back," I offer.

He refuses because he doesn't want me falling behind, so we sit side by side, me trying to work and him playing on his phone until the early hours of the morning.

CHAPTER FIVE

"Let's get out of here," Jay says the second I open my eyes to find him looking down at me the next morning.

"Yes." I jump out of bed and start gathering up my stuff. He doesn't need to ask me twice to leave this shithole.

I make quick use of the bathroom before Jay grabs our cases and we sneak out. The place is in darkness, and thankfully it's silent.

We jump in the car and both start laughing uncontrollably. I'm not sure why he's so amused, but I'm just grateful we got out of that place alive.

"Where are we going?" I ask when it seems he knows what directions to take.

"I discovered I could get some 3G when I was sat on the toilet whilst you were asleep last night. I managed to get a map up."

"You left me alone in that room in the middle of the night?"

"It was either that or piss out the window."

"I think I'd have preferred that."

"I've found a route that will take us past some of the places you mentioned, and I've booked a room for the night."

"You're doing a lot of planning for someone who didn't want any."

"I thought you deserved to know you're going to be sleeping somewhere decent tonight."

"I appreciate that more than you know. You deserve that, too; you're on holiday, after all."

"That place was a million times better than some of the hellholes I've slept in in the past. Having you beside me made it feel almost like a posh hotel, much better than the sweaty men I usually wake up with."

"Is there something you need to tell me?" I ask with a laugh.

"Definitely not. I'd lay my life down for those guys but they aren't coming nowhere near my junk."

Jay quickly changes the subject after glancing over at me. My fears about his job and the memories of losing my dad must be written all over my face.

He efficiently navigates us to a fancy hotel in Windermere and treats me to a wonderful breakfast, consisting of an all-you-can-eat continental buffet before a mouth-watering plate of American pancakes, while he polishes off a giant fry up.

He drives us around the lake once we've finished and I spend the whole time staring out the window at the incredible views. I knew it was going to be stunning up here from what I've seen on the TV, but it really is amazing.

"What are we doing?" I ask when Jay pulls off the road into a small parking area.

"I thought we could experience the lake close up."

I hop out of the car and follow him down the track to a small beach-like spot at the edge of the water.

The sun's shining, and in this secluded little corner, we're sheltered from the cold wind.

"If I ever win the lottery, I want a view like this from my house."

"I could live with that," he agrees as he rests back on his elbows next to me.

We're both silent as we soak it all up; the sound of the water, and the birdsong from the trees above us. I allow myself to get lost in the peace this place has to offer.

Jay scares me when he suddenly jumps up. "What's wrong?"

"Nothing," he says as he pulls his hoodie and t-shirt off at the same time.

"What are you—" My question gets cut short when he slips his trainers off before dropping his jeans.

"Burning off breakfast. Join me?"

"No, I'm okay." He may have got me in the sea before, but it's not happening again. Once was cold enough.

"Your loss," he says before he turns his back on me and drops his boxers.

My mouth falls open as I stare at his naked behind—he has the most perfect arse. I watch as he walks toward the water before his bottom half disappears into what I can imagine feels like an ice bath. It doesn't seem to bother him; he ducks under before swimming off into the lake.

I watch him but the image of his naked arse seems to be burned onto the inside of my eyelids.

Thankfully—or sadly, actually, I'm not really sure—he covers himself when he eventually emerges from the water. To be fair, it must've been so cold that I can't imagine there's much to show off right now.

He quickly dresses before asking if I'm ready to take off.

We spend the afternoon driving around and taking everything in. We stop in a cute little village bakery when we start to get hungry and indulge in gorgeous cream cakes, before getting back in the car to head toward our accommodation for the night.

"You booked a room in Gretna Green?"

"Yeah, I've always been intrigued by the place so thought it was the perfect opportunity to check it out."

To say I'm relieved would be putting it mildly when he pulls into the car park of a fancy looking hotel. "I thought we were keeping to cheap B&Bs?" I ask on our way toward the expensive room Jay had already booked.

"I told you earlier, you deserve it after last night."

"Last night wasn't good, but that doesn't mean you need to spend loads. I'd be more than happy with a bog standard B&B."

"I know you would, but I wanted to treat you."

I can't help but swoon a little at his words. I know I made a bit of a fuss about that place last night, but it wasn't because I expected to be staying in swanky places, just clean ones with a couple more pieces of furniture, and without the epic creep we had to share the building with.

"Thank you," I say sincerely when we come to a stop outside our door. I reach up on my tiptoes and give him a quick kiss.

"I know how you could thank me properly." My eyes widen and my mouth drops. "I'm joking," he quickly adds on. "No need to look so worried."

Was I worried? I wonder as I follow him into the room. No, I'm pretty sure the tingles I felt when he said it were more to do with excitement.

"Oh my God, look at that bath." Sat in the middle of the bathroom is a huge free-standing tub just calling out to be used.

"Knock yourself out. We don't have dinner reservations until nine."

I don't need any more convincing than that. I get the water the right temperature before searching for the complimentary bubble bath. When I find it I let out a sigh of relief that it's not the standard lavender scent I hate. Instead, it's a fresh mandarin and grapefruit scent that makes my mouth water.

I check to ensure I'm covered in bubbles before telling Jay he can come in when he knocks. He opens the door and peeks through before walking in with a glass of bubbles.

"Champagne and a bath full of bubbles. What could be better?"

"Well, technically it's prosecco, but close enough. And you forgot to mention the hot man."

"Must have been an oversight. Thank you," I say, reaching an arm out to take the glass. "What's wrong?" He's got an odd look on his face.

"I'm disappointed."

"Why?"

"I was at least hoping to see some boob."

"Oh, get out," I say, flicking bubbles at him.

"What? It's not like I haven't already seen them." That may be true but it doesn't stop me from blushing at the thought of exposing myself to him.

"Get out."

"Or licked them," he mutters as he steps back. His eyes darken as they drop from mine down to where my boobs are hiding behind the bubbles. I raise an eyebrow at him. "Okay, okay, I'm going," he says with a pout but before he turns, he scoops up the bubbles covering me and puts them on my head. I manage to hold my smile until he shuts the door.

"FUCK ME, YOU LOOK GOOD," Jay announces when I emerge from the bathroom a long time later. Luckily, I packed a dress just in case. It's a classic black prom dress, paired with a thin red belt and red peep-toe court shoes. My only jewellery is a heavy silver bracelet consisting of a series of solid squares; it's one of my favourites but can only be worn with something simple because of its size. My make-up is done—nothing exciting, just a bit of mascara, blusher and gloss. The only thing left to do is my hair.

"Thank you." I run my eyes over him as he does the same to me.

He's wearing a dark pair of jeans and a plain white shirt. He looks incredibly sexy, resting back against the headboard where he's been watching TV.

I sit myself down at the dressing table and pull the hotel hairdryer from the drawer. I feel his eyes on me the entire time; they burn into my skin and ensure the tingles he started when he came into the bathroom earlier continue to simmer just under the surface.

"Keep it down," he instructs when I go to pull my hair back. I mostly get on fine with my hair; it's easy and low-maintenance because it's always straight, but when I get dressed up I always feel like it's lacking because I can't do anything fancy with it.

"Why?"

"Because you look sexy." His eyes hold mine in the mirror and the heat in them ensures I do as he says. "Come on, it's time to go."

The short journey in the lift is torturous with his scent filling my nose while the heat of his hand burns into my lower back. I feel his fingers twitching where I can only assume he's as desperate to move it as I am. The memory of how it felt when he had his hands on me last night is right at the forefront of my mind.

I let out a breath when the doors open and I swear I hear him do the same. He leads me toward the restaurant and pushes the waiter out of the way so he can be the one to pull my chair out. I try not to let his gentlemanly actions affect me but it's no hope, I swoon hard. When I look up into his eyes to thank him, I feel myself fall for him even more than I already have. That's the moment I know I'm never going to be able to get him out from under my skin.

He orders us wine. I'm already buzzing from the two glasses of prosecco I had in our room but I don't argue; it's not every day that I get this kind of treatment so I'm going to enjoy it while I can.

By the time we've eaten and Jay suggests we sit in the bar, I can already feel the room spinning a little, so when he places a cocktail down on the coffee table in front of me, I know I'm making a huge mistake by drinking it, but I'm flying too high to care.

Some amount of time later, I feel Jay wrap his arm around my waist and attempt to get me to the lift. My legs are like jelly and I swear I'm going to hit the floor any second. I wrap my arms around him to stop me from falling.

"I could get used to this," he whispers in my ear as we wait for the lift.

"Hmmm, I think you'd better, soldier boy, because I'm not letting you go."

"And I definitely like the sound of that." His words are at odds with his previous warning about this being a two-week only thing but I'm too drunk to read too much into it.

By the time the doors open, I'm stood in front of Jay, looking up into his gorgeous grey eyes. I feel him push me back by my hips and my legs must do as they're told because a few seconds later, I feel the handrail in the lift press into my back.

Jay doesn't move until the doors shut. Then, he presses himself against me and takes my lips in a hot and dirty kiss. My hands grasp at his shirt as my leg lifts around his waist as I try to get closer to him.

I feel the vibration of his moan all the way to my clit. Fucking hell, this man is like a drug; I don't think I've ever craved something so much in my entire life.

I feel myself being lifted from the floor, and the next thing I know, I'm in his arms as we head down the corridor toward our room.

He sits me on the bed before I feel my shoes being slipped off. Soft kisses run up the inside of my leg before I feel him almost at my knickers. I suck in a breath as I prepare for what's about to happen but he pulls back, and seconds later I feel him undoing my belt and unzipping my dress. Then my bra's gone, and I feel the burning heat of his palms against my breasts. My head falls back as I focus on the sensation of him squeezing and pinching.

I fall back onto the bed when he encourages me to do so. My alcohol-filled brain doesn't let me worry about being totally bare for him when I feel my underwear slide down my thighs and over my feet. The mattress dips as he crawls on top of me, and when I look down I see he's gloriously naked, only I don't get a chance to see everything because he folds himself over me and kisses me senseless. I feel him at my entrance and my muscles clench as they prepare for what it might feel like having him push his way inside me. I watch as he sits back, and he's just about to thrust forward when my eyes spring open.

I STARE AHEAD. The room's light and the side of the bed next to me is empty. What the fuck?

Then I hear something. When I look toward the noise, I find Jay once again doing sit-ups. My heart continues to pound at the same speed as my clit as the images that were just so vivid in my mind continue to play out as I watch him. His muscles stretch and pull with each movement and his damp skin glistens in the morning sunlight.

I'm almost back on level ground by the time he stops and stands. "Sorry, did I wake you?" he asks when he sees I'm watching.

The second his eyes land on me, I feel my face fill with heat. Fuck.

"What?" he asks, a small smirk playing on his lips.

"Nothing."

"Skittles, you're flushed as red as a fucking tomato and your eyes are wide as fuck. That's not nothing."

"I... uh... just woke up all of a sudden and I didn't know where I was," I lie.

His cheeky smile finally breaks free. "Right." I watch as he climbs onto the bed. He's only in his boxers so I get a nice close-up of his chest and stomach. "How about you tell me the real reason?" he says as he runs his fingers over my cheek and down my neck to my collarbone.

"I was dreaming," I whisper.

"Do tell." He's got a wicked glint in his eye.

"I can't really remember it now."

"Liar."

I shift onto my side and realise I'm dressed in his shirt, and I'm wearing knickers. "Did you put me to bed last night?" I ask, because other than the dream I have no recollection of leaving the bar, and I'm thinking it was just that—a dream.

"You don't remember?"

My cheeks flush once again as I shake my head.

"That's a real shame, Skittles, a real shame."

"What happened?"

"I couldn't possibly tell."

"Wanker," I mutter.

He has a little laugh to himself but he doesn't say any more.

It was just a dream, I'm sure of it. He told me he wouldn't do anything until I begged for it so I'm pretty sure he wouldn't take advantage when I'm drunk. Right?

This question rolls around my head the whole time I'm getting ready and throughout breakfast. I'm fairly sure it was all a dream. I'm desperate to ask him more, but at the same time I'm scared he'll make me admit what I think may or may not have happened—or worse, the details of my dream.

When we get to the bit of Gretna Green where they do all the weddings, there's a bride and groom having their photos taken. We stop on a little grass bank and watch the happy couple posing and laughing. They look unbelievably happy about the new chapter of their lives they've just embarked on.

Nothing is said between us for the longest time as we sit and watch the world go by, so when Jay suddenly speaks up, it startles me a little.

"Wanna get married?"

"What?" I ask, thinking I just heard him wrong.

"Let's get married."

"It's weird, because I thought you just asked me to marry you... twice," I say with a laugh.

"I guess I did. What do you say?"

"I say you're crazy. We can't just get married."

"Why not? We're here and this is where all kinds of crazy shit goes down, marriage-wise."

"You can't just turn up here nowadays, say 'I do', and be on your way. You still need to register and stuff beforehand."

"Well, that wasn't a no," he comments with a laugh.

"I'm not going to respond to your craziness with an answer, Jay. It's totally insane."

"But the wedding night," he pouts.

"Seriously, you're nuts."

His focus is still on the couple and photographer in front of us but he has this wistful look on his face that I haven't seen since we started this road trip. The sudden moment of seriousness reminds me of everything I'm running away from and the plans I need to make about my future. It's unrealistic to think I'll finish uni next year and work with mum in her shop, because it's going to be gone unless she makes some drastic changes. I need a plan for me, not her. If I'm going to focus on my jewellery then I need to find more stockists, look at going to trade shows, get my name out there, a million and one things really.

"Ready to make a move?" Jay eventually asks, distracting me from thoughts of my future.

"Yes."

We grab a couple of takeout coffees from a café before getting back in Peggy and heading farther up north.

***

"THERE'S a classic car show this weekend, look," Jay says excitedly as we drive toward Inverness. "Can we go?" I can't help but laugh because he sounds like an excited little child.

"Sure."

"We can stay here somewhere tonight, and then go tomorrow."

His excitement is infectious, and I find myself looking forward to a day staring at old cars—not because I want to, but because more than anything I want him to be happy, and right now he's buzzing.

We spend all afternoon driving around the country roads, taking in the scenery before heading into town to find somewhere to stay for the night.

"What about there?" I say, pointing to a vacancy sign on the side of the road.

We continue up the long driveway to reveal a quaint bungalow. It definitely doesn't have the grandeur of the hotel last night, but equally, it looks loads better than the dilapidated farmhouse from the night before. We may have found a happy medium, even if it does look more like someone's home than a B&B.

We stand hand in hand waiting for someone to answer the door, and eventually an elderly lady pulls it open. She shouts something behind her but fuck knows what she says because her Scottish accent is so strong she may as well be speaking another language. I glance over at Jay, whose eyebrows are raised slightly, showing he has no clue either.

"Good evening, come in," she says to us. Thankfully, it's slower, and easier to understand.

She ushers us into their living room where her husband is sat watching TV.

"Good evening. I'm William, and this is my wife Mary. Are you looking for a room?"

"Yes, we saw your vacancy sign. I'm Jay and this is Erin."

I stand awkwardly as Mary looks us both up and down. She gives her husband a nod before he asks what kind of room we want.

"Double would be great," Jay answers without missing a beat.

"I presume you're married," Mary says, looking down at my left hand.

"Uh... no." Thankfully Jay doesn't elaborate and tell this obviously traditional couple that we've only known each other a few days.

"You're welcome to stay but only married couples will share a room under my roof," Mary says when William fails to do his job by the look of the stare he receives.

Jay looks over at me. The expression on his face makes me smile, because I can tell he's begging for me to apologise and be on our way so we can find a double bed. Unfortunately for him, I do the opposite. I'm not sure if it's for my own amusement or torture, but I tell Mary it won't be an issue and that we'll have a single room each. As the words leave my mouth, Jay's chin drops and his eyes narrow at me. I just smile at him.

"The rooms are next door to each other but there will be no sneaking into each other's in the middle of the night."

"Of course not," I say politely, earning me another death stare from Jay.

We stand by our doors as we watch Mary retreat down the hallway after offering us dinner.

"What the hell, Erin?"

"What?" I ask innocently. "I didn't want to carry on looking for us not to find anything, or worse, another shithole. This will be fine and it's only for one night. I'm sure you can cope."

"You're gonna pay for this."

"Maybe you should have told me what happened last night."

"Oh, so this is revenge, is it?"

"Maybe," I say as I unlock the door and walk into my room. I put a little extra swing to my hips, leaving him muttering about getting me back for this.

When the door shuts behind me and I'm alone in my room, I can't help but feel like I've made a mistake. I suddenly feel lonely and I don't like knowing he's on the other side of the wall. I sit down on my bed and let out a sigh.

I have a quick shower before changing and knocking on Jay's door.

When he opens it, he's only in his boxer briefs, giving me a great show of what I'm missing while alone in my room next door.

"I know what you're doing, and it's not working."

"Really?" he asks as he bends over to put his jeans on.

I want to look away and not be affected by the show he's putting on but it's not working. Damn him.

By the time we get to the dining room, Mary and William are sat waiting for us with a steaming cottage pie in the middle of the table.

"Sorry, he wasn't ready," I announce when we walk in.

We spend the next few hours chatting away. We learn all about Mary and William's five children, as well as their nineteen grandchildren. Yes, they may be a little old-fashioned, but they stay true to what they believe in and they're such a lovely couple, I can't help but warm to them.

"I GUESS THIS IS GOODNIGHT, THEN," Jay says when we stop by our doors.

"I guess it is. Sleep well." I go to push open my door but my wrist gets grabbed and in seconds, I find myself up against Jay's chest.

"I don't think so," he mutters before slamming his mouth down on mine.

I worry for all of about two seconds that we're going to be caught, but as soon as I feel his tongue against mine, all thoughts vanish as I lose myself in his kiss.

When he pulls back, we're both panting with need and the images I still vividly remember from my dream last night are at the forefront of my mind. I desperately want to follow him into his room and let him get his hands on me, but I know we can't, so instead, I bid him goodnight and bolt to the safety of my room before I do something Mary and William wouldn't approve of.

I change into Jay's shirt, because I can't imagine wearing anything else to bed now, and toss and turn as I imagine what we could be doing. I should be using the time to do some work but all I can picture is him looking down at me.

I eventually fall asleep at some ungodly hour, but it's fitful and full of lustful dreams I shouldn't be having in this religious couple's home.

AFTER BEING TREATED to a home-cooked English breakfast, and somehow agreeing that we'll spend tonight with them, we head off to find the car show. Jay's like a kid on Christmas morning as we queue to park in a muddy field. I don't share his enthusiasm as it's cold and drizzly out. The last thing I want to be doing is walking around in the rain looking at cars. I think my lack of sleep—and lack of Jay—has made me a little moody.

I follow him around for just over an hour before he suggests I get a coffee and sit in the café to warm up while he continues to ohh and ahh. I'd love to share his excitement but they're all just cars to me.

I pull my sketchbook out and sit there coming up with ideas as I look out at the cars in front of the marquee.

I get lost in my car-inspired designs and jump a mile when Jay places his hand down on my shoulder hours later. "Sorry," he says, sitting down next to me and grabbing one of the fresh coffees I notice he's placed on the table. "Let's have a look."

I hand over my sketches and he flicks through the pages. "These are incredible. There are loads of female car fanatics who'd love something like this."

"You think so?" I ask sceptically.

"I know so. I know it's none of my business but I think you need to let your mum deal with her business, and you need to focus on this. You've got a talent you could really make something of."

I let out a breath, because the reminder of what I've left behind sits heavy on my shoulders. I've had a couple of texts from Mum telling me she's had more final demands come through. I've been too scared to call her back and find out how things are really going. It's much easier living in denial as I flit around the country with Jay, but with every day that passes, I get more and more aware that I'm closer to going back and dealing with it all once again. Unfortunately, these two weeks will only last so long before I fall back to reality with a bang.

"WHAT ARE you two all dressed up for?" I ask when we arrived back at the B&B later that evening to find Mary and William all ready for a night out.

"Susan's nephew runs a dance class at the village hall on a Friday night. Highlight of our week," Mary says happily. "Oh, you two should come. We've been working on a rhumba; I think you would enjoy it," she adds with a wink.

"Oh, I don't know," I say, thinking Jay's going to tell them where to go, because I can't imagine him wanting to go ballroom dancing.

I almost get whiplash when I turn to look at him so fast as he says, "Sure, sounds like fun."

"Fantastic. We need to leave in ten minutes, so go and get changed quickly."

"What the hell?" I ask Jay once we're out of earshot.

"What? I thought it might be fun, seeing as we'll be sleeping apart again tonight. I'll get to have my hands all over you."

A shiver runs through me at the thought. Okay, so credit where credit's due, he does have a point.

"Doesn't seem such a bad idea now does it?"

"I guess not," I say on a sigh, trying to appear less excited about it than I really am. It's been years since I danced properly, but the prospect of doing it with Jay definitely piques my interest.

I quickly change into my black dress and red shoes. Mary and William are looking dapper, ready for their night on the tiles, so it was my only option. When I meet back up with Jay in the hallway, I find him in the same outfit as that night as well.

He comes to a stop in front of me and runs his eyes from the top of my head all the way to my toes. He gives me tingles without even touching me.

"You look hot as fuck in this dress," he whispers in my ear when he steps up to me. "Do you know what's sexier, though?"

I shake my head, knowing he's about to tell me anyway.

"Taking it off you."

My mouth goes dry, and I have the sudden urge to drag him into my room and demand he does just that when I hear a voice asking if we're ready because we're going to be late.

"Fuck," Jay mutters before I watch him rearrange himself in his jeans. He must feel my stare because he looks up at me. "What? I can't help it. Have you seen yourself?"

I shake my head at him because I don't want him to know how happy it makes me to know I affect him so much.

The village hall is exactly like I was expecting. Every surface is covered in pine panelling, and the chairs and tables around the edges of the room look like they should have been replaced about thirty years ago. At the far end of the room, there's a guy who stands out amongst the elderly couples, not only because of his age but because he's wearing skin-tight black trousers and a shirt undone almost to his belly button. I guess he's the instructor.

"Are we ready to go? Do you all remember the moves?"

"Wait!" Mary shouts. "We've brought some friends."

The guy's eyes light up when he sees us. I can only presume it's because we're close to his age.

"The more the merrier. We'll soon get them caught up."

He starts the music and the sounds of Aerosmith's 'Don't Want To Miss A Thing' fills the hall, and all of a sudden each couple pairs off and starts a well-choreographed rhumba routine. I had plenty of dance lessons as a kid so I know what a rhumba looks like, but I was not expecting these elderly churchgoing couples to move quite like this. This instructor must be having a whale of a time getting couples of this age moving their hips quite like that.

"Holy shit," Jay mutters next to me.

"It's quite a thing, huh? You're never too old for a little bit of that," the instructor says, wiggling his eyebrows and nudging Jay's arm. "How about we get you some tonight?"

"U-uh..." Jay stutters as the instructor grabs both our hands and pulls us on to the makeshift dance floor.

"I'm David, by the way," he says. He teaches us the first few moves as the couples continue with their dance. I'm amazed when I find that Jay's a natural dancer and we move together flawlessly.

"How much Viagra do you think is in this room tonight?" Jay whispers in my ear when David walks off to see how the others are doing.

"Oh God, don't," I say with a laugh as I look to the side to see the couple closest to us grinding away against each other.

"It's a good job they're all past it. Otherwise, there could be more than ten kids conceived tonight."

"Oh, please stop." The image that brings into my head is too much. "Anyway, where'd you learn to dance?" I ask, because this clearly isn't his first time.

"Promise you won't laugh."

"Of course."

"A year or so ago, my sergeant was getting married. He'd been having lessons with his now wife but when we got deployed a few months before the wedding, he needed a partner."

"Oh my God," I mutter quietly, trying not to smile. "You took her place while he practised?" I really want to laugh at the image of two strapping army men ballroom dancing around whatever war-torn country they were in, but what he did was too cute.

"That was so nice of you."

"You never say no to a favour when the next day that man could be the one to save your life," he says, but I can see he instantly regrets bringing his reality into this.

"Well, you're very good."

"What about you?"

"I had dance lessons until I was about fourteen."

"That's it, perfect hip action," David says as he stares at Jay's arse a little too intently. Jay narrows his eyes at him and I try to hold in my smile.

The dance class goes on for two hours. I never would've thought some of those old couples would've lasted that long, but they all look more awake than I feel.

"Right, one last time, all the way through from the top," David announces after everyone's had a quick drink.

Jay pulls me flush against him and places one hand on my waist and the other in my hand. He lowers his head so our noses are touching and he looks deep into my eyes as we wait for the music to start. We're not saying any words, but I feel like we're having a conversation, communicating just through our eyes how much we've come to mean to one another after only a few short days.

I don't hear the music start, I'm too lost to him, but when he starts moving I quickly catch up.

"Don't step away from me," Jay warns when the song comes to an end and the other couples separate.

"Why? We've finished."

"Unless you want David and everyone else in the room to know as well as we do how much I want you right now, you'll stay here." To nail his point home, he flexes his hips and pushes his erection into my stomach.

"We can't stay like this all night."

Once all the couples have walked past us, Jay pushes me in front of him and we head over to join them, me acting as his human shield.

"I can't believe we've got to sleep in separate rooms tonight," he whispers in my ear. "You've no idea how badly I want you right now. The thought of making you come again is fucking painful." His words don't help the throb that's going on between my thighs, nor his hard-on that's now pressing into my back.

Jay fidgets the whole journey to the B&B in the back seat of Mary and William's car. I feel for him because he must be uncomfortable, but I'm equally amused by the situation.

"Would you two like a nightcap before turning in?" William asks once we're all inside.

"That's very kind of you, but I'm exhausted," I respond, thinking Jay won't be up for it, but to my surprise, as I say no, he says yes.

I watch as William pours Jay a generous glass of whisky, but I decline when he offers it to me. Instead, I say goodnight to them all and head to my room. Jay watches me leave and I know he's desperate to follow me, but it's best we're separated right now.

CHAPTER SIX

I stand under the spray of the shower for the longest time as I think about Jay and our time together. I still can't quite figure out why it all feels so natural. It's like I've known him my entire life. Everything is so easy and relaxed when we're together, and I can't help thinking I'm starting to enjoy it a little too much.

I think again about how fast the last few days have gone, and try not to focus on how quickly the rest of our time together is going to pass, because that leads me to the question of what next? What comes after our little road trip? Does he go back to army life, wherever that may be, and do I go back to trying to save an inevitably doomed business just because it's Mum's and I can't bear to see her lose her dream?

I'm in a bit of a sombre mood when I get out and start getting ready for bed. I pull the other cami and short set I brought with me from the bottom of my case, but at the last minute, I shove it back in favour of Jay's shirt. The desire to be encased in his smell all night again is too much to deny. I give my hair a blast with the dryer before jumping into bed. I'm exhausted after everything, and surprisingly, I find myself dozing off to sleep much quicker than most nights.

When I wake up, it's pitch black in my room. I expect there to be a noise as I feel like something woke me, but as I lie there, everything's silent. I'm just falling back to sleep when I hear something, and I instantly know exactly what—or should I say who— it is. I've no idea how I know, but my body seems to be aware whenever he's close. Seconds later, I feel the bed dip and his lips brush mine. It's gentle at first. I guess he has no idea if I'm awake, but as soon as I respond to him, he turns it into something else entirely. It's like he's trying to consume me, and as my hunger for him reignites, my actions match his need.

I free my arms from the duvet and run my nails down his back as he continues to kiss me. He doesn't part our lips even as he pulls the duvet away from my body so he can begin running his hands over my skin.

Eventually, he breaks our kiss, but his lips stay connected to me. He kisses and sucks a trail down my neck and across both sides of my collarbone. His hands come up to the top of his shirt and as his kisses descend, I feel him undo each button. Once my breasts are free, he runs his tongue over each one before flicking my nipples and sucking them into his mouth. He starts off gentle but it's not long before he's sucking harder and harder, making my back arch off the bed with the need for more. I hear myself moan and whimper as he continues to torture my body with just his mouth. Tension builds in my lower belly just like before, only he hasn't touched me down there, but fuck if I don't need him to.

It seems like forever but eventually I feel him start to move down my ribs before kissing around my belly button. My muscles clench as I think about where he might be going. I'm panting and squirming with need, and the image I'm conjuring up in my head of him between my legs only makes it worse.

I hold my breath when I feel his fingers wrap around the fabric at my hips before they slowly descend, and just like in the dream that's still haunting me, he starts kissing up the inside of my legs. Tingles shoot around my body every time he makes contact, and they only get stronger the higher up he gets. I should be embarrassed; he's inches away from my most intimate part and I don't know if it's the effect he has on me, or the fact I know he can't see anything, but I don't care. If anything, I want him closer. I want to know what it feels like to have his mouth on me.

I don't have to wonder for long, because seconds later, I feel the heat of his mouth against me before the sensation of his tongue licking me makes me melt into the bed.

Oh fuck, that's good.

I grab onto the sheet below me as he continues. I whimper, moan and writhe beneath him so much he has to put his arm across my hips to keep me still.

My hands let go of the sheet in favour of grabbing his head; unfortunately, his shaved hair is too short for me to thread my fingers through, although I've no idea if I'd want to pull him closer or push him away.

He changes his angle slightly and sucks hard on my clit as I feel his finger begin circling my entrance.

Oh shit, oh shit. A small voice in my head tells me I need to be quiet, to at least try to be respectful of where we are, and as my orgasm crashes into me, I have to fight to not let go and scream out in pleasure.

Jay continues sucking until my body stops pulsing and I somewhat come back to myself.

Holy shit, that was incredible.

I expect him to do something else, or at the very least climb back up to kiss me, so I'm shocked when I just about see him wipe his mouth with the back of his hand before he gets up and walks out, almost as silently as he came in.

What the fuck?

I lay totally still and bare for a long time after he's disappeared. I know for a fact that wasn't a dream, but why did he just leave like that? There could've been more, I could have…

I eventually move when my previously hot and sweaty body starts to chill. I get myself back in the shower before powering up my laptop and getting some work done. I know my body and I know I'm not going to be sleeping now, so I may as well do something useful.

I lose track of time and end up late for breakfast; I'm surprised Jay didn't knock to make sure I was up. I'm even more surprised when, after getting no response when I knocked for him, I find only Mary and William sat in the dining room.

"Good morning. Did you sleep well?"

Flashbacks play out in my mind and I have to clench my thighs together. "Yes, thank you," I reply politely, even though it's far from the truth. "Have you seen Jay?"

"No, not yet, dear. Is there a problem?"

I shake my head and sit down as Mary pours me a coffee.

I manage a little bit of the breakfast but I've got this feeling in my gut that something's very wrong, so eating is the last thing on my mind. After a while, I excuse myself and head back to my room. I knock on Jay's door. I know it's stupid because we'd have seen him come in, but I feel the need to try.

After packing all my stuff, I sit myself down on the edge of my bed and try not to worry. I'm sure he's just gone for a drive and lost track of time or something.

We had planned to move on today, but as the time starts to get closer to lunch, I decide that I'll probably be sleeping in here again tonight and it stops me packing my last few bits. I look down at my phone and remember his warning from when we first met, *this is only a two-week thing, no promise of a future or swapping phone numbers.* My heart drops knowing that our time together is slowly coming to an end.

I'm just powering up my laptop in the hope of finding a way to get home when I hear a car engine outside. I lean across the bed and pull the net curtain back to reveal what I hoped I would see. Jay's

Peugeot has pulled up in the space we've taken over the past few days. He's in the driver's seat but the scene isn't what I was expecting because he's leant forward with his forehead resting on the steering wheel. I may not know that much about him, but the last few days have given me the impression that what I'm seeing isn't normal, that he doesn't get down very often.

After a few more seconds, I allow the curtain to fall back into place so Jay can have his moment in peace, whatever it is.

Footsteps echo down the empty hallway and the second I hear his door open, I do the same. He must hear me but he doesn't react. I just about manage to get my foot in his door before it slams in my face.

"Jay?"

He walks over to the window but doesn't turn around or acknowledge me in any way.

"Jay, what—" I don't get to finish my question because he turns and looks over his shoulder. His eyes are dark and tired and there's a deep line between his eyebrows. He looks stressed. "What's wrong?" I finally ask when I'm able to find my words.

Jay continues staring at me as if he wants to say something important, but no words leave his mouth.

"It's—" he pauses and takes a breath, but in the end he just shakes his head and says, "nothing."

"You can tell me. Maybe I can help."

"No," he snaps harshly, but one look at my shocked face has him apologising for his abruptness almost instantly. "It's not something you can help with, Skittles."

"Okay. I could listen at least, be a sympathetic ear," I offer.

"It's fine. Honestly," he adds when he sees I'm not falling for his blatant lie. "Anyway, what are we doing today?"

I sit on Jay's bed whilst he gets himself ready. It didn't escape my notice that he was wearing the same clothes as last night. When we emerge a while later, we bump into Mary in the hallway, who insists on making Jay something to eat as he missed breakfast. I can see that he wants to get away but the lure of her home-cooked food is too much.

"You can drive," Jay says, handing me the keys to his baby as we walk toward where she's parked.

"Uh…"

"You can drive, right?"

"No."

"No," he repeats, like it's the craziest thing he's ever heard. "How?"

"It's not that I don't want to, I've just never got around to it. Public transport's pretty good in Bristol and there's no parking at uni." The way Jay's face screws up as I say the words *public transport* makes me laugh.

"How about some driving lessons?"

"Here? Are you serious?"

"Why not? Once we get out of town, the roads will be practically empty. It's perfect."

"But they're all windy," I say in a panic. I don't want to be responsible for wrecking his beloved Peggy.

"You'll be fine, trust me."

I stare at him for a few seconds as I wait for him to tell me he's joking, but his eyes don't waver, so eventually I grab the keys he's still holding out and unlock the car.

My nerves tremble once I'm sat in the driver's seat. My palms are sweating and my feet are shaking.

"I'm not sure this is a good idea," I admit, looking over at a tired Jay who's getting comfortable in the passenger seat.

"You'll be fine."

He talks me through the basics, most of which I already know. I may not have had any lessons but I'm not a total idiot.

"Okay, gently ease off the clutch as you press down on the accelerator."

I do as I'm told and in seconds, the car begins to move. My heart bangs in my chest as we slowly start to back out of the space.

Once we get on to the country roads, I relax a little, but only slightly because although there's less chance of me hitting another car, there's a pretty high chance we could end up rolling down a cliff if I were to come off the road.

"See, I told you you'd be fine. You're a natural," Jay says with a beaming smile.

His praise makes my confidence grow and I press the accelerator a little harder. He may be egging me on but it hasn't meant I've missed his whole body tense up a time of two at his lack of control.

I'm buzzing by the time I pull into an almost empty car park in Inverness town centre.

"Did you enjoy that?" Jay asks with a smile on his face. I'm relieved to see he's lost the sad, stressed look from an hour or so ago.

"Yeah, I really did. Thank you."

"You're welcome."

After getting a coffee, we wander off through town, looking in shop windows.

"Have you been here before?" I ask, when I get the feeling Jay knows where he's going.

"No." He's got a twinkle in his eye that makes me question his answer but I leave it there.

Once we're happy we've soaked up enough of the town centre, we hop back in the car—Jay driving once again—and we head out to the couple of spots Mary and William suggested we visit.

We arrive at Brodie Castle just as the sun's beginning to descend for the day, and it's beautiful. After walking around the grounds, I drag Jay inside. He looks bored as hell, but I love all the old furniture and patterns. As we walk, I sneak a few pictures for inspiration for some vintage-style jewellery.

We have the most amazing day together. His mood when he returned this morning has vanished and he's been back to the Jay I've known the last few days.

"Aren't we heading back for dinner?"

"Nope. I told Mary I was taking you out tonight."

I look down at my ratty jeans and scuffed boots. "I'm not dressed for dinner. I look a mess."

Jay turns to look at me briefly, his eyes run over my face. "You look perfect," he whispers before turning his focus back to the road.

The compliment warms my body and ignites something inside me only Jay's been able to. I squirm in my seat as memories of my midnight visitor assault me.

"I'm sorry about last night," Jay says so quietly I almost think I misheard him. "I shouldn't have pounced on you like that."

"It was fine."

His eyes come back to me. "It was fine?"

I can't help but laugh at the look on his face. "Yep."

Turning away from him to look at the countryside beside me, I smile to myself. It was a lot more than fine.

"What's this place? It looks fancy." I say as we stand in the entrance to what I thought at first was a church is actually a restaurant.

"The Mustard Seed," Jay says, reading the sign in front of us. "It's meant to be incredible."

"I love this building, it's stunning. I'd love to live in a converted church or something one day. I love all the history."

Jay smiles at me, although he looks to be miles away; it's a reminder of this morning and whatever it was to cause such a serious reaction from him. I'm just about to question him when we're shown to our seats.

The food's incredible but it's slightly overshadowed by Jay's mood. I can tell he's trying to push through whatever it is that's bothering him. I wish he'd talk to me, even if it's so I can be a listening ear, but I can tell it's not going to happen. If I've learnt anything about Jayden Baxter over the past week, it's that he's stubborn and always gets what he wants.

THE KISS he gives me before we part into our separate rooms causes even my toes to tingle. I desperately want to drag him inside with me and try to take his mind off his worries, but I do what I should and wish him goodnight before shutting my door behind me.

I don't get a midnight visitor. I don't hear anything from him at all, so when I wake up the next morning, the first thing I do is pull back the net curtain to make sure he's still here. I let out a huge breath when I see Peggy sat where he parked her last night. It's not lost on me how gutted I would've been if he'd gone in the middle of the night. I both love and hate the way he seems to have crawled inside me, but at the same time, our impending separation is never far from my mind. I can wish this trip's going to last forever as much as I want, but I know that's impossible. Real life is just a few days away now, waiting to throw God only knows what at me.

I reluctantly pull my phone out from under my pillow and open up the messages from Mum I ignored last night. I reply with similar words of encouragement I usually say when she tells me how quiet the shop is, but the words are all fake, my enthusiasm that things are going to turn around holding no weight. The only way to save her beloved shop is to make some major changes I don't think she's ever going to agree to.

I drop my phone onto my chest and think about what we should be doing—looking for different premises, streamlining our products, online shopping and marketing.

When I pick my phone back up, I notice I have another message. I click on the icon and Frankie's name appears. I open it and then regret it instantly. It's a photo of her and Dean, obviously naked in bed, and the caption says 'me and my sexy soldier'. As I stare at Dean's face, I swear I see a little glint in his eye. Cheeky little shit. Frankie's going to skin him alive when she finds out.

I fire back a message telling her how happy I am that she's enjoying herself before getting up and showered. We'd agreed we'd move on today and I'm excited about our next destination—

Edinburgh. It looks like the most stunning city and I can't wait to discover it with Jay.

After a quick breakfast we say our goodbyes to Mary and William and head off, hoping to get into the city before lunchtime. As it's Sunday, the roads are fairly quiet and the drive's straightforward.

As the scenery starts to change from countryside to city, butterflies start up in my belly. This is somewhere I've wanted to visit for a long time and I'm more than ready for the adventure to start.

We park at one of the hotels I found on the drive here and secure a room for the night, although we can't check-in until later.

"What do you want to do?" Jay asks as we walk out of reception. The hotel's in a central location to almost everything, which is why I chose it, and I know exactly what I want to do.

"Just walk. I want to see everything, I want to feel the city, soak up the vibe."

Jay's eyes sparkle at my response. I know he's trying to contain a laugh at my over-excitement about being here. "You're so cute, Skittles," he comments before kissing the end of my nose. The smile he gives me as he pulls away lights up his face. Thankfully, when I met him for breakfast this morning, he was more like his old self again; there was no sign of yesterday's stress.

"How long can we stay here?" I ask. I hate to bring up anything that involves our ever-ticking clock, but I need to know how much I can squeeze in.

I watch his gorgeous face as he has the same realisation. We're into our second week and our time is running out. Fast.

"Two days," he answers after a few seconds. "I'd love to give you longer but we really need to start heading south."

"It's fine. I understand." I look back out over the stunning city below so he can't see what I really think about us heading back. My eyes fill with tears threatening to break free. I'm not ready for this to be the end for us yet; I feel like we're meant to have so much more time together. The word *forever* floats around in my head but I bat it away because thoughts like that aren't going to help me. This was always going to be a two-week thing, I knew that from the beginning, but it's a shame my heart didn't get the message, because it seems to be getting more and more attached to Jay as our time together continues, and I know that it's going to shatter into a million pieces when he leaves.

I push my depressing thoughts away and try to focus on the here and now. We're stood in the incredible Edinburgh Castle, looking down over the city below as the sun sets and the lights of the city begin to bring it to life.

I let out a sigh and soak it all in. I want to remember how this moment feels because I know what I have ahead of me isn't going to be easy. Jay must sense my mood because he stands a little closer and wraps his arm around my shoulder. He doesn't say anything but I know he's thinking the same.

CHAPTER SEVEN

"Skittles, wake up. We need to get going," Jay whispers.

I stretch out my aching legs and groan at the prospect of getting out of this incredibly comfortable bed. "Another hour?"

"You've already had that."

I groan again.

"Come on, you can sleep in the car."

I begrudgingly swing my legs out and pull my aching body to a sitting position. I have a quick, hot shower to try to freshen myself up but I'm still sleep-fogged, which is seriously unlike me. There's something about having Jay sleeping next to me that seems to solve my sleeping issues. I'm not looking forward to my long sleepless nights returning when he's gone.

The last forty-eight hours were by far the best of my life. Exploring a city as amazing as Edinburgh with Jay was a thing dreams are made of. I've wanted to see the city for years and I'm so glad I never made the effort before, because this has been perfect;

even with my now exhausted body after walking God knows how many miles. Jay doesn't seem to be affected one bit, but then I guess he's trained for a little more than just walking around a hilly city; his toned body certainly points that way. He looks as limber as ever while I hobble my way out to the car to start our long journey back down south. He hasn't told me where we're going next, and I'm more than happy for it to be a surprise.

I think I make it about an hour into the journey before I'm asleep again. I've never been able to sleep when travelling before and I put my new ability down to Jay's presence.

I wake up and fall back to sleep more times than I can count; songs on the radio blur into the next one and the view hardly changes as we fly down the motorway. The only constant is Jay sat next to me, silently driving. He feels my stare every time I glance over and immediately looks back at me. It makes me sad because although he smiles, I can see the dark clouds he's been trying to keep hidden resurfacing. He's had a couple of phone calls over the last two days that he's excused himself to answer, and when I've asked about them, he's tried to play it off like it's nothing, but I can tell it's not. I asked if it's his mum but he said as far as he knows she's fine, but the only way to tell for sure is to turn up because she doesn't answer the phone unless it's her dealer. I'm not sure if he was exaggerating, but I'm hoping so.

"Are you sure you're okay?" I ask for the millionth time.

"Yes, stop worrying. We're nearly there."

I sit myself up and look out the window to see a *Welcome to Cambridge* sign approaching.

"Cambridge?"

"Yep. You loved Edinburgh and this place has some great history too, so thought you'd like it."

"Jay, what the hell?" I ask when he starts heading up a posh driveway I would assume is to some fancy manor house, only the hotel sign at the entrance was a bit of a giveaway.

His answer is to shrug at me. I've tried my hardest to pay my way but other than the odd meal and a couple of coffees, I haven't succeeded. It bothered me in the cheap B&Bs we stayed in, but this place looks like it's going to cost a bloody fortune.

I let out a sigh as Jay pulls the car to a stop in front of the grand building. As I take in its vastness, I feel the weight of our impending separation pressing down on my shoulders.

"Hey," he says, reaching up to grab my cheek. His hand encourages me to look at him, and when I do, I see his face drop at the sight of the tears in my eyes. "I want to treat you, okay? I want you to have something to—"

"Remember you by," I whisper, cutting him off.

He instantly gets this guilty look on his face so I know I hit the nail on the head.

"I'm sorry, Erin."

I'm not entirely sure what he's apologising for. It could be a number of things but I feel the need to do the same. "Me too."

"Come on then, I've already reserved a room."

"Jay, it's too expensive. Let's just go and find a B&B."

"No," he snaps, a little more harshly than intended if the look on his face is anything to go by. "I've got this all planned."

"Okay."

"I HAVE A ROOM BOOKED UNDER BAXTER," Jay says to the lady behind reception.

They continue chatting about the booking but I zone them out in favour of looking at the interior of this incredible hotel. The building's ancient and inside's just as gorgeous as the exterior. The decorations around reception are all deep ruby and gold. Butterflies flutter in my stomach as I take in the appearance of a couple of guests. I don't fit in here in my worn jeans, scuffed boots and slightly bobbly jumper. I pull my sleeves down over my hands as I start to feel more and more out of place.

"Come on then, our room's waiting," Jay says, stepping up to me and distracting me from my extravagant surroundings. He grabs my hand and pulls me toward the lifts. I don't realise he doesn't have hold of our cases until a very well dressed employee wheels them in behind us on a trolley. It all seems a little much for Jay's duffel and my tiny suitcase but I go with it.

Jay keeps a tight hold on my hand the entire ride to the top—yes, the top—of the hotel.

"Jay?" I question, when the bellboy backs out of the lift.

"Shhh... come on, you're going to love it."

He's not wrong, because from the second I step foot over the threshold, I'm in love. The room—or should I say suite—is incredible; totally over the top for the two of us, but still incredible.

Jay thanks the bellboy and I watch as he smoothly slips him some money before he quickly leaves us to it.

"Jay, this must be so expensive."

"Stop going on about the money. It's fine. I'm usually stuck on base and spend nothing. I want to enjoy ourselves, make tonight special."

The question about this being our last night together is on the tip of my tongue, but I don't want to know the answer so I snap my mouth shut and nod at him.

"Just so you know, I'm not one of those girls you need to spend money on to make something special."

"I know you're not, Skittles. I didn't do this because I thought it was what you wanted. I've done it because it's what you deserve."

My heart flutters and I know in that moment the last little bit I was holding on to has gone. I stare into his grey eyes and in one sense I can see my entire future, because I know he's going to stay with me forever, but at the same time I feel like I'm looking at the end.

"Don't get upset." His hands drop mine in favour of holding on to my cheeks. "I want to show you how much our time together has meant to me, how much you mean to me."

Thankfully, he doesn't give me a chance to answer because I

probably would have burst into tears. Instead, he lowers his lips to mine. We stay motionless for a long time with our lips connected. As nice as the connection is, I need more of him. Our hours are counting down and I'm desperate to spend them as close to him as possible.

He must have the same thoughts because within seconds I feel his lips move against mine before his tongue sweeps in. He kisses me deeply, passionately, until my entire body is alight. My nipples peak and every time his chest presses against them, little bolts of lightning shoot off around my body. Jay's hands slide down my neck before descending until he grabs on to my arse. He pulls my body tightly against his, allowing me to feel his hardness pressing into my stomach.

When he pulls back, we're both breathless. "Jay, I—" I start, but a phone ringing stops me.

I stand and watch as he walks over to answer it. I can't help but smile when I see him try to rearrange himself in his jeans—kissing me caused that. This man is gorgeous, strong, kind, brave, and he wants boring ol' me. Even after all the time we've spent together, I still can't quite get my head around it. He has the most exciting life, shipping off all around the world, saving people's lives, yet he's spent the last ten days or so being the kindest and sweetest guy.

"Yes, she's on her way," he says, pulling me from my thoughts.

"Where am I going?" I ask when he's put the phone down.

"I've booked a couple of surprises for you."

"Isn't this enough?"

"Nowhere near." He's in front of me again and before I realise he's moved, he's pulling me back to him for a short but amazing kiss. "I told you I wanted to show you how much our time has meant to me, how much you mean to me."

After grabbing his duffel bag, he takes my hand and together we head back into the lift—only this time, we descend to the basement.

It's obvious what he's done when the lift doors open because we're greeted by a giant spa and well-being centre sign.

We just step out when he tugs my arm and pulls me up against him. "You go and relax, I'll be in the gym next door. I'll meet you back up in the room when you're done." He presses a second room key into my empty hand before giving me a slightly inappropriate kiss and pushing me toward the spa entrance.

"Erin?" the lady behind the desk asks.

"Yes."

"Okay, if you head through that door you'll find a robe to change into and some lockers to put your clothes in. When you're ready, come back out and have a seat on one of the loungers. Kristy will come and get you."

I glance over to where she pointed and see a series of loungers in a garden room looking out over the grounds. "Okay, th-thank you," I stutter. This has taken me by surprise and I feel totally out of place, having never stepped foot in a spa before. I need Frankie here; this kind of thing is a weekly occurrence for her. As I walk through to find the robe, I realise how much I miss my best friend. We've hardly spoken since I left with Jay, and the only thing I know about what's going on with her is that she's shagging Dean, Jay's non-soldier mate. Before getting undressed, I grab my phone from the back pocket of my jeans and write her a message.

> Erin: You would not believe where I am! Jay's booked us a suite in this insane hotel in Cambridge and I'm currently stood in the spa. I've no idea what I'm doing. I think this is our last night.

I'm surprised when I immediately see three little dots on my screen.

> Frankie: Make the most of it; you deserve it. Is tonight going to be the night?

Butterflies erupt in my belly as I think about what's in store for us tonight. That kiss earlier sure pointed toward more. The memory of him coming into my room in Inverness still haunts me, and I'd kind of hate to not have the chance to experience that again, only I'd like to be able to see him this time.

> Erin: Only time will tell.

Frankie: If he's half as good my soldier, you're in for a good night.

I still don't have the heart to tell her over the phone that Dean's a liar, but I'm going to have to as soon as I get back.

> Erin: See you soon. Love you. x

Frankie: You're not going to get away that easily without telling me the details once you're back. Love you too. x

I stare down at my phone and let out a sigh. Sharing what Jay and I have done together seems weird somehow. It's been about us, and part of me wants to keep it that way. I feel like we've experienced something no one else is going to understand. I know most people are going to think I'm crazy for going with him in the first place, let alone falling for him when I don't really know much about him, but I have, and I think it's time I stopped denying how much. I try not to think about it because then it leads to me thinking about him leaving. I really want to ask about where he's based, what he's going to be doing and when his next leave is, but it makes everything too real.

I'm stood there with my phone in my hand staring at the blank screen for so long that eventually there's a knock on the door.

"Are you okay in there?"

"Shit," I whisper. "Yes sorry, I had a call. I'll be two minutes."

I quickly strip out of my clothes and stuff them and my phone into the locker before slipping into the thickest, softest robe I think I've ever worn.

When I step out, two women are chatting at the reception desk.

The door shutting behind me alerts them to my presence and they both turn to look at me. I feel my face heat. "I'm so sorry."

"Don't worry. Come this way." I follow Kristy down a short corridor, spending the whole time wondering how she gets her blonde hair quite so perfect, before heading into a softly lit room full of candles and the same relaxing music filtered throughout the spa.

"Have you had a massage before?"

I shake my head, too busy looking around the room at everything to answer.

"Okay, well in a minute I'll leave you to get comfortable. You can remove your robe and lie face down on the bed, and cover yourself with the towel here."

"Okay," I whisper.

"We'll do your facial afterward."

Kristy does as she said and disappears out of the room and I stand there feeling totally overwhelmed. She may have only given me a couple of instructions but I have no idea what I should be doing.

I follow my instincts and get onto the bed.

"Are you ready?" I hear her ask in a soft voice.

"Yes."

I'm face down and it kills me not to be able to see what Kristy's doing. I'm too damn nosy for this.

It's only a minute or two before she softly starts telling me what she's going to do, and then I feel her warm hands on my feet; I all but jump from the bed.

"Sorry, are you ticklish?"

"Yes," I say, trying to squirm out of her hands.

Thankfully, she changes her technique before swiftly moving on to my legs. It takes a while but eventually the soft music and her repetitive actions relax me.

"Erin?"

"Huh?" I ask, lifting my head from the hole.

"We're done."

I blink a couple of times as I try to figure out where I am. Kristy looks at me with an amused but knowing smile. Clearly, I'm not her only client to fall asleep on her table.

"I'll give you a couple of minutes to relax and then we can start your facial. You'll need to be on your back for that one so you can again cover yourself with a towel. I've put a clean one over there. I've left you a glass of water but would you like anything else?"

"That's perfect, thank you."

I just about manage to stay awake to enjoy the facial and I soon realise why Frankie does this kind of thing regularly. By the time Kristy has finished, I feel amazing. I swear my face has never been so clean.

"Thank you so much; that was incredible."

"You're welcome."

"Is that it?" I ask, seeing as she hasn't talked about anything else.

"No, you have appointments with Charlie and Ronnie, but you need to go and get showered first as I'm sure you won't want to once Charlie's done your hair."

"My hair?"

"Yes. If you go back to where you got the robe, you'll find showers. All the products you need will be in there. Then, just wait out on the loungers."

I follow her instructions and in a couple of minutes I find myself stood under a waterfall shower, silently thanking Jay for organising this for me. As much as I want my hair done, I'm also desperate to see him. Is it crazy that I miss him? I'm also kind of desperate to see him working out in the gym. I've loved waking up in the mornings to find him doing his sit-ups next to the bed.

My thoughts run away with me and I once again find myself rushing to get back out before someone has to knock for me.

I've barely sat my arse on the lounger before I hear my name being called. When I look over my shoulder, there's a young slim guy with the silkiest locks I think I've ever seen stood smiling at me.

"Are you ready, darlin'?"

"Sure am."

Charlie leads me to a hair salon at the end of the corridor, sits me down and hands me a glass of bubbles. I could get used to this.

"So, darlin', what are we doing?"

"It could do with a trim."

"Okay, what else? How do you want it for your big night?"

"My big night?" My mind runs away with me and all I see is Jay and I in a huge bed. Embarrassment flushes my neck and face.

"Yes, I'm presuming you have dinner reservations with a sexy young man, and if your blush tells me anything it's that the plans don't end there," he whispers, making me flush more. "Just as I thought."

I change the subject and explain to Charlie how my hair doesn't do anything so it's not worth his effort, but he tells me that's rubbish because he can work magic. I give him permission to do whatever he wants and sit back with my bubbles.

"Tell me about this sexy man, then," Charlie says, once I'm back from the basin.

I hesitate for a second but when I meet his soft, kind eyes in the mirror, I find our story falling from my mouth. I tell him everything about meeting Jay in the nightclub to our road trip that has found us here.

"OMG, that's so romantic," he coos as he cuts a few millimetres off my ends. "A two-week road trip with a sexy soldier. Sounds like my kind of week," he adds with a wink.

I find it way too easy to talk to Charlie, because without realising it, my fears seem to fall from my lips. "What's going to happen next, though? We never talked about what would happen when our time was over."

"You've fallen in love with him, haven't you?"

I avert my gaze because Charlie's stare is too intense. It's as if he's reading my thoughts.

"Yes," I whisper. "What am I meant to do now?"

"You need to talk to him, darlin'. See if he feels the same way."

"What if he doesn't? I mean, he says all the right things, but what if this really was just two weeks of fun for him whilst he's on leave? What if this is it?"

"From what you've said, I don't think that's the case."

"I don't even know where he's based," I huff, thinking of all the times I've tried to bring the subject of his work up only to have him sidestep it.

"What do you think?" Charlie asks when he holds up a mirror behind me.

"It's gorgeous. I don't know how you did it."

"Pure genius."

I stare at my reflection with perfect curls framing my face. Charlie's not only cut and curled my hair to perfection, but he also added some highlights that give it a real sun-kissed look. It's stunning, it really is. "You are. Thank you."

"You're welcome, darlin'. I hope it knocks his socks off."

Charlie has just walked off when a slightly older woman approaches. "Erin, I'm Ronnie, I'm going to do your nails and make-up for you."

"Okay." I get up and follow her to her station at the other side of the room.

"Nails are to be red," she states. "Let's see your hands then, love."

I do as I'm told and lift my hands so she can inspect my nails. They're not in bad condition per se; I don't chew them or anything but I don't exactly look after them. "Why have they got to be red?" I ask.

"That's what I've been told."

"By whom?"

She shrugs, but it's kind of obvious, really.

Ronnie's easy to chat to as well—not as easy as Charlie mind you, and thankfully she steers clear of any talk of relationships. By the time she's finished with me, my fingers and toes are fire engine red and my face is flawless. I thought Frankie had a way with make-up, but this woman seriously has skills. As I stare at myself in the mirror, looking better than I ever have in my life, I have the sudden desire to take a selfie, which is very unlike me.

"Do I need to pay for all of this?" I ask before leaving the spa.

"Nope, it's all sorted." I'm torn between being really grateful for what Jay's done and annoyed that he's spent even more money on me.

As I make my way to the lift, I see the frosted windows hiding the view of the gym goers behind. Something tells me he's right there on the other side of the glass, and I wish I could see him. I'd love to watch him putting everything he has into his exercise, watching his muscles bulge and the sweat pour from him. I shake my head to clear the thoughts. Who is this woman I'm turning into? I've never before even considered what a guy would look like working out.

I hit the button in the lift for the top floor with frustration, although I'm not sure if it's fuelled by my straying thoughts or still lingering after our kiss earlier.

I let myself into our room and just as I expected, I'm alone. I take the opportunity to explore the suite, as the only thing I explored before was Jay. I walk through the living area to find a bedroom with the biggest bed I've ever seen in my life. Seriously I think about ten people would be able to sleep in it. It seems totally over the top for two; we're gonna have to shout at each other, we'll be so far apart. Through a door on the other side of the bedroom there is one impressive bathroom with a two-man Jacuzzi bath in the centre. I may have just had the most relaxing couple of hours of my life but still, my body aches to be laid out in that with the jets massaging my muscles.

Regretfully, I turn and walk back into the bedroom. Something catches my eye that I didn't see before. Hanging in front of the mirrored wardrobe door is a black dress. I walk over and run my fingertips down over the satin fabric. It's plain, simple, and way too slinky for my liking. It's more like something Frankie would pick, not me.

I lift it from the wardrobe and turn it around, and not only do I find that it's almost backless, but there's a label hanging from it.

"Wear me."

I put it back and take a step away. I look at the dress before looking down at myself. It's going to look awful clinging to all my lumpy bits. I glance in the mirror at my perfectly done hair and make-up, and the sight gives me some courage.

After quickly stripping out of my clothes and changing into a fresh pair of knickers, I pull the dress on. Thankfully, it doesn't cling like I was expecting it to; it skims over my skin perfectly.

I spin to look at my back and notice the most horrendous VPL. "Shit."

I rummage through my small case but only find what I was expecting: more cotton knickers. Fuck.

I lift the skirt and regretfully pull my knickers down my legs before smoothing the fabric back into place. It looks much better but I'm hyperaware of my bare skin.

I slide on my red court shoes, telling myself there's no way Jay will know I'm not wearing any underwear. I spritz myself with some perfume before sitting on the edge of the bed. I'm just about to grab my phone to take a photo of myself to send Frankie when I hear the door open.

My heart begins to pound as I wait for him to round the corner into the bedroom. I listen to his footsteps for a few seconds before he begins to get closer.

My breath catches the moment he appears in the doorway.

"Wow," I breathe, taking him in from head to toe.

He's dressed in a perfectly pressed white shirt with a slim black tie and black trousers. It's a million miles away from how he's looked in his jeans and hoodies.

"I could be saying the same thing. You look stunning," he says, his eyes running over every inch of my body. "I knew that dress was made for you."

"When did you get it?"

"That morning I went off in Inverness."

"Oh."

"I saw in it a window and it had your name written all over it."

"It's gorgeous."

"You are."

He steps up to me and cups my cheek in his hand. "How was I so lucky to find you?" Tears pool in my eyes. "Hey, none of that. We've got reservations." He leans in to kiss me but when he glances at my red lips, he changes his mind at the last minute and goes for my neck instead. He kisses and nips down my neck and across my chest until he's skimming the swell of my breasts with his soft lips.

"I wish you understood how sexy you look to me." As he says this, he runs his hands down my back and squeezes my arse. I feel his head lift from my cleavage and when I look up, his dark, hungry eyes are gazing at me. "Skittles?" he questions as he continues caressing my arse.

"Shit." My face flushes, knowing I've been caught without underwear.

"Oh, no. Never apologise for being this incredibly sexy. If I wasn't so fucking hungry I'd have made you come already; I can still taste you from the last time. I was so fucking desperate to have you that night but caving to it has only made it worse."

He drops to his knees and presses his nose between my legs. I want to be embarrassed but one look in his eyes when he glances up and I feel anything but. He presses his nose in a little harder and sparks shoot from my clit. My knees threaten to buckle but thankfully, Jay stands and pulls me to him.

"Dinner?" he asks, as if that didn't just happen.

"Uh... sure."

DINNER WAS AMAZING—FROM what I can remember of it. Having those grey eyes looking at me over the table had me pretty distracted. Every time I looked at Jay, I was back upstairs with his hands and lips on me. It doesn't help that every chance he gets, he places his hand high up on my thigh or runs his foot up my leg. I'm sat here just about ready to combust.

I thought we were done and was eager to get back upstairs to have him alone when he accepts the waiter's offer of coffee.

"Didn't you want coffee?" he asks, although I can see a glint in his eye.

"Sure."

"Or is there something you want more?"

I squirm in my seat and a slow, sexy smirk appears on his face.

"Tell me what it is you do want, Erin."

I break my eye contact, too embarrassed to vocalise what I'm thinking.

"Now's not the time to be shy, Skittles. If you want what I think you want, you're going to have to tell me. I told you I'd only do anything once you were begging. Well, now's the time to start, baby."

My chin drops open and I look back into his eyes. Am I about to beg for more of Jayden Baxter? Yeah, I'm pretty sure I am. A little voice sparks up in my head; it's now or never. I swallow down the *never* part because I don't want thoughts of our fast approaching end ruining tonight, and I focus on the now.

"I want you."

He raises his eyebrows as if he wants me to continue.

"I want you to do what you did before."

Another eyebrow arch.

"With your tongue," I whisper as I fight to keep eye contact.

"And..." he encourages.

I drop my eyes down to his crotch before slowly climbing back up to meet his amused yet hungry eyes. "I want all of you."

He stares at me, looking totally unaffected, but his darkening eyes tell me he's very much interested.

"Thank you," Jay says, confusing me, but seconds later two coffees are placed on our table.

I sit back and glance around the room as I try to relax. I jump when Jay's hand lands on my thigh. "Come on, drink up," he says as his little finger starts to stray until it's gently rubbing against my mound. "I'm not opposed to getting you off right here," he warns before sipping on his coffee.

I have two sips of mine before I push my chair out behind me, grab my bag, and begin to walk off. I feel him behind me in seconds, his heat warming my bare back and his hands landing on my waist.

"I didn't think you were ever going to move," he whispers in my ear.

Jay crowds me into the corner of the lift once the doors open and he's just about to lean in to kiss me when I feel someone else step into the small space. Jay looks into my eyes before reluctantly stepping back from me. That one look holds a promise, a promise that makes my insides quiver.

As soon as the doors open, he grabs my hand and pulls me to our room and through to the bedroom.

"Jay, slow down," I complain, when my heels stop me from moving as fast as him. "What the fuck?" I squeal, when my feet leave the floor.

"Can't wait for you," Jay mutters once he has me over his shoulder.

One of his hands squeezes my arse while the other one shoots up under the fabric of my dress and slowly starts to slide up my leg. Heat pools between my thighs with every inch closer he gets.

I just about manage to contain my moan when he stops and throws me onto the bed. "Hey," I complain, but when I look up to see him pulling at his tie, I shut my mouth in favour of watching him strip.

His tie hits the floor before he starts working on his shirt buttons. I follow his hands as he makes his way down. The white fabric soon joins the tie and I expect him to start on his trousers, but to my surprise he drops to his knees instead.

He grabs one of my ankles and gently slides my shoe off before it drops to the floor with a thud, followed by the other.

"You have no idea what kind of images have been running around my head with you looking like this tonight. The things I want to do to you..."

I groan at his words. He could suggest almost anything right now and I think I'd say yes.

When his lips touch my ankle, I fall back onto the bed in favour of focusing on the sensation. Before I know it, he has my dress around my waist and my legs spread. I'm totally exposed to him.

"Beautiful," he mutters between kisses up my inner thigh. As he gets closer, my muscles start to clench in anticipation. "I've dreamt about doing this every minute since I first tasted you."

"Jay," I moan just as his tongue connects with my sensitive skin. "Shit, ahhhh."

It's as good as I remember but when I open my eyes and see Jay between my legs, it becomes so much more. I scratch my nails over his short hair as I moan and rock against his mouth.

"Come on my mouth," I hear him say against me, and the vibration of his words gets me right on the edge of my release. He presses his thumb to my clit before sliding his tongue inside me, and it's the final straw. Light bursts behind my eyes and my entire body twitches and shakes as my release hits. Jay says something again and the vibrations make my orgasm stronger.

I'm panting when he pulls away from me and stands. I feel his stare but I can't open my eyes, not yet.

"Fuck, you're beautiful." I'm not sure I believe him in this instance, as I'm sweating with my dress hitched up around my waist. "Erin, look at me."

When I do as I'm told, Jay is gloriously naked before me. I take my time running my eyes over every solid but perfect inch of him. I've never seen a man naked in the flesh before, so when I get to his waist, I'm not sure where to look. That is, until he takes himself in his hand. Then, I'm fascinated.

"Get up," he demands, and I do immediately.

I step up to him so my breasts brush his chest and he wastes no time in taking my mouth. I can taste myself on his lips. For a second, it makes me want to pull away, but as soon as I feel his tongue against mine I forget all about it. His hands lift to my shoulders and he pulls the straps down over my arms, allowing my dress to pool at my feet. The second it hits the floor, he pulls his lips away from mine and stands back.

"Fuck," he mutters as he runs his eyes over me. "So fucking perfect." My skin ignites as his eyes burn a trail into me. "You ready for this?"

I nod, because the way he's looking at me renders me speechless.

"You sure you want it to be me? You don't want to wait for someone special, someone who can give you everything you deserve?"

I'm desperate to tell him he is special, that he's given me everything and more during our time together, but the words get stuck on my tongue. So instead of speaking, I step back into him and show him. I run my hands up from his waist, across his chest and over his shoulders so I can pull him to me. I kiss him as I walk us back to the bed. When I feel the mattress against my legs, I fall back and pull him with me.

Jay allows me to scoot up the bed before crawling over me, ensuring he kisses every bit of skin he can on the way up.

"I don't think this will last very long," he admits as he runs the tip of his tongue around the shell of my ear. "I've been waiting for too long."

"Don't care."

Jay's fingers run down my stomach until he finds my swollen clit. He teases me until I'm squirming under him again before pumping his fingers inside me to ensure I'm ready.

"Okay?" he asks when he's in position between my open legs with his cock in his hand.

I nod. I know what he's really saying, *this is going to hurt*, but I'm okay with that. This is right; there's no one else I'd rather be here with right now, no one else I've ever really considered. I didn't know it before, but I was waiting for him.

A second later, I feel myself stretch as he presses inside me slowly. It doesn't hurt like I was expecting. It actually feels nice, and I'm seriously relieved.

"Okay?"

I nod and he presses farther, and just as I think everyone exaggerates about the pain, it hits me.

"Argh," I grunt.

"I'm sorry." Jay leans forward to kiss me before he quickly thrusts forward again. I moan against his lips and dig my nails into his back. He continues to kiss me as the pain subsides.

"I know you're hurting right now but you have no idea how fucking incredible you feel," he whispers in my ear.

"I'm okay," I say as I flex my hips slightly.

"Yeah?"

"Yeah."

"Thank fuck." His hips are moving before he finishes speaking.

Just like he warned, it doesn't last very long. It's only a few thrusts before he groans; his entire body goes still, and then I feel him releasing inside me. The look on his face as he comes is an image I'll never forget as long as I live.

When he's finished, he falls on top of me, panting; he's heavy, but I love the weight of him on me. I wrap my arms around his back and make the most of this time.

After a minute or two, he pulls his head from my neck and sweeps away the hair that had fallen across my face. "Are you okay?" he asks, so softly it makes tears sting my eyes.

"Yes. Was that...?"

"Incredible, Erin. Fucking incredible."

I smile wide.

"Next time, I'm going to make you scream," he promises. "But first," he says, as he gets up and walks to the bathroom. The sound of running water gets me moving and in seconds, I'm stood in the doorway, watching him leaning over the bath, adjusting the water temperature.

"Hey," he says when he turns around and sees me watching.

"Hey."

He looks at me like he wants to say something else, but he must change his mind because after a few seconds, he walks over, lifts me into his arms, and kisses me before gently placing me in the soothing warm water.

"Where are you going?" I ask in a panic when he starts to leave the room. I thought this was going to be a two-person bath.

"I'll be back," he says before disappearing and leaving me alone. Reality hits me hard in that moment. After the high of tonight, knowing this is all about to come to an end is a hard blow to take.

"What's wrong?"

I look over to see Jay stood a few feet from the bath with a concerned look on his face and a bottle of bubbles and two glasses in hand.

"This is our last night together, isn't it?"

"Erin," he says, setting the bottle and glasses down and getting in with me. He pulls me to him and starts kissing me.

For a few hours, I forget all about what's to come, and focus everything I have on him.

CHAPTER EIGHT

"**M**orning, Skittles," Jay says with a wide smile from the floor where he's doing his daily sit-ups when I wake.

"Morning." I try to sound all chipper. Although he never confirmed it last night, I know I've just woken up to our last day together and I'd rather cry than smile right now.

He gets himself up, then crawls over to me.

"Morning breath," I complain.

"Don't care." He bats my hand out of the way and presses his lips against mine. "I've ordered breakfast to the room. We need to be out by eleven."

"Okay," I mutter sadly as there's a knock at the door.

When Jay reappears, it's with a trolley full of food. My stomach grumbles right on cue, and we both tuck in. We may have had a three-course meal last night but we did plenty of exercise to burn it off after. My face heats as I recollect everything we did together. Once Jay was happy I'd recovered from our first time, he made sure to show me how it should be, and true to his word, he'd had me screaming—more than once.

"It was pretty incredible, right?" Jay says when he looks over and notices my blush.

"Yeah. Jay—"

"I can't put it off any longer, can I?"

I shake my head. "It's our last day, isn't it?"

"I'm sorry, Skittles. I've got to head back."

"Where's back?"

"Germany," he admits.

"WHAT."

"I'm based in Germany."

My heart sinks. I've no idea if carrying this on is even a possibility but I was under the impression he at least lived in this country. "Oh."

"That's not it."

I look up at him as a ball of dread starts to grow in my stomach. The look on his face isn't showing he's about to share some good news.

"I'm about to go on a six month tour of Afghanistan."

I drop the pastry in my hand and I vaguely hear the thud as it falls from the bed.

"We fly out on Monday from base. I'm so sorry," he says when he watches my first tear drop. "I didn't want our time to be tainted by it. I was so looking forward to going, getting back into the thick of it and then... and then I met you." My first sob erupts. "Erin," he whispers as he grabs my hands. "I wasn't expecting this to turn into anything. I thought we'd have a little fun and that would be it. I wasn't expecting to..."

"To..."

He looks up to the ceiling and lets out a long breath. "To... fall in love with you."

I collapse onto his chest and cry. I cry like I haven't in years, since that day we found out my dad had been killed. The thought of that brings on another round of sobs. Jay holds me the whole time and whispers sweet things in my ear, rubbing my back.

"I... I love you, too," I manage to admit eventually. And for the first time since I met him, I see Jay get a little choked up. It does nothing for my fragile state to see tears in his eyes.

"I'm so sorry. I should have told you."

"No. I don't think you should have. If I knew before we left, I probably wouldn't have come with you, and then I wouldn't have ever experienced any of this. I wouldn't have experienced you."

"Fuck. I wasn't expecting this," he repeats. "I don't know what to say. I don't know what to do next," he admits, looking totally lost.

"I'll wait for you."

"I can't ask you to do that."

"I'm not asking you to. I'm telling you it's what I'll do. This has been everything to me. You are everything to me. I'll wait."

I watch as Jay chews everything over. I can see all his thoughts and concerns rolling around behind his eyes, and I sit quietly and allow him the time he needs.

"Come on, let's get moving. We still have time to figure this all out."

"When are you leaving for Germany?"

"Tonight. Johnny's picking me up in town later this afternoon."

"Okay," I whisper, trying my best to keep my emotions locked down. It won't do him any good, knowing how affected I am by all this. I don't want him to leave, knowing I'm so upset. I'm going to have plenty of time once he's gone to fall apart.

It's just before eleven when we walk out of our fancy suite hand in hand. The journey down to reception and then out to his car is a total blur. I want to cling on to every second but they seem to speed by too fast, and before I know it I'm sat in the passenger seat waiting for Jay to start the car for the trip home.

The car roars to life before I hear a loud clunk.

"Fuck."

"What?"

"The clutch has just gone."

"What do you mean it's gone?"

"It means it's fucked," he snaps.

"Well, can't we just get it fixed?" I'm not stupid enough to realise it will probably take longer to find a new clutch for his car than we have, but the words are already out of my mouth.

He turns to me and is just about to snap at me again when his face softens. "Sorry, this isn't your fault. Fuck, I need to get back. Shit."

"It'll be okay. Can we get a train or something?" I grab my phone to start looking at other options.

"WHERE ARE YOU MEETING HIM?" I ask as the train pulls to a stop.

What was meant to be a three-hour drive has turned into an almost six-hour journey. Jay is seriously agitated. I don't think these kinds of last minute issues sit right with his strictly planned army life. He's had to put his friend off and I know he's here in the city waiting on him. I can see Jay's trying to keep himself in check for my benefit, and I appreciate it, but I wish he'd chill out a little.

He grabs both of our bags and I try to keep up with him as he finds us a taxi and barks at the driver to head toward Cabot Circus.

"I'm so sorry. This has totally ruined our time together."

"It's fine, Jay. There's not a lot we could've done about it. We're almost there."

Jay pays the driver, and hand in hand we walk past the shops down Broadmead until he pulls me to a stop by the seating area in the centre of the walkway.

"I need you to know how much this all meant to me, Erin," he says sincerely as he places his hand over my heart.

"I know. Me too," I say, trying desperately to keep my tears at bay.

"But I need you to promise me something."

"Anything."

"If someone better comes along, I want you to go for it. Don't put your life on hold for me."

"Don't be crazy, I won't—"

"Promise me," he repeats, a little harsher.

"Okay, I promise," I say, but I have no intention of following through on it because I know for a fact there won't be anyone else.

"But if in six months' time you still want me, then I'll be here, right here in this very spot, waiting for you."

I lose my battle and my tears fall. Jay reaches up and catches them with his thumbs.

"I have something for you." He drops his duffel bag on the floor and pulls something from the pocket. My breath catches when I see a little black box in his hand and my eyes widen in shock. "It's not *that* kind," he says with a sad laugh. "But it's a promise. A promise that I'll be here waiting for you no matter what you decide."

Jay grabs my shaking hand and slides the stunning vintage ring onto my finger. I choke back a sob as I study it. "It's my birthstone," I say, looking at the opal sat in the centre.

"BAX." I hear shouted, but Jay doesn't turn around or even acknowledge it.

"Here," he says, popping a piece of paper inside the ring box and handing it over. "I love you, Erin, and I'll be back for you. I promise."

"I-I love you, too," I stutter out as a guy I vaguely recognise steps up to us.

"I've got to go." He pulls me into a tight hug and we hold each other for a long time before he lets go and gives me the most incredible kiss. "I promise," he repeats again before stepping back.

It happens all of a sudden and I know it's how we both need it to, but he grabs his bag, turns, and marches away. Johnny's hot on his tail and the only thing I hear him say is, "Whoa, mate, it looks like you had fun."

I stand on that exact spot for the longest time after they've left. I feel lost. I don't want to go home, I don't want to go anywhere, not without him.

I feel like half of me just left.

I don't notice the people walking around me or the sun starting to set and night descending. All I can focus on is the empty feeling in my chest that only seems to be getting worse the farther away I know he's getting.

I lift my hand holding the box and open it before pulling the piece of paper out.

13/10/2012

I promise. x

With that piece of paper gripped in my hand, I make my way home, toward an unsteady few months and one very long wait.

CHAPTER NINE

6 months later...

I understand why Jay said he wouldn't be in contact, that he wanted me to live my life, and if we were meant to be then we would be. But fuck, these last six months have been the hardest of my life.

The shop is right on the cusp of going under, Mum's health is deteriorating by the day, but she still point blank refuses to give it up. I get that she's chasing her dream, but there has to come a point where it's just not worth it, and I'm pretty sure we're there.

I swipe a coat of gloss across my lips and as I put the cap back on, my ring catches my eye. I haven't taken it off since the second he slid it on my finger six months ago.

I try to keep my butterflies under control, but as the days have been counting down, they've been multiplying faster and faster. I'm excited as hell but I'm also nervous. What if it's not like I remember? What if it was only meant to be those two weeks? All these questions

118

fly around my mind as I step out the front door and look at Peggy sat on the drive.

Two weeks after I got back, the last thing I was expecting was to find Dean stood at my doorstep with Peggy's keys swinging from his fingers.

"He told me to drop it off here." Dean said, handing them over. "There's this, too."

When I opened the envelope, there was a receipt inside for an intensive driving course, and a note telling me to look after his baby until he got back.

I jump inside and start her up. She purrs just like she did when Jay drove her. I've made sure I've kept on top of all her maintenance and she's perfectly clean, ready for his return. I have to admit, I'm going to be sad to see her go. Since setting up my website and getting my jewellery into more stores across the city, I've managed to get enough orders to have a little stash of money put away ready to buy myself a car of my own. Mum hated that I was no longer selling exclusively through her shop but I can't go down with her. I need to think of my future, now more than ever.

I'm a nervous wreck as I sit on one of the benches waiting for him. The town is packed, as there's some kind of event going on. There were signs on every post on the drive here, but none of them held my attention. There are street entertainers on every corner, and people chatting, laughing, and joking as they go about their day. They have no idea the importance of who I'm waiting for as I sit here.

I wait.

And I wait.

I look around through the hordes of people waiting for his face to appear, but it doesn't.

I check my phone. I have no idea why, because as he promised the night we met, we never swapped numbers.

Maybe he's delayed, so I wait a little longer.

I sit there until the sun's long set and the street's practically empty, still holding on to a small shred of hope that he's going to appear, while trying desperately hard not to think he changed his mind—or worse. Not one second of the past six months have I been able to forget that he left me to enter a war zone. No, I can't think like that. He's strong, nothing will have happened to him.

He's coming.

I know he is.

Something deep inside me tells me he's fine; I have to trust my instinct.

Eventually, I need to move. I'm stiff from sitting on the same bench practically all day, and I'm starving after having eaten through the snacks I brought with me hours ago. I stand up and stretch my back out before rubbing my hand over my ever-growing belly. He's been kicking the whole time I've been sat here waiting for his daddy, but I can only wait for so long. In my last ditch attempt in case he's really late, I pull a piece of paper from my notebook and scribble out a message for him before tucking it into the bench. I have one last look around the dark street before I walk away.

I've got to be strong, I tell myself. This isn't just about me anymore. But the second I shut the car door—*his* car door—I break down and cry like I've never cried in my life.

EPILOGUE

I take one last look in the mirror before opening the bathroom door to join Alex in the living room.

"Did he go down okay?" Alex asks.

Denny hasn't been great at going to bed for the last few weeks and it usually takes me having to lie with him until he drifts off—that's after his nightly story, of course.

"Yeah, he was okay."

"E, what's wrong?" he asks when he looks up at me.

"Nothing, babe. I'm just tired."

Alex has always been able to tell when something's wrong; he's too perceptive. I knew I shouldn't have gone and dug that scrapbook out, but something about talking about Jay with Denny tonight had me wanting to remember. I've never told Alex the whole story about Denny's dad, just that I had a fling with a soldier, and I don't intend on telling him the details now. What's the point? Denny's going to be five soon, and it's not like he's ever coming back.

Most days, I'm okay, and I feel like I dealt with everything that happened after Jay didn't come back, but others threaten to break me.

I look up to the last photo I have of Mum and me on the mantelpiece. She has her hand on my pregnant belly and is smiling up at me. She died a couple of weeks later. The stress of it sent me into early labour. Denny was in hospital for weeks before he was strong enough to leave. Everything went to shit pretty quickly but Denny saved me. Every day, he saves me, and now we have Alex, and life is good.

"Come and sit down, baby. You need to relax a little, you're working too hard."

I fall down next to Alex and give him a kiss when he leans in.

Life's good. I've got a good boyfriend, a great business and an amazing son. My only problem?

I'll never forget *him*.

***

Keep reading for more Jay and Erin!

NEVER
FORGET US

PROLOGUE

Jay

I was there that day.

Just out of sight, on the corner, watching her.

She was even more beautiful than I remembered. From where I was stood, I could see the excitement in her eyes as she scanned the crowd, looking for me. Her hair, longer than when I first met her, blew around her face in the breeze. She was wearing a grey heavy knit poncho that hid her gorgeous curves, and as desperate as I was to go over there and pull her to me, I knew it wasn't the right thing to do.

I stayed in the shadows all day, not once taking my eyes from her. It was going to be the last time I saw her.

The sun had long set when I saw her turn her back on me and leave. The stabbing pain in my gut as I watched her walk away is something that will stay with me forever. I made my way over to the bench she'd occupied all day. I plucked the neatly folded up piece of paper I saw her leave and my hands shook as I tried to prepare myself for what she could have written.

After a few seconds, I found the courage to open it. The moment my eyes landed on her handwriting, they filled with tears. I couldn't remember the last time I cried. It wasn't when my dad left or when my mum overdosed. It wasn't when I lost any of my mates on tour, and it definitely wasn't in the last few months, as I've dealt with what happened. But as I looked at those four little words, my eyes filled faster than I could control.

I'll never forget you.

CHAPTER ONE

"Oh fuck! Denny, get up!" I shout in a panic when I see the time on the alarm clock next to my bed. "Denny?" I repeat when I don't hear any movement.

I pull on the pair of leggings I discarded before falling into bed last night, and grab a hoodie from the chair.

"Denny," I shout again as I wrestle with my hoodie and burst into his room. Because it's so bloody late, his room is light, and I see confusion in his eyes.

"Mummy?"

"We're late. Get dressed, I'll make your breakfast."

I throw his uniform at him and run down to the kitchen. I knew I shouldn't have accepted the contract for a nationwide store, but the thought of having my jewellery in shops across the country was too big an opportunity to turn down. I think I eventually got into bed sometime after four this morning.

I yawn as I butter Denny's toast.

"I'm ready."

"Okay, here," I say, shoving the toast toward him. "Have you got your PE kit?"

"Yes."

We both run toward the car. Denny stuffs toast into his mouth and I try to keep hold of his school bag and PE kit as I find the right key.

He looks over at me when he's finished his breakfast, his face sleepy and sad.

"I'm sorry, baby."

He shrugs at me and I instantly feel awful. He's my number one priority, he has been since the day I found out I was pregnant, but lately everything is getting on top of me. I know I only have myself to blame.

I wave him off as he runs through the playground at just gone nine. If I wasn't so angry with myself for making him late, I'd be proud of the fact we went from sleeping to school in just under forty minutes.

I climb in the car and rest my head back. Alex is already annoyed that I'm working so much, and now it's affecting Denny's education. I hate to even consider it but I'm going to have to ask if the delivery deadline can be pushed back.

Pulling the sun visor down, I stare at my tired eyes, yesterday's lingering make-up only making them worse. I wipe at my skin to try to tidy it up but it has little effect. Nor does running my fingers through my hair, which looks like there should be a bird nesting in it.

I blow out a long breath before deciding to stop at the coffee shop around the corner. I need caffeine—and now. I hate spending money on takeout coffee since Alex convinced me to buy insanely expensive machines for both home and shop, but today's an emergency.

I just about hold my body upright as I wait in line to be served. Maybe I was wrong; going straight back home would've got me caffeine quicker.

I'm eventually served and waiting for the largest cappuccino they can give me when I get the weirdest feeling. I tell myself it's just sleep deprivation, but the nagging that I need to turn around won't budge.

Giving in, I glance over my shoulder. There doesn't seem to be anything exciting going on; everyone's drinking their coffee and reading the papers. I go to turn back around when a figure in the corner catches my eye. His head's down, but I don't need to see any more.

My body knows instantly.

That weird connection, one I remember all too well, slams into me. I stumble back, bumping into another customer and causing them to tip their drink down themselves. I mumble my apologies and run out of the coffee shop. I hear the barista calling after me that my coffee's ready, but I don't stop. I can't. Instead, I run. I run until my legs burn and my heart pounds. I crash into the shop door and the wind chimes Frankie insists on having above clatters with my force.

The shop is empty but it's only a second before my best friend pops her head around the corner. Her eyes widen as she sees the state of me.

"Erin? What is it? Is Denny okay?"

I bend over and brace my hands on my knees as I try to catch my breath. I go to pull a stray piece of hair from my face to find it's stuck down by the tears I didn't realise I was crying.

"Erin?" Frankie asks again, her tone a warning.

"He's fine, Denny's fine," I whisper to put her mind at rest.

"Then what?"

"I saw him," I say when I've somewhat got my breath back.

"Who?"

"*Him,*" I repeat, but it's clear from her drawn eyebrows she hasn't got the foggiest idea what I'm talking about. "Jay."

"What?" she screeches. "You couldn't have."

I think after Jay didn't come back, I was the only one who believed he was still alive. To this day I can't explain it, but I had this feeling deep down that he was out there somewhere, and that his untimely death wasn't his reason for not coming back to me. I explained my theory to a couple of people who thought I was crazy, so I buried it down and went along with everyone else. I had too much going on with the death of my mum and Denny's premature arrival to deal with that too.

"Here," Frankie says, handing me a pack of wipes from her handbag. "You look like shit."

I take them and attempt to do something with my face as Frankie makes us both coffees.

I sit myself behind the counter and tip my head back as I run through the events of my morning.

"Go on then," Frankie encourages as she places a steaming cappuccino in front of me.

I tell her all about being late for school, and the whole time she gives me the evil eye. She's been lecturing me about how many hours I've been working for weeks. I've got everything under control but Frankie's obsessed that I'm going to work myself into the ground just like Mum did.

"He was just there, sat in the corner with his head down."

"How did you know it was him if you couldn't see his face?"

"I didn't need to see his face to know it was him, Kiki. I felt it."

"You felt it?" she repeats sceptically.

I know it sounds nuts, and if someone was telling me this story I'd probably have the same reaction, but that's how it was.

"Yes."

"What did you do?"

"I ran."

"You ran all the way here? It's like, three miles."

"I had to get away. I wasn't ever meant to see him again, Frankie. I prayed for months that one day I would open my front door to find him stood there. Fuck, I even dreamt it a few times and woke up *at* the fucking front door. He didn't come back for me that day. He didn't want me," I manage to get out through my sobs.

I drop my head into my hands and break down. Frankie wraps both her arms around my shoulders and holds me while I cry. The pain of that day washes through me once again. The utter devastation I felt, knowing he didn't come back for me when I was pregnant with his child. Everyone told me he was killed and it wasn't his fault, but I knew differently. I knew he hadn't chosen me.

"Don't shout at me, but are you 100% sure it was him? It wasn't your mind playing tricks on you? It wouldn't be the first time," Frankie asks when I've calmed down.

She's right, of course. For almost a year after that day, I thought I saw him everywhere. I stopped so many guys with dark shaved hair in the street I lost count, and every time I realised it wasn't him, the pain of losing him would engulf me once again.

"You haven't been sleeping properly. How many hours did you get last night?" she asks to prove her point. I don't answer; she doesn't need me to. My tale from this morning and the bags under my eyes are evidence enough. "Exactly. What are the chances after all these years of you just bumping into him?"

She's got a point, and although I'm convinced I saw him today, her words do make me question myself.

"Take the weekend off. Get some sleep, recharge your batteries, and see how you feel about it all then. If you really think he's here, you have to decide what you want to do about it. Go find him, or leave it buried in the past."

I SPEND the rest of the morning with Frankie before she locks up and takes me back to the coffee shop to collect my abandoned car.

"Do you want to come in and get some lunch?" she asks when she pulls up directly in front of the one place I certainly do not want to go in.

"I'm good, thanks."

"You sure? You look like you could do with a salted caramel muffin," she says, trying to tempt me with my favourite.

"I need to get home."

She gives me a long hug before I start toward my car. I feel her watching me and I know she's worried, but I'm fine. Everything is fine.

Once I've showered, I feel a little more human again. Frankie never commented on the fact I'd clearly fallen into the first items of clothing I could find this morning, and I was grateful. It was bad enough looking at her preened to perfection; I didn't need it pointed out.

I grab my phone and diary and make the call I've been hoping to avoid.

TWENTY MINUTES and a lot of grovelling later, I just about manage to add another month to my deadline. She wasn't impressed as it's going to be cutting it fine to get my range into their stores for a spring launch, but it was that or nothing. I'd hate to cancel, but at the end of the day, Denny comes first, and I seem to have lost sight of that the last few weeks.

I spend the afternoon taking stock of where I'm at. I write myself a new to-do list and schedule with my extended deadline, and by the time I need to leave to pick Denny up from school, I'm feeling a little better about everything. Well, everything apart from *him*, of course. I have absolutely no clue about what to do about that, and I'm pretty sure I never will.

In only two weeks, Jay changed my life in ways I could never have imagined, and I will be forever thankful for what he gave me. But at the same time, I don't think I'll be able to forgive him for what he took away from me. Him.

DENNY'S FACE lights up when he sees me stood at the school gates. I've been late more times than I want to admit recently, and I hate myself for it.

I desperately want to make it up to him, so instead of heading straight home like he's expecting, I drive us into town so he can spend his pocket money before a very rare visit to McDonald's.

The joy on his face warms my heart, and for an hour or two it pushes aside everything I've been battling with today. This little man is everything. He doesn't care if I have jewellery in one or a million stores. All he needs is me, and I feel like I've let him down.

"Don't forget Dawn's looking after you tonight," I remind him on the way home.

"Yes, I can show her my new racetrack," he says excitedly, clutching the box I've told him he can't open until he gets home.

It's Alex's weekend off. He runs a nightclub in town, and he's lucky at the moment if he gets more than one weekend off a month. When he is off, he insists on taking me out and spoiling me.

The last year with him has been incredible. He's been the family both Denny and I were missing. He helped me to see it's okay to be me as well as a mum, and he's helped bring joy and laughter back into the house. But above all else he's been there every time I needed a shoulder to cry on, or to cuddle me after a long day. He's been hinting about us taking our relationship to the next step recently, but I'm not sure I'm ready for him to move in just yet.

"You look pretty, Mummy," Denny says when I find him and Dawn, Alex's mum, sat on the living room floor playing.

"Thank you, baby. Are you going to be good for Dawn?"

He smiles and nods before going back to his beloved trains.

"Thank you," I say to Dawn.

"You're welcome," she says tightly.

Alex pulls up out the front right on cue. I grab my coat and bag before repeating my warning about being good to Denny as I step out into the cold.

"Hey, baby," Alex says softly as I get in his car. I lean into him and give him a quick kiss. "I've missed you."

"Me too," I mumble against his lips.

Seeing and hearing him brings everything that happened this morning right back to the front of my mind.

"Where are we going?" I ask when Alex pulls off in an attempt to distract myself from my thoughts.

"We've got a table booked at Chiquito's, then tickets for Thor."

I put everything I have into looking excited but I fear I fall a little far from the mark.

"I thought you wanted to see it?"

"I do," I lie. Honestly, I have no interest in watching Thor; I only made it look that way because he wanted to.

"WHAT'S WRONG?" Alex asks as we wait for our dessert. I should have known he'd notice my despondence; he's too attentive not to.

"Nothing."

"Don't give me that. It's like you're not even here." Hearing his concerned voice doesn't help. I think I'd prefer if he were angry with me.

"I'm sorry. I worked so late last night that I didn't get up in time to get Denny to school this morning. I rang Stella and insisted she put my deadline back," I admit.

"At bloody last. I've been telling you to do that for weeks." He reaches over and squeezes my hand.

"I know," I whisper.

"Don't you feel better now? Like a weight has been lifted?"

"I guess." He's right, and if it wasn't for everything else that's happened today, I'm sure I would be relieved, but all I feel right now is sick and confused.

Frankie can tell me all she wants that it was my imagination, but I know it was him. Every fibre of my being knew it was him sat in that dark corner.

Thankfully, Alex changes the subject to his hunt for a new assistant manager. I do my best to agree and nod in the right places, but fuck knows if I was successful.

The film passes me by in a blur. If Alex questions me about it later I'm fucked because I didn't watch a second of it. The whole time, thoughts of Jay floated around my head. Our time together played out like my own personal movie as I wondered what to do. Just ignore it and try to get on with my life knowing he's here? Or do I try to find him?

Was he just visiting Bristol, or does he live here? Was he on leave? Has he met someone else? And then the question that's been in the back of my mind for years... why didn't he come back that day?"

By the time I make it into my en suite to take off tonight's make-up, I'm utterly exhausted. I left Alex downstairs to say goodbye to his mum in favour of getting into bed. I feel awful even thinking it, but if I can pretend to be asleep, maybe he won't touch me. I've never once even considered getting out of having sex with Alex before. Usually his moves work wonders, and by this time on our dates he's got me right where he wants me.

Not tonight, though.

Tonight, I have another man taking up space in my head. One I should have forgotten about years ago.

CHAPTER TWO

It's been two weeks since that morning in the coffee shop. I'm trying to keep busy as a distraction from thinking about him. I almost feel like I'm back on level footing again. I've found a better balance between work and Denny, and I'm feeling much more relaxed about meeting my deadline.

I'm off to a meeting with Stella so she can show me the final designs for the marketing of my jewellery. One of my stipulations of signing her contract was that I had the final say on how my designs were displayed and advertised. To say she wasn't happy about it is probably putting it mildly, but those pieces of jewellery are an extension of me and I need it to be right. If I want to continue growing in this industry, I can't leave important aspects of my work to other people.

I'm almost at the motorway junction when everything stops.

"Fuck."

I press my foot down on the accelerator but nothing happens. I steer the car onto the verge and turn the key. Slamming my hands down on the steering wheel I let out a frustrated breath. I try to start the ignition again. Nothing.

"Fuck, fuck, fuck."

I scramble around in the footwell to grab my bag, and pull my phone from the bottom. I swipe the screen and curse myself for forgetting to charge it. I chance my luck with only 5% battery and call Alex.

"Hey, baby, what's up?"

"Hey. My car's just died. Any chance you could help?

"I'm about to start interviewing, babe. How about I call someone to come and rescue you?" he offers.

"Okay, yeah, that'd be great as my phone's about to die." I explain where I am and he promises to get someone out to me as soon as possible.

I hang up and go to find Stella's number, but my phone dies loading up my contacts. *Well this is sure to piss her off*, I think to myself as I throw my useless phone back into my bag.

I pull out my notebook and a pen in the hope of wasting a bit of time. Fuck knows how long I could be here waiting.

I get lost in what I'm doing but it can't be much more than an hour later when someone knocks on my window, scaring the crap out of me. I throw my book and pen onto the passenger seat before taking a couple of deep breaths to steady my racing heart.

Stepping out of the car, I smooth my skirt down my thighs before standing at full height to speak to the guy who's come to help.

I come face to face with a familiar pair of dark grey eyes.

My eyes widen in shock, my heart starts pounding, and my stomach turns over. He looks equally as shocked to see me, which makes me feel marginally better. My instincts tell me to run, but unlike last time, I'm in the middle of nowhere.

We stand staring at each other as I battle with my emotions. I want to scream at him and ask him why he did it. I want to shout about the pain he caused me. But standing here, on the side of the road, locked in his stare, I can't find the words. Every single thing I should be saying to him right now dies on my tongue.

So instead of revisiting the past, I say the only words I can manage. "I've got a meeting. Please fix it so I'm not too late."

Jay's eyes soften and his mouth opens like he wants to say something, but after a couple of seconds he closes it and just nods.

I watch as he walks around me to the bonnet. I don't miss the obvious limp that never used to be there.

He must be aware of my attention because as he props the bonnet up, his eyes meet mine. I look away instantly and chastise myself for being caught.

Looking around at my options, I spot a cleanish patch of grass on the verge and wander over to take a seat.

I suck in a slow, deep breath through my lips as I sit down. I close my eyes and lift my head to the sky as I try to find some kind of balance. My world feels like it just tipped on its axis.

My heart continues to pound and my hands shake. I'm not sure what emotion is ruling my body right now—shock, hurt, or just pure anger. As I think back to that day, the anger starts to take over. My hands tremble violently and my eyes sting as I struggle to contain it. I don't want to look like this is affecting me as much as it is.

It's been five years. I should be over this by now.

I have a good life, a great boyfriend, and an amazing son. That should be enough. Yet the longer I sit here, the more I yearn for the guy currently bent over my bonnet. The only one who's ever penetrated my heart, and the only one to have shattered it into a million pieces.

By the time he starts walking over, I feel like I've talked myself down from the emotional cliff I was teetering on the edge of.

"You're not getting any fuel to the engine by the looks of it. Could be a number of things. I'm going to need to get it into the garage to look over properly." I keep my head down as he talks, too aware that the second I look into his eyes, I could lose the battle with my emotions. *I will not allow him to see the mess I'm really in,* I repeat over and over. "Erin? Did you hear me?"

Fuck.

I take one more breath before I look up. I almost laugh, because not only is he just as gorgeous as the day I met him, but the way the sun's shining on him it makes him look like an angel.

"Yeah, I heard," I confirm.

"Okay... so I'll tow you back, then."

"I'm sure I can find someone else to do it," I say, getting up and beginning to walk away. I don't need or want anything from him.

"Don't be like that."

The feeling of his fingers wrapping around my wrist burns. I forcefully tug my arm from his grasp.

"Don't be like what, Bax?" I see his eyes widen at the use of his nickname. I'm well aware I haven't used it since the moment he told me his real name, but that was then. Now, I have no right to use a name that's personal to him. He made sure I lost that the day he didn't return.

"Erin," he says on a large exhale, as he tips his head back and looks up to the sky for a brief moment.

"No. You don't get to do this. You don't get to come in and rescue me from the side of the road. Not after everything."

"I'm sorry," he whispers.

"Not good enough," I snap, managing to regain my composure. "Just leave."

"Just leave you on the side of the road with a broken car? Yeah," he laughs, "like that's ever gonna happen."

"Bax," I warn.

"Erin."

I set my feet solidly onto the ground and place my hands on my hips, attempting to show him how serious I am. The only response is a smirk.

"I'll just be over here hooking up your car. Join me whenever you're ready." He leaves me with his signature heart stopping smile before heading to his truck.

I want to fight. I want to scream at him, demand he leaves me here, but what good will that do? I've got no phone, and a broken car. As much as my heart wants to run the fuck away, my head knows that I need him right now.

I fucking hate it.

In only a few short minutes, Jay has my car attached to his pickup, waiting to be towed.

"You ready?" he shouts over, his smirk still in place. He knows how much I need him right now, he's clearly loving every minute of this.

"Come on, get in," he says as I make my way toward him.

He holds the door open and allows me to get settled before resting his forearm against the door frame and leaning in. His scent fills the car and its familiarity hits me deep inside. I try to keep control of my actions but the smell is too much to ignore. I look up, finding him staring down at me with dark, stormy eyes.

Close up, I can see some faint lines around his eyes, highlighting the time that has passed. They're so familiar—almost like home. When he blinks, it breaks our connection, and I'm reminded of everything that has me on the edge of an emotional meltdown.

After clearing his throat and backing away a little, he gives me some instructions before walking back to his truck. The limp I noticed earlier catches my eye again, but the second I hear his engine start, I disregard it as I concentrate on steering.

Nostalgia hits me the second we pull up to Arthur's garage. In my panic, I'd missed the *A. Hartwell's & Son* sign on the side of the truck. The last time I was here, it was the beginning of our journey. Do I regret the decision I made to go with him that day? No. But I do wish I hadn't put all my hopes and dreams into him coming back. Maybe if I'd been a little more realistic and pulled my head from whatever happily ever after cloud it was shoved in, it wouldn't have hit me so hard.

I shake myself from my thoughts when I see Jay jump down from the truck and start heading my way. I planned my speech on the drive here. I'm going to thank him for rescuing me, then ask to borrow his phone so I can get the hell out of here and away from him.

"It looks like the ramp is empty so we can get it straight up and find out what's going on. I can sort you out with a car for the meantime, if you need it."

His words knock me for six and my speech goes flying out the window as I think about my only other option, a certain white Peugeot covered in tarpaulin in my garage.

I haven't driven that car since its owner disappeared, and I have no intention of doing so now.

"U-uh..." I stutter as I try to look anywhere but at him.

"Erin," he whispers, and I feel his fingertips brush my cheek as he tilts my head so I have no choice but to look at him. His eyes are soft, and I know the words about to fall from his lips are going to gut me.

"No. No, I don't want to hear it. I've got a meeting I'm insanely late for and things I need to do, of which none are this," I say, gesturing between us.

"But—"

"No buts. You've had five years to say whatever it is you feel the need to say now," I snap. "I'm not interested."

It's a big fat lie, of course. I'm desperate to know the truth, but I'm not sure I'm ready to hear it.

"Just get me a car. I need to get out of here."

He opens his mouth like he wants to say more, but changes his mind at the last minute. I watch him walk over to the garage entrance and disappear.

I feel like I can breathe for the first time since getting out of the car, but it only lasts so long because in a matter of seconds, he's back.

"Is there anything you need from your car?"

"Uh... I don't think so." A sudden feeling of relief washes through me that Dawn is picking up Denny from school later and has my car seat. That's something I really don't have the strength to explain right now.

"Here," he says, walking us over to an old, yet perfect, white Porsche 911.

"This is your courtesy car?"

"For you it is," he admits softly. The way he says it gives me tingles I used to love. Today, though, they only fuel my anger.

"I'll be in touch when I have information."

I nod at him. "Good." I jump into the driver's seat and slam the door, shutting him off from me. I turn the key and rev the engine. It purrs under my control but I don't get the thrill I usually would, because my focus is on getting away from here.

I drive about a mile down the road before I see a layby. I pull over and slam the brakes on. My body jolts forward with the force before I rest my head back and take a few long, slow breaths.

What the fuck just happened?

I grab my phone. My gut instinct is to call Frankie, but the second I lay my fingers on it, I remember it's dead.

"FUCK." I shout as I pound my fists down on the steering wheel, attempting to lose some of the frustration and anger flowing through me.

I knew he wasn't fucking dead. I knew it. But I didn't for one minute believe he would be living his life on the other side of the fucking city like I never existed. I imagined us being reunited one day. But not like this.

I stay in that layby for the longest time as I try to make sense of everything. I eventually give it up as a hopeless job, because when it comes to Jayden Baxter and the way he affects me, even after all these years, I'm pretty sure I'm never going to make sense of it.

STELLA LOOKED LESS than impressed when I rocked up to her office hours later and on another planet. I tried to get my head in the game but Jay had done a number on me. All I could see was him, our time together, and the way he looked at me this morning. It was like five years hadn't passed, and he knew me just like he did back then.

By the time I get home, my head's pounding, and I'm on the verge of throwing up. It's a welcome sight to find Alex in my kitchen cooking dinner for Denny when I eventually stumble through the front door.

"Erin, what's wrong?"

"Long day," I mutter, walking over to the cupboard that contains the painkillers.

I feel his eyes on me as I pour myself a glass of water and neck a couple of tablets. His eyebrows are drawn together in concern as he watches my every move.

"I'm so sorry I couldn't come and help you out earlier. Was everything okay with the guy I rang?"

"U-uh..." I stutter. Even the thought of bringing Jay into conversation with Alex has panic settling in my stomach. "Yeah, he was fine. Said it was something to do with the fuel and engine, or something. He'll be in touch."

"You get a courtesy car?"

"Uh-huh." I sit myself down at the table and put my head in my hands.

"Anything good?" he asks, as I hear his footsteps head toward the window. "Fucking hell, baby. He must have liked you," he adds with a laugh.

I just about manage to contain the groan that threatens. "I dunno, it was just what he gave me," I say, trying to sound as nonchalant about it as possible. "Are you okay here? I need to go lie down."

"Of course. I'll do ours for a little later."

"Thank you."

Alex is in front of me before I can take a step. He pulls me to him and squeezes me tight. Tears sting my eyes and a giant lump forms in my throat the longer he holds me.

"I'm here if you need anything," he says softly, before pulling back. "Erin?" he asks when he sees tears in my eyes.

"I'm fine, honestly. Today's just taken it out of me."

"Okay." He leans forwards and kisses away the one tear that drops.

As I leave, I'm hit with a stab of guilt. I look back at him and he smiles.

THE SECOND MY phone rings with an unknown number, I know it's him.

After leaving Alex in the kitchen last night, I decided to run myself a bath. I lay there until the water went cold, running the events of the morning through my head.

It didn't occur to me at the time, but I never gave him my number. He told me he'd be in touch and I just slammed the door in his face. I told myself I was going to wait until lunch time, and then I would contact him, but as I stare down at my ringing phone, I see that's not going to be necessary.

"Hello," I say quietly as I press it to my ear.

"Erin?"

"Yeah."

"It's... me."

"I know. How'd you get this number?"

"I..." The silence between us stretches for over a minute. I'm just about to ask if he's still there when he starts talking. "It's your fuel pump. You need a new one. Actually, if I'm being honest, you need a new car. That thing's the pits."

"I know," I admit. It was Mum's car. I used it after putting Peggy in the garage and vowing never to touch her again, so when Mum died, I just carried on. I've since had other, more important things to worry about than the heap of junk I've been driving.

"I can do the work if you want, but if it were me I'd put the money into a new one. It'll be more economic, not to mention safer." The advice is at odds with his obvious love of old cars. But then, I guess his classics are a long way from my clapped out old Ford Focus.

"Great," I mutter. Thinking car shopping is the last thing I want to be doing right now. I let out a huff before asking, "What should I do about that one then?"

"I can scrap it for you."

"Okay, do that." It's perfect because I don't have to go back to the garage or see him again.

"Consider it done."

"Thank you." I'm just about to hang up when I hear my name.

I blow out a breath, "Yeah?"

"You've still got my car." I can hear the humour in his voice.

"Shit."

CHAPTER THREE

I sit in the car park of the dealership, wondering how the fuck I agreed to this. I went from being happy I wouldn't have to see him again to waiting for him to help me pick a new car.

I get lost scrolling through Facebook, seeing what Frankie's been up to, when there's a gentle tap on the window.

I give it a second or two to prepare myself for seeing him before stepping from the car.

"Was this really necessary?" I huff, slamming the door.

When I look up, I feel like someone slaps me around the face. The second I look into his eyes it's like it's five years ago. A sudden wave of safeness and familiarity washes through me. I allow myself to feel comforted by it for a second before I use it to fuel my underlying anger toward him. Why exactly am I here? I never should have agreed to this.

"I'm sorry. This was a mistake," I say, reaching for the handle.

Just as my hand connects with the plastic, his connects around my fingers.

"Skittles, please," he begs, his voice cracking ever so slightly.

The quiver in his voice makes me look up. I hate that it affects me.

Since the moment he appeared back in my life yesterday morning, he's seemed so unaffected by everything, but that one small waver tells me he hasn't forgotten. My sudden reappearance in his life has rocked his foundations just as much as he has mine.

"This is a bad idea."

"I want to help."

I see red. "A bit fucking late for that, don't you think?"

He drops his gaze, favouring the ground. "Please."

"Ugh, fine." I step away from the car and march toward the dealership entrance. I feel weak giving into him, but damn it, I need a car. I'll allow him this, then give his flashy courtesy car back, and that can be the end of it.

"Why this one?" I ask as we wander around the models on display, waiting for a sleazy salesman.

He shrugs before saying, "I just always saw you as an Audi kind of girl. I was thinking this." He points toward a sporty little white thing. "No?" he asks when he sees my reaction.

"I'd like something bigger." A small three-door is definitely not ideal with a young child in tow.

"It comes in a five-door, look."

I check the price tag. "How much?"

"I'm sure I can get you a good deal."

"I'm more than capable of doing this myself, you know. I'm not some pathetic little woman who needs a man to be able to live. I'm not that shy twenty-year-old you first met."

"Oh, Skittles. Trust me, I can see that." His eyes run down over my body.

With a little help from Frankie, I've completely overhauled my wardrobe since having Denny. The main issue to begin with was that nothing I owned fitted my new motherly curves, but I also found I was no longer comfortable in my old ratty jeans and jumpers. I glance down at my burgundy tailored trousers, white shirt, and black blazer. The second I knew I'd lost the argument about meeting him here, this was the only outfit I considered wearing. Not only is it my favourite, but it fits me perfectly. I shouldn't be dressing up for him, but the excited twenty-year-old within me who remembers everything couldn't help it.

I open my mouth to put an end to his perusal of my body—just because his attention warms me from the inside out and ignites tingles I haven't felt in over five years, it doesn't mean it's right—when the salesman joins us.

AS MUCH AS I insisted I could have done it myself, Jay got a much better deal than I think I would've been able to. He was playing the salesman at his own game; his balls were definitely bigger than mine would have been.

Just over an hour later, I walk out of the dealership, the proud owner of an almost brand new five-door Audi A1 with all the bells and whistles I really don't need, but Jay insisted on. And the colour... white, of course. I didn't even get the chance to argue. The look I got from Jay told me there was no space for discussion; I was having a white car. I don't really care about the colour, other than the fact that for the past five years, every time I've seen a bloody white car of any kind I've had to do a double take at the driver, just in case.

"Let me buy you lunch," Jay offers as we come to a stop by the Porsche. He steps a little closer than usually deemed appropriate between two people. I try to step back but only manage to bump into the car.

I keep my focus off into the distance. This close proximity already has my heart pounding and my temperature peaked. If I look at him, I know all those old feelings are going to come rushing back to me at full force. His smell is enough to put me back inside his old

Peugeot as we travelled up north on our road trip to everywhere and nowhere.

"Erin," he whispers, as I feel the warmth of his fingertips connect with my chin.

I'm powerless the second he touches me. It's like no time has passed. He has the exact same effect on me now as he did that very first night in the club.

He moves my face so I should be looking at him but I keep my eyes downcast. That is, until I feel him squeeze my chin. The shock has me looking directly into his stunning grey eyes. They're not as bright and joyful as I remember, and it suddenly reminds me that I have no idea about what the last five years might have been like for him. I'm quick to remember the pain he caused me, but clearly there was a reason he made the decision not to meet me that day. The way he's looking at me right now, the hunger, the lust, all point to the fact it wasn't because he didn't want me.

I'm pulled from my thoughts as his fingers brush across my cheek before pushing a strand of my hair behind my ear. It burns as his touch slowly runs around the shell before he continues down my neck.

I want to look unaffected, but the goosebumps pricking my skin and my panting breaths say otherwise.

Jay leans in toward me, and I'm at the point where a serious decision needs to be made, when my phone rings.

Reality instantly makes him jump back.

"I'm sorry, I've got to get this," I say in a rush when I see it's Denny's school.

My hand shakes as I bring my phone to my ear.

"Miss Roberts?"

"Speaking."

"We've got Denny here in the nurse's office. He's been sick a couple of times. Would it be possible for you, or someone, to come and collect him, please?"

"Of course. I'm on my way now."

I quickly hang up and turn to Jay. I can tell by the look on his face he knows I'm about to leave, but I need to get to my baby.

"I'm sorry. As soon as my car's delivered next week, I'll return this one," I promise, unlocking it and getting in.

"Erin?" he asks, making me look up with the key halfway to the ignition. "Can I see you again?"

I'm torn. Half of me is desperate to scream yes, to see if what we had is still there, but the other more rational and angry half wants to drive away from him and never see him again. He may have been the best thing that ever happened to me five years ago, but at the same time, he ruined me, and I can't risk that happening again.

"I don't think that's a good idea."

I watch the light extinguish from his eyes and it almost makes me want to change my mind. But I can't. This is the right thing to do.

IT TURNS out there's a sickness bug going around Denny's school. The second I pull out onto the main road to get him home, he pukes all over himself and the Porsche.

All three of us end up confined to the house for the next four days as we pass it on to each other. It's not ideal, but the enforced family time is exactly what I needed to remind me of what I have.

Alex is incredible. He's kind, caring, dependable, and nothing is ever too much to ask of him. I couldn't imagine a better father figure for Denny.

I sit and watch them both on the floor with Denny's trains and I can't help but smile. This is how my life is meant to be. Alex is my future. I need to get my head out of the past and focus on the here and now, and our future as a family.

"Alex?"

"Yeah," he says, coming to sit next to me.

"I think it's time."

His face lights up, and I know I'm making the right decision. "Really?"

"Really. I think you should live here, officially."

He's on his feet in an instant. He pulls me up off the sofa, into his body, and spins me around while Denny watches and laughs at us from his seat on the floor.

"We need to celebrate. I get off early Friday. Let's go out."

"Okay," I say excitedly. "I should have my new car by then; could we drop the Porsche off at the garage before we go out?" I ask. I need to get rid of that bloody thing as soon as possible.

"Perfect." Alex grabs my empty mug and disappears off to the kitchen, muttering about where we can go for our meal.

DECIDING I've spent enough time inside the house this week, I booked myself a hair appointment for this afternoon to get myself glammed up, ready for our night out. It's not often I go to so much trouble, but seeing as Alex has booked us a table in a posh restaurant, I feel like I should push the boat out.

"Mummy, you look so pretty," Denny says when he comes running out of school.

"Thank you, baby. Did you have a good day?"

"Yes, Peter brought his new train in..." Denny excitedly tells me all about playing with his friend's new toy the entire journey home. I hear nothing about how school went; apparently, it pales in comparison.

"Is Frankie still coming over tonight?"

"She is," I confirm, and his little face lights up. From the day I found out I was pregnant, Frankie has been my rock in a way I never could have imagined. She's an incredible aunt to Denny, even if she does fill his little body full of sugar every chance she gets.

"Yessss," he hisses, doing a little fist pump.

As predicted, when Frankie arrives it's with an arm full of chocolate.

"What? Some of it's for me," she says with a wink to Denny, as I take in her stash.

"Whatever," I mutter. "Denny, why aren't you in your pyjamas, little man?"

"I'm going," he says, before disappearing.

"Whoa, looking hot, Momma!" Frankie says when she inspects me properly.

"Thank you."

"It must be a big night—your favourite dress has come out for the occasion."

I look down at my most prized possession, a black Alexander McQueen dress I discovered in a charity shop a year or so ago. I couldn't believe my luck when I saw it still had the tag hanging from it.

"Any excuse to wear it."

"What time are you going?" Frankie asks as she starts unpacking like she's staying all weekend. She puts her bottle of wine in the fridge and turns my oven on like she owns the place.

"Alex said he'd be here by seven-thirty."

"It's seven-thirty now, isn't it?"

I look over at the clock and see she's right. "Any minute then."

Nervous butterflies flutter around my belly.

It's another ten minutes before my phone rings.

"Where are you?"

"I'm so sorry, baby. One of my night staff is running late. I'm gonna be about thirty minutes. Are you okay to wait?"

I look out the window at my new Audi sat next to the old Porsche and let out a sigh.

"Yeah, no problem. I promised I'd get this car back before eight. Could you pick me up from there?" That's not true, of course. Jay didn't give me a deadline for having the car back, but I need it gone, and dropping it off at night means there's much less chance of bumping into him. I can drop the keys through the letterbox and run.

"Okay, that's actually perfect," he says, as it's closer for him.

"Well?" Frankie asks when I rejoin her in the living room. I haven't said anything to her about Jay. She's convinced he's dead, and that I was losing my mind when I said I thought I saw him that day in the coffee shop. To save myself the pain of talking about it, I've just ignored it.

"I'm meeting him at the garage."

"At eight o'clock at night?"

"I promised it would be back tonight."

"Okay," she says, grabbing her wine and taking a sip. The way she's looking at me over the rim makes me nervous. "If he abandons you at some garage, I'll have his balls."

"He said he'll be there, so he'll be there."

"Have an amazing night," she says as I go to leave the room. "Keep the noise down when you get in, please. I don't want to be woken up by your celebratory fuck fest."

"We'll do our best," I say with a laugh as I pull my coat on and grab my bag.

I jump in the Porsche and take a deep breath. I'll just park this up, drop the keys through the letterbox, and that'll be it. Alex can pick me up, and we can start celebrating him moving in. I'll be able to put this whole thing back in the past where it belongs.

Five years ago, I thought Jay was *the one*, but a lot has changed in that time—mostly me. I'm not the person I was back then. Jay isn't the person he was back then. We probably wouldn't even work now.

The garage is in darkness when I pull up. I park the car in an empty space before double-checking that I have no personal possessions inside. The last thing I need is to leave something in it that has him hunting me down to return.

Confident I'm leaving it just as I found it, I grab my bag and lock it up. The tarmac is full of potholes and lumps and bumps so it takes me a while to navigate in my heels. I'm soon stood at the main door, about to mentally say goodbye to Jay. It's the right thing to do.

Unfortunately, I only get the letterbox open when there's a bang from inside and the door is pulled open. My heart jumps into my chest as I look up to the person stood before me.

My eyes widen and my mouth drops open. He looks pretty shocked too, if his expression is anything to go by. His gaze drops to take me in and I do the same.

Jay's white t-shirt and pale jeans are covered in grease and grime. His hands are almost black, and he has smears all over his face.

When he looks back up at me from under his lashes, it's like my world stops. His eyes are dark and he has this incredibly sexy smirk playing on his lips.

My heart continues to race and a gentle throb starts between my legs. The memory of our last night together slams into me. How it felt to have his hands on my body, how he felt inside me.

"H-how did you..."

"The engine," he answers.

"Oh."

"Erin..." He blows out a breath as his eyes drop once again. "Fuck, Skittles... I..."

I squeal when he grabs my wrist and tugs. I hear the door slam behind me as I come to a stop, chest to chest with him.

"Fuck," he mutters again before his fingers entwine in my hair and his lips slam down on mine.

The second we connect, I totally lose myself. I'm taken back to when we were two lost people who found something they didn't know they were looking for.

I have no idea I'm moving until I feel my bum pressing against something behind me. It's not until I feel Jay lift me from the floor and push me up that I realise I'm on the bonnet of a car.

Our lips never stop moving, nor do I want them too. Kissing him was always incredible, but after waiting all these years to experience it again, I realise I never want it to stop.

My fingers alternate between scratching at his head and pulling at the fabric covering his shoulders, and a loud groan rumbles up my throat. I can't get enough of him.

Somehow he gets me out of my coat before I feel his hands running up my thighs. Moans ring out around the garage but I've no idea who they're coming from as he slips his dirty fingers inside my underwear, finding me wet and desperate for more.

"Oh fuck," I curse against his lips as his fingers plunge deep inside me.

He continues to kiss me, fucking me senseless with his fingers until I'm right on the edge. Moments before I crash, he pulls out and steps away. It takes my body a second to adjust, and when I open my eyes, I'm greeted with the sight of Jay undoing his jeans.

He fists his cock as he looks down at me with an intense expression on his gorgeous face.

My chest heaves as he stares at me, spread out on the bonnet of his car waiting for him. He searches my face as if he's looking for something, or committing me to memory.

I'm not left waiting long. His fingers dig into my thighs as he slides me down to the correct position before I feel him tug my knickers to the side and press at my entrance.

There's none of the soft and gentle I remember from our first time, no waiting to allow me to adjust to his size. Instead, he slams into me. He hits so deep I almost want him to stop, but when he thrusts again and again I lose all train of thought as sensation crashes through my body and threatens to break me in two.

Lifting up his t-shirt, I go to run my hands up his back, needing to feel him. His body stills as I touch him. Before continuing, he grabs my wrists and pins my hands above my head.

I slide up and down on the car as he resumes, straining to keep my eyes open to watch but it gets harder and harder the closer my orgasm gets. Jay's eyes are closed and his face and neck are straining. Sweat begins to dampen his hairline.

I soon lose my fight and my eyes close as my release edges ever closer.

Jay releases my hands and lifts my arse from the bonnet, the angle change ensures he gets even deeper. It's only three thrusts before I scream out as pleasure races through my body. He follows with a roar of his own a few seconds later, before falling limply onto me.

My body begins to cool and my heart rate returns to normal. The feel of him starting to soften inside me has reality slamming into me.

"Fuck," I say in panic as I try to push him from me. "Get off."

"What?" When he pulls back, he looks like he's in a daze.

"Get off. That should never have happened."

I see an emotion I can't quite read flit over his face.

"You could have stopped me," he snaps.

He's right. I could—*should*—have stopped him.

"If that wasn't what you wanted, why did you come here looking like that?" he barks over his shoulder as he begins to walk away.

I suddenly feel very exposed. I quickly right my underwear before getting myself on my feet, the evidence of our actions immediately dripping out of me.

"I didn't come here for you," I shout. "I came here to give you your fucking car back so I can get on with my life."

He spins back to me, looking like I just slapped him.

"So you thought you'd do that wearing a dress like that. Just like the one…"

I look down at my black prom dress and I suddenly feel stupid. It's not all that different to the one I wore when we were away. The one he told me he loved so much.

He must see my shame when I look back at him, but he doesn't make it any easier.

"AND YOU'RE WEARING MY FUCKING RING," he bellows, the volume making me cower slightly, his words echoing around the open space.

My fingertip runs over the ring, the one he gave me the day he left, as he promised me he'd be back.

I'm just about to respond, although I have no idea what to say, when my phone rings.

The second the sound hits my ears, my mouth waters like I'm about to throw up. It's Alex, I know it is.

"Shit," I whisper as I pick up my bag from where I dropped it on the floor some time ago, and rummage through to find it.

That sick feeling only increases. I stare at the photo of him on my screen until it rings off.

What the fuck have I just done?

It immediately starts ringing again, and after taking a deep breath, I answer and put it to my ear.

"I'm outside the garage, baby. Where are you?"

"I'm just coming. The owner's here and let me wait inside so I didn't get cold," I lie.

I feel Jay's stare but I can't look at him. Instead, I tell Alex I'll be right there before pulling a mirror from my bag and attempting to sort out the state of my face.

I look different. I don't know if it's the shame or guilt of what I've just done, but it's plain as day in my reflection.

I give myself a pep talk as I put everything away and go to leave. This is it. I have to put Jayden Baxter behind me. I have a life, a good one. One I don't want to screw up because of a memory.

"Erin," I hear when I reach for the door. "Please don't leave."

I don't look back. Seeing the look on his face right now is going to break me.

"I can't. Everything's changed, Jay. Goodbye."

I square my shoulders and do my best to walk out of there like I'm unaffected, like that moment of weakness didn't happen. Unfortunately, in reality, it's like it's five years ago all over again, and my heart has just shattered into a million pieces.

"Sorry about that," I mutter as I get into Alex's car. The second I saw him sat out here, I felt like I was dying inside. How could I have just done that to him? He's the most kind and caring guy, and I've just betrayed him on the night we're going out to celebrate us moving in together.

"Is everything okay?" I can feel his eyes burning into me but I refuse to look at him. I'm convinced what I've just done will be written all over my face. All I want to do is get out of here and forget any of that happened.

"Yeah, why wouldn't I be?" Fuck, my voice doesn't even sound like my own.

"You're all flushed."

"It was hot in there." I feel my cheeks heat even more as the words I've just said register in my head, along with images of what I just did.

Alex continues staring at me for a few more seconds and I'm powerless to do or say anything. I continue to stare out in front of me as I feel the reminder of my betrayal leaking out of me.

"If you've changed your mind, Erin, just tell me." Alex's sad voice tugs at my heart and I turn to look at him. His soft, dark eyes urge me to tell him he's wrong, that we have a future together.

"What? No, of course I haven't changed my mind." His expression visibly brightens once again and he smiles. His excitement is written all over his face.

"Good. Let's go celebrate." He gently grabs my neck and pulls me to him. His lips press softly against mine and I fight to keep mine from trembling.

CHAPTER FOUR

I'm pretty sure this feeling is self-hatred. Every time I've looked at Alex, my stomach has turned over. I feel dirty thinking about having Jay all over me, inside me, leaving his mark in my body. I feel weak. I should've been able to say no, to put a stop to such ridiculous behaviour. Since the moment I met Jay I made decisions I never thought I would. Disappearing off on a road trip with a guy I'd just met. Falling in love with him when I told myself I'd never be in a relationship with a soldier, and then waiting for him to return from tour like everything was going to be perfect. And then there was that night. The night I cheated on my perfect boyfriend.

"Woohoo, Erin," Frankie says, amusement dancing in her eyes

"Sorry, what?"

"Are you okay?" Her amusement fades in favour of the concern that's been there the past couple of weeks.

I want to say no, to break down, cry, and confess all. But I can't. Admitting it would make it even more real than the images on constant repeat in my head. It would mean other people knowing what I've done and hating me like I already do.

"Yes, honestly. I'm fine."

Frankie looks at me for a few more seconds before she changes tact. "So you're just tired then from all the fucking, now Alex is officially moved in."

"Something like that," I mutter, because what she's just said is about as far from the truth as it can get.

We haven't had sex since that night. I can barely stand him touching me, let alone anything else.

I'm a mess, and I don't know how to make it any better. I haven't seen or heard from Jay, but he's in my head constantly, taunting me, teasing me, driving me fucking insane.

"We need a girls' night," Frankie suddenly announces.

"Really?" I ask with no enthusiasm. She knows I love going out drinking as much now as I did back then.

"Yes. You forget that I know you almost as well as I know myself, and there's something up. I'm thinking letting your hair down for a night will fix the issue, or I'll get you good and drunk and you'll actually tell me what the fuck is going on."

My response is just a groan, because I'm pretty sure her first point won't make any difference to my state of mind, and her second... well, that just isn't happening.

Once Frankie has told me the arrangements of our night out, she bids me farewell and flounces out the door to meet a client.

When Mum died and Denny made his early appearance, I really thought that was it for Mum's gift shop. I made the awful decision to shut down from the hospital, and with Frankie's help we cleared it out and boxed everything up. I had no idea that while I was nursing my tiny baby, she was busy setting up an online shop and giving our social media platforms a thorough onceover. I was floored when I got home to find there was a little bit of hope for my mum's dream.

Frankie's plan, as far as I was aware, was to work for her stepdad, so I never put any thought into her doing anything else. But by the time she finished uni, she'd announced her desire to become a freelance social media consultant. While she built up her client base, she told me she'd help with whatever I needed. And that's kind of how it's stayed. She works part-time in the shop while managing all her clients, and I make up the other hours around my jewellery business. I don't think I'll ever be able to convey to Frankie how much I appreciate everything she's done for me. We now have a thriving gift shop Mum would have loved, along with our own successful businesses.

"YOU LOOK BEAUTIFUL, BABY," Alex says when I emerge from the bedroom. "I think tonight will do you good after all the work you've been doing." I feel guilty at his kind words, something that seems to be becoming normal.

"Me too," I confirm. Yesterday was my deadline. I've worked my arse off all week to ensure it's done.

"I don't think you should do any more for Stella. It's taking too much out of you," Alex says as he entwines his fingers with mine and kisses my knuckles. "I don't feel like you enjoy it like you used to. It's not like we need the money."

"I'll think about it." His worried expression makes me feel bad, and he does have a point, although I'm not sure I could turn down that sort of opportunity.

I slide my feet into my heels when a taxi beeps its horn outside. "Any problems, call me," I say to Alex. I know he's capable of looking after Denny, but I still worry about my baby.

"Everything will be fine. Go and enjoy yourself." He gives me a quick kiss on the cheek to avoid ruining my lipstick and opens the door for me.

Frankie waves like a lunatic from the back seat of the taxi and I can't help but get a little excited about our girls' night out.

Frankie squeals like a schoolgirl when I climb into the back of the car. The appeal of a night out drinking and dancing never did lessen for her. I now feel a little too old to be doing this sort of thing, but Frankie always tells me I'm being stupid.

"Where are we going?"

"There's this new bar in town everyone's raving about," she announces excitedly. I notice the driver is watching her in his rear-view mirror with an amused expression.

I shouldn't be surprised when Frankie grabs my hand and pulls me past the queue to get in. The salacious smile she receives from one of the bouncers tells me everything I need to know about why we get special treatment—and if the look wasn't enough, watching him shove his tongue down Frankie's throat and molest her certainly hammers the point home, and also slaps a big fat 'taken' sign on her for every other guy in line to see.

I roll my eyes at her behaviour before following her in.

"Who was that?" I ask, although I'm probably going to regret it.

"Brett. He's a musician really, but works the doors for extra money. He's the one I was telling you about." When I raise my eyebrows for her to explain, it all comes rushing back to me. "You know, the one who does that thing with his tongue—"

"I remember. Please don't repeat it," I beg. The explicit detail she went into the first time was enough.

When we get through to the bar, I'm relieved to see this place is quite classy compared to where Frankie usually drags me. It's definitely more bar than club, and I couldn't be more grateful that we're not going to spend all night shouting at each other over the music.

"What ya drinking?"

"White wine."

She orders, but in true Frankie fashion, someone else offers to pay. "Courtesy of the guy at the end," the barman says as he hands the drinks over.

I look to where he gestured but there's a giant post blocking our view. Frankie doesn't seem too bothered about missing out, because she starts flirting with the barman instead.

I eventually get bored of listening to them and drag her off toward an empty table.

"Hey," she pouts. "He was cute."

"Yeah, and the doorman would flatten him in a second if he knew."

"Aw, Brett doesn't mind sharing."

I sit back and take a couple sips of my wine as I look around. It's modern and everything's glass. It's definitely not the kind of place Frankie usually chooses to drink in.

"What's wrong?" Frankie asks, dragging my gaze away from a very well dressed couple a few tables over.

"Nothing. Just checking the place out."

"It's nice, huh?"

"Yeah, different."

"I do have taste, you know," Frankie snaps, but her smile tells me she's only winding me up. Her taste in most things is way better than mine. It's only her usual choice of nightclub that lets her down. "Plus, we got in for free, and I know if all else fails I can take Brett home with me tonight."

"So it's not serious then?"

"I'm serious about his tongue, but that's about it," she says with a wink.

Silence falls over us again and my gaze drifts off.

"Seriously, E. You need to tell me what's bothering you. I've kept my gob shut up until now, but I'm worried about you."

"It was just work."

"No, it's not. It's more than that. Whatever it is, you can tell me."

A huge wave of guilt washes through me. I know I can tell Frankie anything, and I know she wouldn't judge me. Shit, she's made enough bad decisions when it comes to men that she can't judge anyone. But if I tell her, it'll make what happened, what I did, real. As it is, I can try to put it to the back of my mind and pretend it was a dream, that I didn't cheat on Alex. Imagine that I didn't let Jay fuck me on the bonnet of some car in the garage. Just thinking about it all turns my stomach.

I can feel Frankie's stare burning into me and it only makes the sick feeling worse.

"Erin," she warns.

"It's... It's just..."

"Fuck, are you pregnant?"

"What? No!"

"Really, because you look pale and like you could barf at any moment. Just like when you were—"

"I'm not pregnant," I snap, cutting off what she was saying.

"Then what is it? What's so serious it has that sad puppy dog look on your face 24/7 at the moment? Oh my God, have you changed your mind about Alex moving in?"

"No, of course not. It was the right thing to do." I love having Alex live with us, and I'm sure if it wasn't for Jay fucking everything up, I'd be enjoying it much more.

"You don't sound convinced."

"I am. It's great."

Frankie raises her eyebrows at my attempt to sound enthusiastic.

"Hmmm..." She brings her cocktail to her lips as she continues thinking. Suddenly her eyes widen before she tries again. "Isn't he getting you off? Is that the problem?"

I groan and put my head in my hands as everyone around us looks over. Not only did Frankie say that at an unnecessary volume, but the music dropped out at the exact same time.

"No, he's more than capable," I mutter, once we're no longer the subject of everyone's attention.

Frankie looks me up and down. "I should bloody hope so. So what gives then, E? He's seeing to your needs, you say you love living with him... what's the issue?"

We stare at each other across the table. Her eyes are pleading with me to tell her, that she won't judge, whatever it is, while mine are begging her to stop. Stop digging because I'm so ashamed of the truth I can't bear to say it out loud.

Eventually it gets too much. I lean forward and Frankie does the same, sensing I'm about to say something big. "Promise you won't say anything, Kiki." She nods and her eyes stay focused on mine. "It's J—"

"Well, fuck me gently, if it isn't Miss Frankie!"

I look to my left and my chin drops as I take in the man stood at our table.

"Fuck me," Frankie exclaims. "What happened to you?"

"You broke my heart, sweetheart. I had to find something to fill my time."

His cheesy line makes me want to puke. It also doesn't have the desired effect on Frankie.

"That's fucking rich, Dean, you lying piece of shit."

"Ouch, that hurts," he says with a pout as his hand comes up to cover his heart.

After Jay left to go on tour, the first place I went was Frankie's, and once I managed to stop crying, I had to explain to her that the 'soldier' she'd been sleeping with the whole time I was away—the 'soldier' to fulfil all her fantasies—was a liar. To say she didn't take it well would be the understatement of the year. Once she knew I was okay, she called him and verbally ripped him a new one for lying to her. I wasn't the one she was shouting at, but by the end of it even I felt the need to apologise to her. Safe to say she never saw Dean again, and we never spoke about it again, either. That only confirmed my suspicions that she was a little more invested in him than she'd ever want to admit. If I wasn't so heartbroken about Jay, I probably would've made her talk about it. But with everything that happened after, it kinda got brushed under the carpet.

"Good. It was meant to. Now fuck off back to wherever it was you came from," she snaps with a dismissive wave.

"Come on, now. Play nice. I bought you ladies a drink and everything."

Frankie pushes her cocktail across the table like it's poisonous.

"You may have got all ripped and shit," she says, "but you had your chance here, *soldier,*" she seethes.

Feeling like I'm intruding on their moment, I look away and cast my eyes around the bar. They suddenly stop, though, when they find a familiar face staring back at me.

I suck in a breath as my stomach turns over, and I start to panic. I knew coming out was a bad idea. I lose sense of everything around me as our eye contact holds. As I stare at him, all my anger and frustration from the last time I saw him comes barrelling back into me.

"For fuck's sake," I mutter, dragging my eyes away.

I grab my glass and down what's left of my wine, hoping it'll distract me from his burning stare, although I know it's hopeless. The only thing that's going to help right now is leaving.

I put my hand on my bag to excuse myself when I feel my phone vibrate inside. I immediately pull it out, stupidly thinking it could be Alex, but I instantly regret it when I see that unknown number again. Curiosity gets the better of me and without realising what I'm doing, my finger swipes across the screen.

> Unknown: You look even more beautiful than the first time I saw you across a bar.

Heat rushes to my cheeks and my temperature spikes. I angrily close the message and shove my phone back in my bag. I jump down from the bar stool and look up just as Dean pulls back from kissing Frankie.

"You okay?" Frankie mouths, indicating she's about to leave with him.

"Sure." I force my lips into a smile before pushing my bag over my shoulder and heading toward the toilet sign.

I knew it was a mistake. I should've gone straight for the exit and flagged down a taxi.

"Erin," he growls as he grabs my arm and stops me in my tracks.

"Let go." I refuse to turn and look his way, trying to pull my arm from his grasp.

"No chance."

I let out a breath as I try to see through my anger to find the words I need. "You sent him over, didn't you? You know exactly what he did to Frankie but you sent him anyway so you could get to me," I fume, turning to look at him for the first time. He's just as breathtaking as always, but I don't allow it to affect me. I stand chest to chest with him, my heels giving me a few more inches and making me feel more confident.

The guilt is written all over his face. "I needed to see you."

"So what? You're stalking me now?"

"What? No. We were already here when you walked in. It's just a lucky coincidence."

"Just like how you have my phone number."

I watch as he swallows slowly and glances away for the briefest second.

"How long have you had it, Jay?"

He continues to stare at me but refuses to answer.

"How long?"

"Let's not do this here," he says after a long stretch of silence. He turns to leave but I don't move. Going anywhere with him is a bad idea. He soon notices he doesn't have company, because he turns back and grabs my hand.

Tingles shoot up my arm the second our skin connects and I pull my hand out of his as if I've been burned.

He looks at me and raises an eyebrow as he waits for me to make a decision.

"Fine," I say with a huff. "But then I'm going home."

Silently, we walk down the street and away from the crowds, but the farther we get, the more I regret it. I shouldn't be alone with him. I can tell myself nothing will happen as much as I want, but it's Jay. My brain seems to lose the ability to function when I'm anywhere near him.

"Here's fine," I say, refusing to walk any farther.

I watch as he looks around. "Here?"

"Yes. Now tell me, how long have you had my phone number?"

He puffs his cheeks out as he thinks about the answer.

"Don't fucking lie to me," I warn.

"I've always had it."

I don't realise I've moved until my palm connects with his cheek. His eyes widen in surprise as he lifts his own hand to rub the sting.

"I'm sorry." If my anger wasn't getting the better of me, I might feel bad about the truly mortified look on his face, but that's not the case because I'm fucking livid.

"You've had my phone number the whole time?" I ask, just to clarify I'm understanding correctly. He doesn't respond so I continue. "So all this time, all you had to do was pick up your phone? You left me sat there waiting for you, thinking you were fucking dead, and the whole time you had my fucking phone number? Do you have any idea what you did to me? Any idea what my fucking life's been like since that day?"

I take in his pained face and lowered shoulders.

"Looking sad and pathetic isn't going to help right now, Jay. Maybe if it was a week later, maybe a month with a good fucking excuse. But five fucking years! You suddenly reappear in my life and act like nothing's happened, turning my world upside fucking down, and all you do is stand there and look a little bit guilty. Not fucking good enough."

"Do you think that's what I wanted, Erin?" he roars at me, clearly more affected by my words than he's letting on. "Do you think I planned to leave you there, waiting for me? You were the only thing that got me through those months. The thought of seeing you again, having more time together. That was everything to me."

"Then why the fuck didn't you come back?" I scream, tears starting to sting my eyes.

"I did," he admits quietly.

"Excuse me?"

"I did come back. I was there."

"What?"

"I came back for you, but I wasn't the person you'd have remembered. You didn't deserve that."

"So what, you just turned up to see if I would for your own amusement?"

"Trust me, there was nothing amusing about it."

"You were actually there?" He has to be joking. Right?

"Your hair was down. You had on a grey poncho with black leggings underneath, and a giant black handbag. You looked gorgeous." His eyes darken a shade as he falls back into the memory. Pain I've never seen before flashes through them.

A thought suddenly hits me. I was very obviously pregnant; surely he'd have noticed. Is that why he didn't show his face?

"So you saw me, thought I looked gorgeous but decided against it?"

"It wasn't like that," he pleads.

"So tell me what it was like then?"

"Shit happened in Afghanistan. Bad shit."

"You're alive, aren't you? Don't you think that whatever it was I deserved to make the decision for myself? I could have dealt with it, Jay. All I wanted was you. You left me sitting there, believing you either didn't want me or that you were dead, and I didn't know which option was the better."

"I'm sorry."

"I don't want your fucking apology," I shout. My hands shake and tears roll down my cheeks. "I want to know why, Jay. I want to know why you left me and why you now think it's okay to just turn up and send my world into a tailspin. I have a life now. A life I can't just up and leave like I did back then. I have people who depend on me. I can't do this kind of shit to them."

My words obviously register with him because his eyes widen and he steps back from me a little.

"You've got a boyfriend?"

"Yes, I've got a boyfriend," I confirm.

"But—"

"Exactly," I snap. "You aren't a part of my life anymore, Jay. You made that decision for both of us that day, so you're going to have to live with it."

"FUCK," he shouts as he rubs his hands over his face before running them through his short hair and looking up to the sky.

He stays that way for the longest time. I'm wondering if I should either say something or walk off when he brings his head down and looks at me.

His eyes are dark and tired, and there's pain etched into every inch of his face.

"Have I lost you?"

His words gut me.

I wrap my arms around my middle tightly because the words I'm about to say feel like they're going to rip me in two.

"You lost me when you decided not to come back for me."

I WALK around the city for hours. The pain in my chest is all-consuming. I don't notice the cold or the blisters my shoes are causing. None of them match the pain of telling Jay it's over between us, and the look in his eyes as I walked away from him.

Every part of me knows I made the right decision. I'm not a free twenty-year-old now. I'm twenty-five with an almost five-year-old son, a serious boyfriend, and two businesses. I can't get so lost in a memory of what could have been and ruin the life I've built for Denny and myself. Because that's all this thing with Jay is—a memory. I knew him for a measly two weeks of my life. He shouldn't have this kind of power over me. The thought of never seeing him again shouldn't wreck me from the inside out like it did back then. But it does. More than ever.

When I eventually walk up my driveway sometime after the sun's started to rise, the last thing I expect is for Alex to come rushing out of the front door looking panicked. "Where the hell have you been?" he asks in a rush as he checks me over, looking for God knows what.

"What's wrong? I'm fine," I say, walking up to the house.

"Frankie rang me hours ago. She couldn't find you."

"I thought she left with a guy," I say, like it explains everything.

"Well, clearly she didn't. She came back into the club to find you and you weren't there. She rang me thinking you'd come home just to make sure you were okay."

"Shit," I mutter under my breath.

"What?"

"Nothing. I've got a lot on my mind and I decided to go for a walk. I just lost track of time."

"What the hell, Erin? I've been worried sick."

"I'm sorry. I didn't mean to worry you."

"You need to talk to me, baby. Ever since I moved in it's like we're drifting further and further apart. What's going on with you?"

The guilt's almost enough to swallow me whole as I look at Alex's concerned face. *What the fuck am I doing?* I ask myself for the millionth time.

"Sorry, it's nothing really. It's just been five years since Mum died and it's Denny's birthday soon. I think things just got on top of me with my deadline and everything." I feel like the worst person on the planet using the anniversary of my mum's death to get me out of telling the truth. I truly hate myself right now.

"I'm sorry, I didn't even think," Alex whispers as he pulls me into a tight hug that kickstarts the tears I've been holding in for the past few hours.

CHAPTER FIVE

"So you just walked the streets all night?" Frankie asks, like it's the most insane thing she's ever heard.

"Yes, how many times?"

"It just doesn't sound like you, E." She looks over her laptop and stares into my eyes like she's going to be able to read the truth.

"Well, that's what happened."

"You're really pissing me off, you know that?"

I shrug my shoulders and continue fiddling with the jewellery on display in the shop. I'm desperate to confide in her but at the same time I don't want her to look at me with disapproval and disappointment in her eyes. She might not judge me but that look will still be there regardless.

She already grilled me for over an hour on the phone yesterday about my disappearing act. How was I supposed to know she hadn't left to hook up with Dean and only gone out with him for a fag? If I'd have known they were coming back, I wouldn't have left—no, I would have left, but I would have told them. I had no desire to stay in the same building as Jay.

As I think back to Saturday night, the look on his face when I told him there was nothing between us is the only thing I can see. The devastation. When I told him I had a boyfriend, I thought I'd hurt him, but the look when I said we were done is going to haunt me forever. The girl from five years ago desperately wanted to tell him I was lying and that he was the only one for me, but the sensible adult in me knew it wasn't the right thing to do—even if every fibre of my being was screaming at me to do so.

"Erin?" Frankie asks as she places her hand on my shoulder. When I glance at her she looks extremely angry. "If you refuse to tell me what's wrong, I can't do anything to help when whatever it is blows up in your face. I may not know what it is, but I can read you like a book, Erin Roberts, and I know you're in the shit, and it hurts that you won't confide in me." She pulls her coat on and throws her bag over her shoulder. "Call me when you figure your shit out," she snaps before storming from the shop.

A ball of guilt engulfs me. I rush to the door and twist the lock before flicking the sign over to 'Closed'. I don't make it out the back before my first sob erupts.

This wasn't meant to happen. I'm doing what's right. I'm staying away from him but I'm still hurting everyone around me.

I sit out the back of the shop for over an hour as I pull myself together and try to figure out what the fuck I'm doing. I decide I'm going to ring Frankie this evening and arrange to see her, at her place, away from any possible prying ears. I need to be honest with her; at least that way she might be able to talk some sense into me.

I open up the shop again for the afternoon but it's fairly quiet, as is the norm for a Monday afternoon. I manage to get some paperwork done before my unwanted thoughts overtake my mind once again and I have to put it to one side.

Picking Denny up from school and listening to him tell me all about his day lifts my spirits a little. I can always rely on my little man to cheer me up, even if it feels like I get a sledgehammer to the chest every time I look at him. There's no denying who his dad is, and that's even more reason I can't have Jay hanging around. Maybe I'm wrong and I should allow Denny to meet his dad, but he has a great relationship with Alex. I'd hate for him to feel rejected if Jay isn't interested. If he decided being a father isn't for him, I know it'll break Denny's heart. I've never told him his dad's dead, but I've also never said he's alive. I know the question is coming though, as Denny gets more inquisitive, but what he does believe is that his dad is a hero. He has him on this incredibly high pedestal, and I would hate to ruin that for him if Jay didn't turn out to be what Denny has made him out to be in his head.

The sound of Denny playing trains, talking to the train conductor in the living room makes me smile as I chop onions for dinner. I may have fucked everything up but I have him, and the most important thing is that I do right by him.

"Hey, baby. That smells amazing," Alex says as he walks into the kitchen.

"Thanks," I say as I turn toward him. "Wow." Alex is carrying the biggest bunch of bright and colourful flowers. "What are they for?" I ask with a laugh.

"Work is sending me up north Thursday to train staff in a new club." The tone in his voice expresses how unhappy he is about it.

My heart sinks. I don't want to be left here alone.

"I'm sure it'll be fun," I say, plastering on a smile.

"It's for two weeks. I don't want to be away from you and Denny for that long. I've only just moved in," he says, placing the flowers on the table and coming over to me.

"It'll be fine." I'm not sure who I'm trying to convince. "You'll be back before you know it."

"I'm going to miss his birthday."

"We can put it back," I offer.

"No, you can't do that to him. He's so excited."

"Well... we'll just have to celebrate when you're back."

"I'm so sorry. I didn't have a choice."

"It's fine, really."

"How long's dinner?"

"Twenty minutes. Go on, I know you're dying to go play trains," I say with a laugh.

"Not so much. There is something I'm dying to do though." He pulls me to him and emphasises the *do* with a thrust of his hips. My stomach turns over. I've been making excuse after excuse about having sex after what happened with Jay. I hate it but I'd feel like I was cheating on him by allowing Alex to touch me. It's fucked up, I know.

Thankfully, Denny choses that moment to poke his head into the kitchen. "Alex, come play," he demands.

"Please," I remind him.

"Please."

"Good boy."

Alex follows behind as Denny pulls him from the kitchen but I don't miss the slow perusal of my body and the quick wink as he leaves. That look used to do things to me. Now, I feel nothing.

"Fuck," I mutter under my breath as I lean back on the worktop and look up at the ceiling like it might have the answers to all my problems.

"I'LL WASH UP, you go bath shorty," Alex says to me when we've finished eating.

"Hey," Denny complains because he hates the nickname. He makes no secret of his hatred of being the shortest kid in school. I'm fairly confident he'll catch up. He takes after his dad in almost every way, so I'm sure it'll happen.

Denny's just getting into his pyjamas when there's an almighty bang downstairs.

"What the..." I mutter.

"ERIN, get your pert little arse here right this minute," I hear Frankie shout at full volume.

I make sure Denny's okay before flying down the stairs to see what's going on.

"Alex, you're going out," Frankie tells him.

"I'm sorry, what?" I can't help but laugh at the incredulous look on his face.

"You're going out," she repeats slowly, like he's an idiot, as she hands him his coat.

"But I live here."

"I'm aware. Now off you pop. Oh, and we're going to need at least an hour," she adds.

"Sure thing, boss," he says with a salute that makes Frankie very happy.

The second the door's shut, she turns on me. "You need to start talking. Now."

My heart jumps into my throat. She knows. I can tell by her eyes.

I manage to swallow down the giant lump in my throat to tell her to put the kettle on while I sort Denny out. She calls out as I climb the stairs to tell me it's not necessary because she has wine, and that we're going to need it.

Fuck.

Denny refuses to play in his room until he's seen Aunt Frankie, so I reluctantly allow him downstairs for ten minutes so he can show her his new train. I get death stares from her the whole time. She knows I've only allowed him down here to put off the inevitable.

"Right, bedtime, little man."

"Really?"

"Yes, really. Now give Aunt Frankie a cuddle, then up you go."

He huffs and puffs as he puts his few toys away slowly, before giving us both a cuddle and heading up to bed.

"So, funny story," Frankie says, turning to me. "I was at the petrol station filling up, and you'll never guess who pulled in behind me."

I swallow down the lump that's suddenly reappeared.

"You don't need to answer that, because you already know, don't you?" The stare she gives me pins me to the chair and stops any words forming, so I just nod.

"How long have you been seeing him, Erin? And why the fuck didn't you tell me?"

I stare at her for two seconds before the sobs erupt.

"Fuck," she mutters as she puts her wine down and comes to sit next to me, pulling me into a hug.

"Y-you were convinced he was dead," I stutter out between my sobs. "You th-thought I was crazy when I told you I'd seen him."

"Yeah, but only because the evidence pointed that way. You could have convinced me fairly fast. I can't believe you've been seeing him behind Alex's back, E. What are you thinking?"

And there it is. The look I didn't want to be on the receiving end of. The look of disappointment and disbelief.

"I'm not seeing him, Kiki."

"So you're telling me the love of your life suddenly reappears after five years, a guy you have off the charts chemistry with I might add, and nothing's happened?"

"Well..."

"You've fucked him," she squeals.

"Keep your bloody voice down."

"Erin, seriously. What the fuck are you doing?"

"I have no idea, Frankie. No fucking clue. He disappeared like a fucking ghost five years ago and now all of a sudden there he is, wherever I fucking turn." I explain to her about the car breakdown, and the bonnet incident.

"Fuck, that's hot," she mutters as she fans herself dramatically.

"Not the point, Kiki," I snap. "It shouldn't have happened. But every time he so much as looks at me it's like my brain switches off. What am I going to do? He's fucking up everything."

"You need to decide what you want. Do you want a cushty little life here with Alex and Denny, or do you... Fuck," she suddenly says. "Does he know about Denny?"

I shake my head, slightly ashamed that I've kept it to myself, but I'm pleasantly surprised when Frankie responds. "That's probably for the best right now."

"You think?"

"Yeah. I mean, yeah, it might make him run back to wherever it was he was hiding, but at the same time it might drag him even more into your life than he already is."

I nod because she's right. It lessens some of my guilt about introducing Denny to his dad.

I watch as Frankie falls back into the sofa cushions and downs her glass of wine.

"Wow, sweet and sensible little Erin. I didn't see this coming."

"Not helpful!"

"Everything makes so much sense now," she muses to herself. "Dean suddenly showing up the other night and you disappearing until God knows what time. What happened?"

"I told him it was over," I admit with a pang to the chest.

"Really? How'd he take that?"

The image I've been battling with since Saturday is suddenly front and centre again. "Not great."

"It's not over though, is it?" she asks suspiciously.

"Yes. I told him it was over."

"Erin," she breathes. "Be honest for a moment here. Is it ever really going to be over when it comes to Jay? Not once did you believe he was dead, and not one second has gone by since he left for tour that you haven't been head over fucking heels in love with him. It hasn't mattered that he hasn't been here, because he never left there," she says, pointing at my heart.

"I've got Alex now."

"He may be living in your house and sleeping in your bed, but I think we both know he hasn't got *you*. Not the bit that's important, because that's belonged to someone else since your twentieth birthday."

"For fuck's sake, Frankie. You're meant to be helping," I complain.

"Truth hurts, bitch."

"AM I ALLOWED BACK NOW?" Alex asks sarcastically when he opens the living room door just over an hour after he was sent packing.

"Yes. I was just leaving," Frankie says, putting her glass down and standing up. "Walk me out?" she asks, looking down at me.

Alex grabs my arm as I go to walk past him. I glance up at him briefly, long enough for him to mouth, 'You okay?' to me. I nod and continue behind Frankie. I did the best job I could to try to cover up the fact that I've been crying, but I'm not stupid enough to think Alex won't notice.

Frankie stops when she gets just outside the front door, and encourages me to join her. I pull the door shut behind me but she leans in and whispers anyway. "Whatever you decide, I'm behind you 100%. But..." she pauses for emphasis, "You're gonna have to make a decision here. And it's not just about you. You need to make the right decision for him," she says, flicking her eyes up toward Denny's bedroom.

"I know," I whisper.

I wave her off but I don't rush back in. It might be a cold October night, but for the first time in a long time, the appeal of going into that house isn't there. I'm taken right back to the reason I went on that road trip with Jay in the first place. To get away from here and from Mum, who was hell-bent on ruining herself to keep her business afloat. As I predicted, only one of them survived. I just didn't think it would be the business.

I stand looking out at the darkness before me for so long that Alex eventually comes to find me. Thankfully, the sound of his footsteps breaks through my daze and I rush back inside before he realises I was stood out in the cold on my own.

He looks up and smiles when I turn to him, but it doesn't meet his eyes. He knows something's wrong. "Everything okay?"

"Of course," I lie. It seems to be coming almost second nature these days, and I hate it. "Just the usual Frankie man trouble."

He looks into my eyes as if he's going to be able to read the truth in them. "You've been crying."

"It was nothing. Honestly. Just stupid girl stuff."

Alex looks anything but convinced but thankfully he lets it go.

"Here. Seeing as you already started," he says, handing me a fresh glass of wine.

He comes to sit next to me on the sofa and pulls me into him. I have to really fight not to tense up. Nothing's changed, really, yet I feel totally disconnected to him.

Frankie's right. I need to make a decision. The only problem is that my head and my heart are telling me two different things.

"LET'S GO TO BED," Alex whispers in my ear before he starts nibbling on it. Goosebumps prick my skin where his breath tickles but it's the only response my body has to his advances. I know I can't deny him any longer. It's only going to lead to more serious questions I'm not yet ready to answer.

My head is spinning thanks to the wine and Frankie's demands for me to make a decision as I follow Alex up the stairs, my hand tightly clamped in his.

I haven't had that much experience where sex is concerned, seeing as I've only slept with two men, but I can honestly say this is the first time I haven't been fully present for the act. My mind is well and truly absent. And by absent, I mean on someone else. The guilt eats me alive to begin with, but as he continues, I manage to switch it off. Although it's a relief to not be completely consumed by the feeling, it's also worrying that I'm now able to put it to one side and allow Alex to continue.

Once we've cleaned up, Alex is out like a light. I, on the other hand, lie next to him, the boyfriend who doesn't deserve any of this, and I cry silent tears for hours until my exhaustion drags me under.

CHAPTER SIX

I've never experienced the unease of knowing I can't trust myself. I've always been a very straight-laced person. I've always known my limits and never pushed further than I'm happy with. But as I say goodbye to Alex Thursday morning, that's exactly how I feel. It's not that I think I'm going to jump straight in my car and drive to Jay, because I won't. My concern is if I see him, or if he comes after me. Will I be able to stay strong and do the right thing? It's hard enough when Alex is right here, but with him gone... I just don't know.

I hate it. All of it.

I hated the look in Alex's eyes as he left me. I keep thinking he knows, but he can't, because he'd have questioned me... but he knows there's *something*. I swear he was silently asking me to promise him I'd still be here when he got back. He can feel the distance between us just as much as I can.

I hate that every time I talk to Frankie, she reminds me of the decision I need to make.

And I hate that every time I look at Denny, I feel like I'm keeping the most important thing in the world from him—his dad.

I keep myself together as I drive Denny to school, but the second I shut the front door behind me it hits me once again. The guilt. The confusion.

Deciding against working, I grab a bucket, cloth, and a bottle of bleach. I start on the bathroom before making my way through every room in the house. I wipe away every speck of dust and tidy everything I find in my attempt to clear my head. But by the time I get to the kitchen, I'm as confused as ever.

I drive back to the school in a daze. Denny talks all the way home like usual, but I don't really hear it, and I make dinner while he plays but I don't remember peeling the potatoes or grilling the sausages. Somehow I get dinner on the table without burning it or myself, and I'm just about to call Denny when it happens.

The ceiling gives way right above me, filling the kitchen and covering me in ice-cold water.

I scream in fright and Denny comes careening around the corner to see what's going on.

His chin drops at the sight but I can see the relief on his face that I'm okay. Freezing fucking cold, but okay.

"Shit," I shout, my frustration at life getting the better of me.

"Bad word, Mummy," Denny chastises.

"I know. I'm sorry, baby. Don't listen to me."

He smiles at me as his stomach rumbles.

Water continues to pour down over the kitchen worktops, flooding the floor. My brain suddenly begins to function and I fall down onto my hands and knees so I can turn the stopcock off. When I finally locate it under the units, I can't budge the fucking thing.

I sit up, surrounded by water, and look at Denny as he backs up toward the hallway so his feet don't get wet.

"I'm sorry, baby," I whisper, but he doesn't hear. He's too busy retreating.

I grab my phone, which is thankfully at the dry end of the

kitchen, and Google emergency plumbers. The first one that pops up is A. Harris. I hit call, then explain my issue.

DENNY'S sad face is watching my every move. As soon as I hang up, I call Frankie, hoping she's free and can take Denny out for dinner while I sort this mess out. She doesn't answer so I'm forced to call the only other person I trust to babysit.

"Hi, Dawn. I'm so sorry to call you last minute but I think I've got a burst pipe, or something, and the kitchen ceiling just came down all over dinner. Is there any chance you could take Denny out for some food?"

"Oh no. Of course I will. Paul's at the pub but I could call him if you need some help," she offers.

"No, it's okay. I've got a plumber on his way."

"Okay, I'm just putting my coat on now. I'll be there in a few," she says before quickly hanging up. I hate relying on Alex's mum when it comes to babysitting, but sometimes I don't have much choice.

Leaving Denny watching the water spread across the tiled floor, I run upstairs and grab as many towels as I can find. I throw them all on the kitchen floor in an attempt to protect the carpet in the hallway.

Thankfully, Dawn and Paul only live a couple of miles away, so minutes later I hear her pull up outside. Denny's stomach continues to grumble as I pass his coat over.

"Please can I stay? I want to watch," he begs.

"I'm sorry, baby. You need dinner before it gets too late. I'll make sure Dawn takes you somewhere good." My words don't help as he looks longingly into the kitchen. Denny's a very hands-on kid—I like to think he got that from me, but it could just as easily be his dad. I've no doubt he'll end up fixing or making things for a living, which is why the water pouring through the kitchen ceiling is amazing him right now.

"Thank you so much," I say to Dawn as I put Denny's seat into her car as quickly as I can.

"It's no bother."

"Here." I pull some cash from my pocket.

"Don't be silly," she says, waving me off. "Just let us know when it's safe to return."

I'm just shutting the front door when a white van pulls up behind my car. Relief washes through me. Hopefully the damage will be contained to the kitchen if he can get the water turned off fast.

It's not until he's only a few feet away that I actually look up at him. My mouth drops open as I look at a familiar face.

"Dean?" I ask, my eyebrows draw together in confusion.

"Yeah?"

"Aren't you a mechanic?"

"Technically, yeah. Shall we do the pleasantries when you don't have water pissing through your ceiling?" he asks with a smirk. I'm glad he's finding this entertaining.

"Yeah, sure. Through there."

The sound of another car door shutting hits my ears but I don't think anything of it as I turn and follow Dean into the house.

No sooner is he in the kitchen than he's on the floor in the water and reaching for the stopcock.

"Fuck," he grunts, and pulling back with the handle in his hand. "I'm gonna have to turn this off in the street."

He stands and walks back out past me. I turn to watch him as I wonder how many hours he's spent in the gym over the past five years to transform himself into the beast of a man he is today, when a figure in my hallway catches my eye.

"What the fuck are you doing here?" I snap. I don't mean to be harsh, but he was the last person I was expecting.

His eyes drop from mine and run over every inch of me.

"I wouldn't miss this for the world," he mutters, his eyes still perusing my body.

"For fuck's sake," I mutter when I look down to see my wet,

white, see through t-shirt clinging to me. I reach behind him and grab one of Alex's hoodies hanging on a hook.

I throw it around my shoulders to cover up but I don't miss the narrowing of Jay's eyes as he realises I've put another man's hoodie on.

"Why are you here?" I ask again once his eyes come back to mine.

"I was having a drink with Dean when you rang."

"So you thought you'd come for what? The fun of it?"

"No. Obviously we didn't know it was you. Not that it would have stopped me," he admits, cockily.

"Well, it should have. I said everything I needed to say to you the other night." The effort it's taking for me to stay strong while I say this is incredible. I'm fighting the lump that's trying to block my throat and the wobbling of my chin, which I'm not sure is because I'm angry that he's here or relieved that he is. Whatever it is, it pisses me off.

The sound of running water comes to a stop behind me and Dean's reappearance stops our previous conversation.

"Okay, water's off. Let's see what the issue is. Bathroom above by any chance?" he asks, nodding his head to the ceiling.

"Yes."

"May I?"

"Be my guest," I say, but instantly freeze as I think about what he could see that belongs to Denny.

Neither Jay nor I move, so Dean has to squeeze between the two of us to reach the stairs. I see him glance back over his shoulder at Jay. There's some kind of warning in his eyes, making me wish I was in on their silent conversation.

Jay goes to take a step forward.

"Stop," I say, putting my hand up to halt his movements. "I mean it."

"Erin," he says, ignoring my hand and stepping forward regardless.

I have nowhere to go so I sidestep him. "Just... stay here." He gives me a little nod. I don't need him snooping around my house just as much as I don't need to stay in my tiny hallway with him.

I run up the stairs and breathe for the first time since I found him in my house. I ignore the banging in the bathroom in favour of changing out of my wet clothes.

I have no desire to look good, so I pull on a pair of jogging bottoms and an oversized jumper before piling my wet hair on top of my head. What I need is for him to stop looking at me the way he is, and to forget about me.

"Everything okay?" I ask, poking my head into the bathroom to see my flooring pulled up and the boards stacked by the bath.

"Yeah. You had a fitting pop off. No biggie. I'll have this sorted in no time. Then we just need to hope Dad has a new stopcock in the van so we can get your water back on."

"Your dad?"

"He's A. Harris. Him and Mum are out and left me in charge of the phone in case of emergencies." Dean goes on to tell me all about growing up as a plumber's child but having no desire to spend his day with his hand down other people's shitters—his words, not mine—but he's happy to help out where he can.

"So, is Frankie single?" he asks, changing the subject.

"Frankie's always single."

"Interesting." His lip curls up and his eyes twinkle.

"I wouldn't go getting any ideas. She's likely to cut it off with a blunt knife if you put it anywhere near her after what you did."

"It was just a little white lie, and it was forever ago."

"Hmmm... whatever you say."

"She's smokin'. I wouldn't say no to another chance."

"It's gonna take a bit more effort than last time if you want to show her you're serious."

"Hey now, no one said anything about serious."

That may be true, but it doesn't take a genius to see there was more than just a fling between them.

I make small talk with Dean while he fixes my pipes—anything to avoid going downstairs and dealing with Jay.

"Okay. That should be sorted."

I follow him downstairs and I'm surprised to find the hallway empty when I turn the corner. My heart jumps into my throat and I run for the living room. If he's in there, he'll see all the toys and photos of Denny.

I push the door open in a rush but find the room empty. The kitchen is the same.

"What did you say to him?" Dean asks when he reappears with a new fitting in his hand.

"Nothing he didn't already know."

"You need to give him a break, girl. He's had a rough time."

"He isn't the only one."

"Yeah, so I saw," he says. "Listen, whatever it is you've got going on here is none of my business. But you owe it to him to hear him out, find out the whole story, not just write him off."

"I've got a life now, Dean. I can't just turn back time like none of this exists."

"Maybe not, but you need to talk."

I grunt at his suggestion.

"It may have been a little misguided, but everything he's done has been because he's put you first. Nothing's changed for him, Erin. Well, not where you're concerned, anyway," Dean says, suddenly very serious.

"He's told you all of this?"

"Well, no. He hasn't told me fuck all, but I can tell."

Silence falls around us as Dean finishes whatever it is he's doing. His words are on repeat in my head and I do my best to ignore them, but it's pointless. *Nothing's changed for him, Erin.*

"Right, all done," he announces as he stands and rights his damp clothing.

"Thank you. How much do I owe you?"

"Nah," he says, waving me off. "It's on the house."

"But..."

"You've got to promise me you'll talk to him."

"Dean," I complain. "I'd rather just pay you."

"Sorry, not an option," he says as he gathers up his tools. "Give this a few days to dry out and it should be fine. If not, give me a ring. I've got some contacts."

I nod as he turns to leave. "Thank you. What about the ceiling?"

He grabs an old envelope off the dining table and scribbles down a name. "This guy will sort you out. Tell him I sent you. And Erin?" he asks, making me look up from the paper. "Don't forget to make payment."

"I'll think about it."

When Dean goes to get in the van, the interior light allows me to see a figure sat in the passenger seat. I can't make out any features but he looks defeated. Dean says something to him I can't quite hear, but it makes Jay look up. I didn't need to see his head move because I can feel his stare. It burns into me and makes my heart beat that little bit faster.

There wasn't any need for me to be such a bitch to him, but I need him to leave me to get on with my life. I need him to stop fucking everything up.

I lean against the door frame and watch as Dean backs off the drive. He gives me a little wave, which I return, but Jay doesn't do anything other than continue watching me.

***

I'M STILL MOPPING up water when I hear Denny come running through the front door. His face drops a little when he realises he's missed all the action.

"Did you have a good time?" I ask, plastering a smile on my face.

"Yeah! I was allowed a second trip up to the ice cream factory."

"Wow, you must have been a good boy. It's getting late, can you go up and get ready for bed?"

"Really? Can't I play trains with Dawn?"

"I'm not sure she can stay, sweetie." I have no idea if that's true; it's just wishful thinking.

"Everything sorted?" Dawn asks once Denny's headed off upstairs.

"They fixed the leak so now I've just got this," I say, pointing up to the hole in the ceiling. "And a very soggy kitchen."

"It could have been worse," Dawn comments helpfully.

I think the place burning down may have been better than what happened tonight in some ways.

"DAWN, come and see my new bit of track," Denny shouts as he rounds the corner, still pulling his pyjama top on.

"Just for a couple of minutes."

I listen to Denny's laughter while I finish up cleaning, and it lightens my heart slightly.

A few minutes later, I'm thanking Dawn for helping out once again and waving her off.

"Time for bed, little man."

Denny pouts his small lips at me but does as he's told, and I follow him up the stairs.

"Mummy, tell me my story."

I swallow down the giant lump in my throat. I've managed to get out of telling it the past couple of nights, but I knew it wouldn't last forever.

"Once upon a time, there was a handsome soldier..."

ONCE DENNY'S FALLEN ASLEEP, I sneak out and close his door behind me. I'd do anything for that little boy, but telling that story over and over again rips me to shreds. I wipe my cheeks with the back of my hand and decide a hot bath is in order. I set the temperature before running downstairs for a very large glass of wine.

I lie back and allow the water to soothe my tight muscles. I think back to only a few weeks ago when my biggest issue was meeting my deadline, and wonder if life will ever be that easy again. I hope I made my point tonight, and that will be the end of it so we can both get on with our lives. What we had all those years ago was incredible, but time has moved on. I can't drop everything just because he decided to show up.

I must drift off to sleep because the next thing I hear is the sound of smashing glass. I shoot up, sloshing water everywhere, and look over the side of the bath to see my smashed glass in a puddle of wine.

"For fuck's sake. When's this shit gonna end?" I ask, and I pull myself up so I'm standing. I step over the mess, wrap a towel around my body and hair, and leave the room, deciding I'll get dressed and come back to deal with it.

I pull on my pyjamas and cover them with one of Alex's giant hoodies. I bring the soft fabric up to my nose but instead of the comfort his scent usually brings, sadness washes through me.

As I brush my hair, I stare at myself in the mirror. I look pale, and the black rings around my eyes only make it look more obvious. No wonder Alex is concerned; I look bloody terrible. The fact I'm not sleeping is written all over my face, etched into every pore.

Frustrated with myself and how I've allowed Jay to affect me, I angrily rub moisturiser into my face and coat my lips with some balm.

Not being able to look at myself any longer, I turn my back on the mirror and go to sort out the mess in the bathroom.

"Fuck, fuck, fuck," I mutter when a shard of glass slices my finger. "This is all fucking karma, isn't it?" I ask no one. I've never really been one to believe in all that, but it seems since I made the colossal mistake of betraying Alex, the universe is against me.

I wrap some tissue around my finger and scoop up the rest of the glass gently so I don't end up with any more wounds, and take it all downstairs.

As I walk past the front door, a shadow catches my eye, but thinking it's the trees, I continue to the kitchen. I drop the glass into a bag when I hear a gentle knock. I look up to the front door to see the dark shadow still there.

My heart begins to thud in my chest, and my hands start to shake. I don't need to answer the door because I know what, or who, I'm going to find. My body knows when he's close, just like it did that day a few weeks ago in the café, and all those years ago in that club.

Slowly, I walk over to the door, my head and my heart at war with each other about what I should do when I get there. I should tell him to leave, to forget about me. I can tell myself this as much as I want, but I'm not sure I'd ever be able to convince myself.

As I stand staring at him through the frosted glass, I can feel my pulse in every part of my body.

What's going to happen when I open the door?

I reach my hand out and pull the latch down. The click is almost deafening. Slowly, I pull the door open. I only make it two inches before part of his face comes into view.

His shoulders are squared like he's come to fight, but his head is down in defeat.

He waits a second before he begins to look up through his eyelashes, the sight makes my breath catch and my hands tremble. His eyes are dark, full of hunger, passion, and anger.

I let go of the door when I feel him push against it, and in seconds he has me backed up against the hallway wall and is kicking the door closed.

Those dangerous eyes stare down into mine, ensuring my heart continues to race, and my temperature soars.

Then his lips are on mine. His tongue sweeps into my mouth and coaxes mine to join. My hands go to his head before I feel his fingers dig into my thighs as he lifts me. His hips press me against the wall and I feel his hardness pressing into me. Tingles erupt between my legs and I begin to ache for him.

His mouth devours me as his hands roam around my body, not knowing which part to focus on first. His hips continue moving, making me pant with need for him.

"Jesus, Jay, fuck," I mutter when he moves his lips down to my neck.

My words must spur him into action because I feel myself pulled from the wall and carried toward the living room. His lips stay connected to my skin the whole time.

When we get to the sofa, he lowers me down before moving back slightly and grabbing onto the bottom of my hoodie—*Alex's* hoodie. The thought is short-lived, because when his hands come back to me they're squeezing my breasts and pinching my nipples through the thin fabric of my vest.

Jay drags his eyes away from my breasts and back up to mine. I see my own stress and torment from the past few weeks reflected back at me. The only thing missing is the guilt.

I don't get a chance to think any more because his lips come back to mine and he drops his weight onto me. One of his hands slides up the inside of my vest to tease my nipple. The other threads into my hair while I grab onto his arse and pull him down harder as he continues to drive me crazy. I go to slide my hands up his back but he grabs my wrists and pins them above my head. I'm totally at his mercy.

His hand slides over my breasts and stomach before it slips easily into my knickers once he's lifted himself up. I moan and writhe beneath him and he pushes me closer and closer to my release.

Then the one word that brings my world crashing down around me fills the room.

"Mummy?"

Jay pushes himself off me. His eyes widen as he stares down and regret fills his face. It's the first time I've seen any sign from him that what we're doing here is wrong.

I lay motionless as he slowly climbs from the sofa and backs up across the room. I want to be amused by how skittish he looks right now. But I can't. The weight of what's about to happen presses down heavily on my chest as I wait for the inevitable.

Jay's going to take one look at Denny and know the truth. As is Denny.

My head is screaming at me to get up, to intercept Denny before he enters the room and send him back upstairs, but my body is incapable of moving. It's like it's forcing me to deal with the recklessness of my actions, my stupid decisions.

Slowly, the door pushes open. "Mummy, I can't sleep."

My focus stays on Jay as his eyes widen further. His chest is heaving up and down, and his hands are balled into tight fists.

I see Denny in the doorway in my peripheral vision but I don't look his way. I'm too intent on seeing Jay's reaction.

He's going to realise any second. Then what's he going to do?

"Fuck," falls from Jay's lips as he stands stock-still, staring at his son for the first time.

"Mummy?" I hear whispered from the doorway moments before I feel him come to stand next to me.

I look between them as they stare at each other, two different sized versions of the same person.

"Mummy, is that my—" Denny's words are cut off when a growl erupts from Jay's throat.

When I look up to him, I see his focus has shifted onto me. His stare is hard and angry but I don't miss the utter disbelief and confusion.

"Jay... let me—"

"I can't deal with this right now." His hands come up to his head and he runs them over his scalp and down his face. "Fuck, Erin. This is... this is... fucked up."

I stand, wanting to go to him, but as I do, Denny grabs my hand and I experience something I never thought I would. I'm being ripped apart by the two men I love most in the world. Denny needs me to explain; he's a child and has no clue what's going on right now. But Jay... his understanding of the situation isn't helping him, and I desperately want to go to him, too.

I don't get the chance to make a decision because Jay makes it for me.

No more words pass his lips as he gives me one last stare before marching from the living room, and seconds later the house, leaving behind only the echo of the slammed door in his wake.

"Mummy, was that my daddy?" Denny repeats after a few minutes of silence have passed between us.

I look down at his confused face and pull him onto my lap.

Honesty is the only answer I can give him. "Yes, baby. That was your daddy."

"He's exactly like I imagined." His words push me over the edge and I cling to him as I cry.

Now what do I do?

CHAPTER SEVEN

I explained everything to Denny the best I could before putting him back to bed last night. I told him his daddy had a very important job and that's why he hadn't been here before. It wasn't all that different to his usual bedtime story, other than Denny's now seen more than a photograph. He knows just as well as I do that he's not dead. Now he's seen him, though, it's only a matter of time before Alex finds out, because there is no way he's going to keep this to himself. He's always idolised his dad, even from the few things I've told him, so now he's seen him in person he's going to want to shout it from the rooftops.

Suddenly the decision I've been pushing to the back of my mind is right there at the front with a giant ticking clock beside it.

When I leave Denny and get myself into bed, I find a message from Alex on my phone.

Alex: Sorry I didn't call, everything's a little crazy here. I promise I'll ring you tomorrow. I love you.

I text back a quick *I love you, too* but it's painful to type. While he was worrying about not being able to ring me, I was downstairs on the sofa with Jay. Guilt eats me alive.

"MUMMY, please can I see Daddy again?"

Since the moment Denny opened his eyes this morning, that's all I've heard. He's buzzing with excitement, whereas I'm struggling to find any enthusiasm for what I've got to deal with.

"I don't know, baby," I answer honestly, after deciding I've already told enough lies recently. For all I know, finding out about Denny last night might have forced Jay back to wherever it was he fucked off to five years ago.

I let out a sigh as I wave to Denny across the playground. I'm not looking forward to what I've got to do next but there's no use in putting it off.

I drive straight to the garage, focusing only on the task in hand. If I don't do this right now, I'll find any excuse to put it off.

I'm surprised to see the place all shut up when I get there. As I pull into the small parking section, I see two guys stood by the entrance. I recognise the giant as Dean but the smaller one isn't familiar.

"I'm guessing this is your fault," Dean says with a little smile on his lips when I'm in hearing distance.

"What's wrong?" I ask, not wanting to confirm his suspicions.

"He's refusing to open the fucking door."

Yeah, this is definitely my fault.

"Erin, this is Titch, our apprentice," Dean says when he sees me glance over to the kid next to him. Now I'm close, I can see he probably hasn't even got his driving licence yet.

"Hey... Titch," I say with a smile, trying to be polite. It amuses me when I watch his face flush red before he does a shy little wave.

Dean also sees and makes it a million times worse for the poor kid by roughing up his hair and teasing him about how to talk to women.

Shaking my head at both of them, I stand in front of Dean and knock on the door.

"Fuck. Off," is barked from inside the garage.

"It's me," I call, turning my focus to the door and blocking out Dean and Titch behind me. "Open up, we need to talk."

His response is to laugh.

"I'm pretty sure he's off his face," Dean helpfully adds behind me.

"Jay, please. We need to talk about this."

"You don't fucking say," he shouts sarcastically. "Probably would have been better five years ago, don't you think?" he snaps.

"Don't you think I would have done if I had the chance? For all I knew, you were fucking dead."

"I may as well have been. You've gone ahead and got yourself the perfect little life, haven't you? With your boyfriend and *my* son."

I don't miss Dean's sharp intake of breath.

"Jay, just open the damn door," I demand, beginning to get pissed off with this to and fro.

There are long minutes of silence as we stand and wait to see what he's going to do before we hear a bang and the door opens a few inches. As soon as it's wide enough to squeeze in, I do. It's clear I was the only one being invited in when the door slams shut again.

"We'll stay out here then," Dean calls.

"Go home."

"You don't have to tell me twice, boss."

I stand just inside the door and watch as Jay walks off through the garage toward the office at the back.

When I get there, I see it's not an office like I remember, but a self-contained flat.

"You live here?"

My question goes unanswered. Instead, he swipes a bottle of whisky off a coffee table made from wooden crates, and falls back onto the ancient sofa. He takes a swig, then wipes his mouth with the back of his hand. Looks like Dean's assumptions were correct.

I step up to him and take the bottle from his hands.

"Hey," he complains, reaching out for it.

"It's nine in the morning, Jay."

"And? It's not like I have a kid to look after... Oh wait... I do!"

I fix him with a hard stare. "Don't," I warn, "or I'll walk out right now."

I may not be innocent in this whole thing. I know that I should have told him about Denny sooner—he is his dad after all. But I was trying to protect my son.

His sulky face ignites my anger. I'm not having this conversation with him while he's wasted.

Spinning on my heel, I walk away from him and over to the little kitchenette to make coffee. The sight of the fancy machine brings back memories of our first morning together when he insisted on walking to the other end of the high street just to get good coffee. I smile at the memory and kick the machine into action.

By the time I walk back around the sofa, Jay is out like a light.

I sit myself down on the chair opposite him and watch him sleep. His dark eyelashes are resting down on his strong cheekbones and his full lips are slightly parted. It's the first time I've seen him look peaceful since he came crashing back into my life.

After drinking my coffee and covering Jay with a blanket I found on the end of his bed, I sit back down. I never once got the chance to watch him sleep when we were on our road trip. He was always awake before me in the mornings. It's something I never realised I missed out on, but as I sit here now, I wish it was something I'd experienced back then, because he's only more beautiful when he sleeps.

I sit there for hours, hoping he'll wake up, but it's wishful thinking because it was obvious he'd been up all night drinking.

The time gets so late that eventually I have to leave to collect Denny from school. Placing my notebook back in my bag, I leave the note I wrote for Jay in front of him before softly kissing his forehead and walking out.

I came here to have this all out with him but I still have everything hanging over me. I can only hope he takes me up on my offer later.

DENNY'S still going on and on about his dad until the minute he falls asleep. I'd put money on him dreaming about him tonight.

I hate that I have no answers for him. I was hoping that after seeing Jay today I'd have a clearer idea about if he wants to be in Denny's life. I know it was a big bombshell but it can't be all that different to the day I discovered I was pregnant. I knew the second I looked at the positive test that I was having it, and I already knew I loved it.

I shut his door and quietly make my way downstairs, hoping and praying that he stays in bed tonight. Ideally, I wanted to have this meeting with Jay when Denny wasn't around, but I don't have a lot of options. I know Frankie's busy with clients all week, and it's not like I can call up Dawn and ask her to look after Denny while I spend time with his dad.

I put the vegetables on and pull a bottle of wine from the fridge. I hate to be a hypocrite because I was seriously pissed off that Jay turned to alcohol last night, but I need a drink.

I take a giant swig as there's a knock on the door.

Putting the glass on the table, I smooth down the front of my skirt and straighten my necklace.

My hand shakes as I reach out to open the door, memories of how he greeted me last night slamming into my head. I shake them out and take a big breath to prepare myself.

Tonight's entrance is very different.

"Hey," he mutters when I pull the door open. The heat and passion in his eyes from last night is gone, replaced by apprehension.

I direct him through to the kitchen and offer him a drink.

"Just water, please," he says solemnly.

The atmosphere is heavy as I silently fill a glass for him and hand it over. His fingers brush mine as he takes it, and the tingles have our eyes connecting across the table.

"I'm sorry," I whisper

"Me too."

"Dinner won't be long."

We continue to stare at each other. The words I need to say are right on the end of my tongue, but I just can't push them out.

Eventually Jay fills the silence, and what he says breaks my heart. "If I'd have known… I'd have been right by your side. I need you to know that."

Although that's amazing to hear, it isn't going to help. "Can we not focus on the what-ifs? I'm sure we could both have done things differently in the past five years, but we're here now, so let's just focus on the facts and the future."

"Okay."

"Thank you."

I feel his eyes on me the entire time I'm dishing up dinner. There are a million questions hanging between us, but it's like we're both too scared to ask them.

When our eyes meet, it feels like the weight of all this lifts. For a moment, I forget about all the bullshit surrounding us, and focus on him. On the way he made me feel back then, and the way he still makes me feel now, despite the years that have passed.

As I stare at him with two plates of dinner in my hands, the dam breaks. A sob erupts and tears fill my eyes. This is all too much. The guilt, the emotions, the pressure, the uncertainty, and the lies. It all hits me at once, and I crumble.

Jay catches me just as my knees buckle, but the plates go down with a crash. The ceramic shatters and food shoots across the tiled floor as Jay holds me against him, his hardness against my soft curves. I cling on to him like he's going to disappear again if I don't. Having him back in my life makes it so obvious how much I've missed him, how big a hole he left when he didn't come back.

"I'M SORRY ABOUT DINNER," I say when I feel strong enough.

"I don't give a fuck about dinner, Skittles. I came here for you." His use of my nickname makes a couple more tears fall. I can't even put into words how good it feels to hear him say it again. It's like I suddenly feel whole.

I go to step away from him but he has none of it. Instead, he swings my legs up into his arms and effortlessly carries me from the kitchen, sidestepping the roast potatoes in his path. Laughter takes over from my previous outburst at the sight of the mess we're leaving behind when I look over his shoulder.

Jay walks us to the living room before gently dropping me onto the sofa. Memories from last night set my pulse racing, but unlike yesterday, he sits himself down at the other end.

I watch as he thinks about what he wants to say. It doesn't seem to help, though, because he can't get his words out when he does open his mouth. "How did... When did you... What's his..."

I take pity on him. "Denny. His name's Denny, and he's almost five."

"Denny?"

"It's short for Jayden."

I hear Jay's sharp intake of breath. I'm not sure why he's surprised; why wouldn't I name my son after his dad, who I thought he was never going to see? I knew the moment I walked away that day what I was calling him, but it took me a long time to be able to say his whole name without a wave of grief washing through me. I may have been convinced Jay wasn't dead, but that didn't make the pain of his disappearance any easier.

"You named him after me?"

"Of course. I couldn't think of a more perfect name for him. I wanted him to know everything about you, so you could live on through him."

"Do you still feel that way?" he asks cautiously.

I look at Jay's concerned face and I can't believe he's even asking that question. "More than ever. He idolises you, Jay."

"He's never met me."

"It doesn't matter. You're his dad. That's kind of how parenthood works." I instantly regret my words because the look he gives me says 'how should I know?'.

"You'll be an amazing dad."

He gives a noncommittal grunt.

"What exactly can I offer a kid? The last five years have been shit. I've been to hell and back, barely able to look after myself, let alone a child."

"You have everything to offer him. Kids don't care about whatever it is you're talking about. All they want is love, and I know you're capable of that."

"I was," he mutters, looking away from me.

"What happened, Jay?" I whisper.

He doesn't respond straight away. Instead, he gets up from the sofa and walks over to the mantelpiece covered in photographs of Denny throughout the past five years.

"He was so small," he comments when he comes to one of me holding him in hospital when he was days old.

"He was premature." I don't elaborate, because although I have every intention of explaining every minute of Denny's life to Jay, right now, it's his turn.

"How's your mum?" he asks next, when he comes to a photo of her.

"She's dead." His head spins back to me, a look of shock on his face. "You knew as well as I did that it was coming. It's your turn, Jay," I say.

He looks at me, sadness and sympathy filling his eyes.

"What happened?" I prompt when he makes no effort to start talking.

"I never planned for things to be like this. I was meant to walk up to you that day and sweep you off your feet."

"But you didn't. You watched me sit there like an idiot as I waited for you. Why?"

"Things went wrong in Afghanistan," he admits before taking a couple of deep breaths. "We went out to rescue a truck that had broken down on the outskirts of a town we'd just taken control of. It was meant to be simple. Go there, get it moving, and get back to base. Only, it didn't happen that way. Things didn't feel right the second we pulled up, but I put it to the back of my mind and focused on the job in hand.

"There was no one around. The place was derelict, or so it seemed. We got the truck started, and Johnny and I were walking back to our vehicle when it happened."

"What happened?" I ask on a whisper as I lean toward him.

"The truck exploded. Someone fired an RPG and the whole damn thing went up. Johnny and I were the only ones who survived, as we'd walked just far enough away." Tears fill my eyes as I try to imagine what that could have been like. "He ended up in a worse way than me. We were airlifted to Bastian, and rushed to surgery. He had his left leg amputated above the knee, while I just had a few bits of debris removed and some wounds stitched up."

"Shit," I mutter, because I have no clue what to say. I didn't notice myself get up, but I suddenly realise I'm stood right in front of him. As I look up into his pain-filled eyes, I wonder how I ever could have been mad at him. I should have known something serious had happened.

"Jay," I whisper as I reach my hand out to his. My touch makes him flinch.

"No, Erin," he says weakly. "I should go."

"No, please. I'll tell you everything you want to know about Denny."

"I can't. I need to go. I'm not the man I was back then, Erin. Everything's changed."

I've no idea what he's really trying to say, but the look on his face guts me.

As we stand staring at each other, my phone vibrates on the coffee table. Reality slams into me.

"That's Alex." I don't mean to say it out loud, and I regret that I do instantly, because I watch the last little bit of Jay shatter in front of me.

He stares at me for another second before he turns and begins walking away.

My phone continues to vibrate and my heart breaks in two. I look down at the coffee table, then up to the door Jay just walked through. I don't realise I make the decision until I'm moving.

"Jay," I call down the driveway.

He stops as he hears my voice but he doesn't turn back.

I'm in front of him in seconds. My hands slide into his and our fingers lace together. I see some life come back into his eyes, and before I know what I'm doing, I reach up and kiss him.

He doesn't react straight away, but I know his body well enough to know he's not going to stop this.

When I pull back and give his hands a tug, he effortlessly follows my lead.

I've no idea what I'm doing. All I do know is that I can't let him leave like this. I can't allow him to be alone when he's so lost inside his own nightmare.

I pull him back through the hallway and to the living room. I stay standing before him after pushing him down onto the sofa. As I look at his haunted face and dark eyes, something explodes inside me. Something I'm powerless to control.

I don't bother second guessing my actions because I'm pretty sure nothing could stop me right now. Stepping forward, I watch as some life comes back into Jay's eyes, like he can read my mind.

"Skittles?" he asks, but there's no strength behind it. "What are you—"

His questioning soon turns to a gasp as I hitch my skirt up and straddle his lap. My hands land on his cheeks before my lips crash to his. He's slow to respond; I think it's the shock, but it's not long before I feel his hands squeeze my arse and pull me tighter against him.

I kiss him until we're both breathless, but it's not enough. I need more of him. I need to rid him of his awful memories.

I kiss across his rough jaw before I start on his neck. I feel his pulse hammering against my lips and it only encourages me.

Seeing a small scar on his neck that I don't remember being there before, I trace it with my fingertip before dropping my lips to it. I feel Jay flinch beneath me before his body stills.

When I pull back to look at him, there's heat in his eyes that wasn't there before, but the dark shadows are still present.

I grab onto the hem of my blouse and pull it up over my head. Jay's eyes drop to my breasts, which are just about being contained by the thin fabric of my bra.

Reaching behind me, I unsnap my bra before going for Jay's t-shirt. I want to feel his skin against mine. I just grab the fabric when I feel his hands stop me. I'm about to question him when he moves my hands toward the fly of his jeans. All thoughts leave my head as I make light work of popping the button open.

He helps me out by lifting his arse slightly so I can free him.

As I stare down, an eruption of excitement floods my body.

I waste no time in pulling my knickers to the side and lifting myself up. The desire to have him inside me is too strong.

A loud moan bubbles up my throat as I slide down on his length and I watch Jay's jaw tense.

The second I'm fully seated, I lose control. With the help of his hands gripping my hips, I take him as hard and deep as I can. Sweat covers my skin as I push us toward our releases.

Jay's hands leave my hips in favour of my breasts and he squeezes and pinches until I'm right on the cusp of my release.

"Fuck. Jay, fuck," I pant as I begin to fall. I try to stifle my scream when my orgasm hits.

My movement becomes erratic as my body pulses with release. Jay's hands return to my hips as he pumps up into me a few more times before he lets out his own growl and empties himself inside me.

I fall forward on his chest, my heated skin sticking to his t-shirt as my heart continues to pound.

As my body begins to chill, my brain starts to function again and reality seeps back in.

Pulling myself off him, I keep my eyes averted as the guilt sits heavy on my shoulders.

"Erin?"

"I'm sorry," I whisper.

"Don't ever apologise for that," he says, his voice deep and gravelly. It's sexy as hell.

"I think you need to leave."

He stares at me for a few seconds. I can see his argument forming but at the last minute he agrees. In reality, him leaving is the last thing I want, but it's the way it has to be.

I get myself off the sofa and grab my blouse to cover up. I'm suddenly very aware of my nakedness.

By the time I look up, he has his jeans done up and is standing by the door. The look on his face breaks my heart.

"When can I see you again? I still have so much I want to know," he says, reminding me of what tonight was meant to be about.

I make a snap decision I might regret in the morning.

"It's Denny's birthday on Sunday. We're going shopping for his party tomorrow. Come around for breakfast, and you can join us."

"Really?" The hopeful look in his eyes makes my heart flutter.

"You want to get to know him, right?"

"Of course. I'll be here."

I stand, with only my head poking into the doorway so the neighbours can't see my scantily-clad body, and watch as Jay gets into that familiar white Porsche and drives away. I can't help but smile as I lock the door and go to collect my clothing from the living room.

My happiness is cut short when I see another missed call from Alex.

CHAPTER EIGHT

I toss and turn all night as the memories from my time with Jay tonight mix with my guilt over Alex.

Our relationship over the past year has been perfect. Easy. But is that what I want long term? I've never been able to forget Jay. Is that why I've never jumped into my relationship with Alex with both feet? I've always been aware that I've taken things as slow as possible with him. Was I waiting for Jay?

By the time I hear Denny get up and come running in, I know what I need to do. It's not fair to either Alex or Jay to continue like this. I need to find the strength to admit what I really want and to make the changes needed.

"Good morning, baby," I say when he runs and dives onto the bed. "I've got a surprise for you." Big grey eyes look back at me in anticipation. They're so similar to his dad's it's scary.

"Tell me, Mummy."

"We're going shopping to get all your birthday stuff."

"I know that," he says with a huff.

"Daddy's coming with us." The smile that spreads across his face almost splits it in two. It confirms I made the right decision when I invited Jay last night.

Denny's buzzing as I prepare breakfast. He's running around the house like a maniac, to the point I'm worried he's going to crash before Jay even gets here.

I'm just starting to think he's changed his mind because he's over half an hour late, when I hear a knock.

"He's here! He's here!" Denny squeals excitedly as he runs full speed to the front door.

He's stood staring at the latch he can't quite reach when I get there. I swear I've never seen him this excited.

I suck in a deep breath and open the door.

Jay's eyes meet mine for a beat before they drop to the small person stood practically vibrating next to me. They're softer than I think I've ever seen, and the love I see shining in them melts me.

I continue watching as Jay steps forward slightly before dropping down to his haunches in front of Denny.

They stare at each other, both fascinated by the person stood in front of them.

A giant lump forms in my throat as I watch them.

"Hey, buddy. How's it going?" There's a slight quiver in his voice.

Denny doesn't do anything and Jay's eyes flick up to mine. They widen slightly when they take in my tears. I smile weakly at him in encouragement.

Jay turns back to Denny. "I... uh... got you this," he says, pulling a stuffed knitted dinosaur from behind his back.

I try to contain my sob but it's hopeless, and a couple of tears drop. I never thought I'd get to experience this.

All of a sudden, Denny launches himself at Jay. They almost crash to the floor but Jay manages to put his hand out to stop them. Denny wraps his arms around Jay's neck and I watch as Jay returns the embrace.

I can only imagine how we must look to passers-by as Jay and

Denny stand there clinging to each other and I sob by the side of them.

It's long minutes before Jay slowly stands, Denny still clinging to him like a monkey.

'You okay?' he mouths to me. Concern fills his eyes but when I nod he accepts it.

"Come on, you two. Breakfast's not going to eat itself," I say once I've wiped my cheeks with the back of my hands.

Denny looks up from Jay's shoulder but makes no attempt to move, so he ends up being carried in.

The whole day feels like a dream. I never thought I'd get to experience this but here I am having spent the day with my son and his dad. I have to keep looking at both of them to remind myself it's really happening.

"That's it," Jay says as he places the last of the bags down on the kitchen table.

We spent all day getting everything Denny could need for his birthday party tomorrow. He had it all planned out to be a train-themed party for all his school friends, but since Jay gave him that stuffed toy earlier, things changed pretty quickly, and now everything's dinosaurs.

"Daddy, come on!" Denny calls from the living room.

Jay gives me a look and I can tell he's torn. Denny has lapped up every second of Jay's attention today, and as much as I've loved watching them, I also selfishly need a little Jay time myself.

"It's fine, you go play," I say with a smile.

The sound of their chatter and laughter as they play together in the living room warms my heart as I put everything away and begin dinner. I haven't asked Jay if he plans to stay, but he doesn't seem to be making any attempt to escape yet, so I do enough for three.

"DENNY, IT'S BEDTIME," I announce from my seat, watching him and Jay playing trains on the floor.

"Oh, Mummy… just another ten minutes," he whines.

"It's already late. You don't want to be tired for your party," I say, hoping the reminder of what tomorrow brings will get him moving.

"You're coming, right?" he asks Jay excitedly.

He looks over at me, also wanting to know the answer to that question.

"Of course he is."

"Yessss. Can Daddy tuck me in and read my story tonight?"

"If that's okay with him," I say, not wanting to throw Jay in right at the deep end.

"Uh… I guess. But I've never told a bedtime story before," he admits.

"It's easy," Denny says, as if it should come naturally.

"If you say so, buddy."

Denny comes over and gives me a cuddle before grabbing hold of Jay's hand and pulling him from the room, announcing he can't wait to show him his bedroom.

I sit where I am on the sofa with my legs curled up for a while, trying to get the idea that this is all real to settle into my head.

I listen to their footsteps and the rumble of Jay's deep voice that filters down the stairs.

As incredible as today has been, I can't help the guilt and the feeling of dread over what's going to happen. I'm not stupid; I know the coming days, weeks and months aren't going to be easy, and I know I can't keep putting off the inevitable. But this is so right that I want to stay in the moment, pretend none of that's going to happen.

I hear the recognisable sound of Denny's bed clunk when Jay puts his weight on it and I can't stop myself.

I silently climb the stairs, desperate to hear what Jay's going to do.

"Tell me about meeting my mummy," Denny demands, and my heart pounds in my chest as a lump forms in my throat. He wants his usual bedtime story. Only, it's from Jay's point of view.

"You sure you don't want one about dinosaurs?" Jay asks, and I can hear the apprehension in his voice.

"No."

"Okay... well... I met her one night when I was out with friends. I saw her across the room and I knew instantly—"

"Knew what?"

"That she was going to change my life. She was the most beautiful woman in the room. I couldn't believe my luck when she spoke to me."

"Why did you go away?"

I hear Jay let out a big breath as he prepares to answer that question. "It was my job, buddy."

"All this time?"

"Uh... yeah."

"Are you staying now?"

"Yeah. I'm here to stay now."

The confirmation that Jay's not planning on going anywhere slams into me. I hadn't even considered the possibility that he's still in the army and would be going again at some point. For some reason, I just assumed he was done.

"Good. I'm glad you're here."

"Me too, buddy."

"Daddy?"

"Yeah."

"Do you love her?"

I suck in a sharp breath and my palms start to sweat. The silence stretches on and I begin to think Denny's fallen asleep and Jay's not going to answer.

"Yes. I've loved her from the minute I first saw her."

I put my hand over my mouth but it doesn't stop a loud sob falling from my lips.

"It's time for you to go to sleep now," I hear Jay say, his voice wavering ever so slightly.

He knows I'm here.

I push myself off the wall and race downstairs in the hope I'm wrong and wasn't caught eavesdropping.

It takes longer than I expect for Jay to find me in the kitchen where I'm trying to busy myself with the washing up.

The second I hear his footsteps getting closer, butterflies erupt in my stomach. I don't turn around, even when I know he's stood in the doorway.

"We need to talk," he warns after clearing his throat.

I put my hands on the worktop and lean forward slightly as I try to gather as much strength as possible. Whatever he wants to talk about right now isn't going to be easy.

I spin around. His hard stare is fixed on me but the second he sees I've been crying, his eyes soften slightly.

"This is how it should be," he states, but his words confuse me. "What?"

"This," he says as he gestures around the kitchen. "This is how it should be. Us. Me, you... him. We should be a family, Erin."

"We should." But it's not that easy. An unexpected wave of anger washes through me. "We could have been. All you had to do was come back."

He looks as though I've just slapped him. "I've told you why—"

"Yes, and I get it, I do, Jay. But we were here waiting. We could have been there for you, through all of that. I didn't care about anything other than having you here, with us. That was your decision to make."

"I didn't know I was making that decision. I didn't know about him." His voice starts to rise as his anger ignites. "You could have searched for me. I deserved to know."

"I was pregnant, you abandoned me, my mum died, and I went into premature labour. I'm sorry if hunting down what I thought was a dead man wasn't top of my fucking list. He could have fucking died, Jay. He was so early, and so small. It was the scariest thing I've ever experienced. So I'm sorry if you weren't my first priority."

Regret fills his eyes the second my words register and he crosses the room. He pulls me to him and although I'm fuming, I allow his embrace.

As soon as our bodies connect, I start to calm down.

"I'm sorry," he whispers into the top of my head. "None of this is your fault. I'm sorry."

"You're right. I could have looked for you," I admit, because I'm well aware of all the things I could have done. But every time I considered doing so, the thought of having his death confirmed broke me. So in the end, I decided ignorance was bliss, and I could continue with my life, believing he was out there somewhere.

Jay gently tugs on my hair and I pull back to look at him. The anger from before has gone, his face only showing sympathy and understanding.

"If I'd have found out for sure you were dead, I don't know what I would've done," I admit.

"What are we doing, Erin?"

I go to open my mouth but soon realise I don't have an answer.

"The two people I care about most in the world are playing house with another man." A little bit of his previous anger pushes its way back in, and I realise he's not angry at me, but with the situation.

"I don't know," I admit. "Alex is a good man, Jay. I shouldn't be doing this to him."

"Then don't. End it."

"What, just like that? Kick him out and invite you to fill his shoes?"

"I wouldn't be filling his shoes, Erin. He's in mine." His voice is deep and his sudden possessiveness causes my belly to flutter excitedly.

"But—"

"No buts, Erin. I'm laying it out here for you in the simplest way I can. I want you; I want this. I want to continue where we left off. I want to be a family, and I think you want that too. But you're the one who's going to have to make it happen. I refuse to be the other man in your life, Erin. I should be *the* man in your life."

I stare at him, my mind spinning with everything he's just told me. I should be ecstatic, and I am, in a way, because I do want everything he just said.

"You need to decide what you want, Erin. I hate to do this to you but you need to know that if you choose him, I'm not going to be around to watch him bring up my son."

"That's not fair, Jay."

"I don't give a fuck. He has what's mine, and I will not stand around and watch him live my life."

I swallow as his words settle into my brain.

If I don't choose him, that's it for us. Denny's smiling face from today flashes in my mind.

"You need to seriously think about what you want, Erin."

His arms fall from around me and he takes a step back. Coldness engulfs me and I wrap my arms around my middle.

"If you decide it's not me, I'll walk away and allow you to live your life. But if it is me, then I can assure you, I'm claiming everything that's rightfully mine."

I nod as he continues to back away.

"Denny's party," I manage to get out.

"I'll be here. But I'll be waiting."

I blink and he's gone, leaving behind his heavy words and two possibilities for the future.

I stand there for a long time, staring at the empty doorway where he laid out his ultimatum. As much as I understand his reasons for putting me in this position, I also hate him for it. How can he tell me that if I decide to stay with the man who's been there for me through everything over the past year, he'll be gone? How can he put the decision as to whether Denny will see his dad again on me like that?

I fall down onto one of the dining room chairs as I continue to play out each possibility in my mind.

None of this is fair. Not for me, not for Jay and certainly not for Denny, who is mostly oblivious to what's going on around him and how one decision from me could change his life forever.

Then there's Alex. I only asked him to move in with me recently. He thinks we're going somewhere, that we're a family. How could I possibly tell him it's over? I know I'd have a good life with him.

But is it good enough?

What Jay gave me in just those two weeks we had together was more than good. It was incredible.

"Fuck," I shout, pushing the magazine that's in front of me off the table. "Fuck, fuck, fuck."

I try to put everything to one side as I concentrate on making the birthday cake I promised for Denny. I've been practising icing trains for weeks for this thing, and then Jay appears and suddenly I've got to make dinosaurs. Bloody typical. I guess it's just proof that life with him definitely wouldn't be boring.

I've almost finished when my phone starts ringing.

"Hey, baby. Actually answering my call tonight," Alex says with a laugh and I feel like I'm dying inside.

"Sorry, I've been busy with the leak, and I've started designing for the summer collection." I hate how confident I sound, reeling off those two lies. In reality, I haven't done much of either.

"Everything ready for the birthday boy tomorrow?"

"Yeah, I think so. I'm just finishing off his cake."

"Send me a picture."

"I will," I say, and then wonder how I'm going to explain the dinosaurs.

"I miss you, baby."

"You too."

"I hate sleeping alone again. I'd just got used to having someone to cuddle every night."

"Aw, well, you'll be back soon." I want to sound like I miss him too, but even I can tell that I don't sound all that bothered. "Listen, I've got to get some final bits done for tomorrow; can I call you in the morning?"

"Oh... yeah sure. FaceTime me so I can wish Denny happy birthday?"

"Of course. I'll see you soon."

"I love you, Erin," he says, and it feels like someone's ripping my heart out.

"You, too. Night."

I quickly hang up the phone, achingly aware that I couldn't have made it any more obvious that something's wrong.

My phone starts ringing again before I even have a chance to put it down. My stomach drops, thinking I'm either going to have to come clean over the phone when he's miles away, or lie through my teeth —*again*.

I breathe a sigh of relief when I see Frankie's name on my screen.

"Hey," I say, putting my phone to my ear.

"What's wrong?"

I burst into tears.

"I'm on my way."

CHAPTER NINE

"Happy birthday to you..." I sing when I open Denny's door the next morning. He smiles wide when his sleep-fogged brain registers what today is.

"I'm five!" he announces happily.

"You are, baby," I confirm as I wonder where the hell the past five years have gone. "Now get up and get dressed. We've got a party to prepare for."

"Is Daddy still coming?"

"I think so," I say, because after last night I wouldn't be at all surprised if he avoids it.

"Happy birthday!" Frankie says when we join her in the kitchen a while later.

"Aunt Frankie, why are you here?"

"To celebrate, silly."

In truth, Frankie decided I needed a girls' night in after our brief phone call last night, so as well as bringing two bottles of wine, she packed her stuff and announced she was staying the night.

We spent hours going back and forth over what I was going to do, and I went to bed thinking I'd made my decision. Now I've got a slightly fresher head on my shoulders, I'm not so sure.

Frankie's words from last night come back to haunt me. "If you wait until you're 100% sure, it could be too late," she warned. And I know she's right, but it doesn't make any of this easier.

I make us pancakes for breakfast, and Frankie insists on sticking a candle in Denny's so he can blow it out. "Practice for later," she says, putting the plate down in front of him.

When she looks up at me, she must be able to tell where my head's at because she gives me a sympathetic smile.

"It'll be okay," she says once Denny's left the room.

"I know. I hate this."

"Well, that's what happens when you jump into bed with another man." I fix her a hard stare. "Sorry," she mutters sheepishly. "It's true though."

I can't deny she's right.

THE KIDS ARE due to arrive in thirty minutes. Denny's already running around like he's spent all morning downing Red Bull. I send him to the living room to check for the fifth time that everything is as he wants it and all his toys are tidy, while I plop myself down on one of the dining room chairs with a coffee.

"Remind me why I'm doing this," I say to Frankie when I look over at her sympathetic but amused eyes.

"Because you love him and you'll do anything to make him happy."

I barely have time to take a sip of coffee before there's a knock on the door.

"I'll go," Frankie offers, but I tell her to stay put and go myself. It'll only confuse the parents if she's at the door.

When I pull it open, though, I start to wish I'd allowed her to, because stood in the doorway looking a little unsure of himself is Jay.

"Hey," I say sheepishly. "I wasn't sure if..." I trail off, because he knows exactly what I'm thinking.

"I told him I'd be here, so I am."

"Okay," I whisper, swallowing down my emotion. "Denny, guess who's here," I call out behind me, needing the distraction.

Denny runs out and squeals in excitement when he sees not only Jay but the giant present in his hands.

"You didn't have to at such short—" His hard stare stops my words.

He allows Denny to pull him to the living room, and I just about manage to breathe a sigh of relief when he looks back at the last minute. His eyes are begging me to make a decision. To choose him and our family.

"Was that—" Frankie goes to ask, but she can obviously tell by the look on my face who it was. "Everything's going to be okay, Erin. Get today over with, and then you can get everything sorted."

"Yes, it'll all be fine," I say with a confidence I don't feel.

Jay keeps himself hidden away in the living room with Denny. I'm dying to know what he bought him, but I also don't think us being in the same room as each other is wise if he's going to keep giving me that look.

I busy myself with greeting Denny's friends and making small talk with their parents. All but a couple capitalise on their child-free time and make a run for it the second they've handed over their little darling.

"Everything okay?" Frankie asks from her position of filling up plastic dinosaur cups.

"Yep, so far so good."

FRANKIE, Jay and I are busy dishing out the sandwiches for the kids' indoor picnic when the front door bangs shut.

"Who's that?" Frankie asks. When I look up, I can see she's having the exact same thought as me, because her eyes are wide with panic. She glances over my shoulder to Jay, and then we both look to the doorway and wait. He's completely oblivious as he continues handing out sausage rolls to hungry children.

I feel sick when a shadow falls across the entrance to the living room, and seconds later the inevitable happens.

Alex comes to a stop in the doorway, his hands full with a giant bunch of flowers and a blue gift bag.

"Surprise," he announces. "Happy birthday, little man."

Denny's face lights up at the same time Jay's drops. He was having a hard time dealing with the fact there was a man in my life, but I think it was made easier by the fact he'd never been able to put a face to him.

It takes Alex a few seconds before he notices Jay's death glare, but when he does look up, his mouth drops instantly.

Alex's eyes run over every inch of Jay's face as if he must be imagining things, while Jay's face only becomes harder, more serious.

They stare at each other for long minutes. The kids are unaware of the tension falling around the room and continue stuffing their faces.

I feel Frankie step up to me and her hand wrap around my forearm. "Go talk to him, welcome him home. And unless you want to have this conversation now, in front of an audience, you're going to need to look excited that he's here."

I let out a breath and plaster a smile on my face. "Oh my God, Alex! I wasn't expecting you." My voice sounds ridiculous, all high and squeaky, and I know Frankie is rolling her eyes at my attempt of excitement behind me.

"Let's go and get you a coffee, you must be exhausted," I say once I've given him a very tedious kiss. I can feel Jay's stare burning into the back of my head.

I grab Alex's hand and I'm surprised when I feel him follow me. I was expecting at least a bit of a fight.

We walk through the hallway, past the small bag he dropped by the front door. No words are spoken but I can feel the tension radiating from him.

"Erin?" he asks the second I come to a stop in the kitchen.

I ignore him a while longer as I faff around with the coffee machine and try to gather my thoughts.

"Erin?" he asks again, a little harsher this time.

Turning around, I lean back against the counter before I risk a look up at him. I was expecting to see anger etched into his features, his lips to be in a thin line and his eyes accusing, but I see none of that. All I see is Alex. The guy who's done everything he can to make me happy, to show me he loves me. The man who's told me countless times how he wants to build a life with me, grow our family together.

I let out a giant breath I didn't know I was holding, as I will the tears stinging my eyes to stay put.

"Why didn't you tell me?" he asks calmly. I was expecting shouting, anger, not this.

"It was all a bit of a surprise."

"How long has he—" His question is cut off as Frankie pokes her head into the kitchen.

"Sorry, we need more sandwiches," she says as she tiptoes into the room and grabs them as if her sneaking will mean she's not here.

"I couldn't say no to Denny," is all I say to whatever Alex's question was going to be as I grab the plate of cooling chicken nuggets behind me and practically run from the room.

Fuck.

The next few hours are the most awkward of my life. I do my best to stay away from Jay so I don't arouse Alex's suspicions any more than I already have, but that only means Jay's glances and attempts to get my attention increase. I also don't miss the increasingly cold looks he gives to Alex every time he speaks to me. Jay's doing the best job he can at marking his territory, and it's pissing me off. He may as well just pee all over the room.

For some reason though, Alex is either oblivious to all of this going on around him, or he's playing a very good game by appearing to be unaffected by Jay's presence.

Thankfully, as the party begins to wind down, I notice Jay grab his jacket. I prepare myself for what he might say. Will he remind me of his ultimatum, or will his anger over Alex's appearance get the better of him?

Fortunately—or unfortunately, I'm not really sure—after Jay says his goodbye to Denny, he disappears through the front door. He doesn't even look my way.

"I think there are going to be fireworks," Frankie whispers in my ear after watching Jay's silent departure.

"Not helpful, Kiki."

"Just making sure you know what's coming your way. Alex is too quiet, and Jay's about to blow. It's not going to be pretty."

"I know," I snap.

"THANKS FOR YOUR HELP TODAY, FRANKIE," Alex says when he joins us in the kitchen with more rubbish. The kids left over ten minutes ago, so we're all attempting to tidy up after them. "But you don't have to stay for this. Head off home and enjoy your afternoon."

I look over my shoulder at Alex to see the darkness I was expecting when he first laid eyes on Jay earlier starting to creep in.

"Uh... okay," Frankie says. "I'll... uh... ring you tomorrow, E."

"Okay. Thank you," I say as she leaves the room to find Denny.

Alex takes over Frankie's position of drying up and we work silently side by side. The atmosphere is horrendous. He clearly has plenty he wants to say about the situation, and I wish he'd just come out with it.

Alex is still eerily calm all evening, and as the minutes pass by, I'm more and more on edge. But I refuse to have this out with him while Denny's awake to witness it.

"I've run you a bath," Alex says sweetly once I've got Denny to bed.

"Oh... thank you." I'm more than grateful. After a day dealing with not only hyperactive four and five year olds but also having Jay and Alex in the same room, I'm very ready for some relaxation. But this wasn't how I was expecting our evening to go.

Deciding to make the most of it, I grab myself a glass of wine and settle into the bath. It's anything but relaxing. My head's spinning. What's going on with Alex? Surely he has questions about Jay's sudden appearance. He has to be a little curious as to why I haven't told him he'd be here today—or that he's even alive. Then there's Jay, who's also messing with my head. The look on his face when he saw Alex for the first time. He was devastated. His imagination was obviously only so good, because having a face to put to the man I've been living with ripped him apart.

I end up getting out long before I usually would. I'm all over the place and the anticipation of my impending conversation with Alex has my stomach turning.

He's sat on the sofa with a beer, watching the TV when I appear not long later. He glances over and smiles. Why is he being like this?

"I've ordered Chinese. I didn't think you'd be up for cooking."

"Thank you."

Once I've refilled my wine, I join him. I fall back onto the sofa and let out a big breath.

"Bet you're glad that's over with. Do you think maybe you should have a party somewhere else next year? Soft play or something?" He's got a little smug smile on his face because he told me from the very beginning I'd regret having it here.

"Yeah, I think so. That was exhausting."

Alex looks at me for a few seconds longer, as if he's waiting for me to say something, but when I don't, he starts telling me about the new club he's been helping set up this week.

It's weird. Really weird.

Dinner arrives and we sit and eat like it's any other night. The only difference is that my wine goes down way better than usual.

It's not until Alex suggests we head to bed that I realise something's missing. There haven't been any little touches; he hasn't leant over to kiss me during the adverts like he usually would.

As I climb the stairs, I feel the weight of what I'm about to do press down on me. I need to put a stop to this. I shouldn't be getting into bed with Alex like everything's okay. It feels like the conversation I need to have with him is going to be the hardest thing I've ever done. It seemed simple when I was talking to Frankie about it last night, when Alex was so far away, but now he's here, following me up to the bed we share, it doesn't feel so easy.

I go about my usual routine. I remove my make-up, brush my teeth and hair, and pull on a pair of pyjamas.

The sight of Alex propped up against the headboard, clearly naked, turns my stomach. I hate myself for what I've been doing, for what I've done to him.

"What's wrong?"

My mouth goes so dry I don't think I could get words out even if I wanted to.

I stand frozen to the spot as we stare at each other. The words I need to say are right on the tip of my tongue, but when he flicks the covers back, encouraging me to join him, I do just that.

I lie flat on my back with my arms pinned to my sides. It's only then I realise my head's spinning from the three large glasses of wine I've had.

My eyes are shut but I feel Alex peering down at me. My heart pounds so hard I can feel it in my fingers.

The second his hand lands on my waist, I flinch. My eyes spring open in surprise but I soon shut them again. Being able to see him only makes this worse.

His lips press to mine but I don't respond. He doesn't seem to notice, or he doesn't care, because he trails soft kisses across my jaw and down my neck. He whispers how much he's missed me the past week, but his words don't have the effect they usually would.

It's when he starts kissing down over my collarbone that I start to panic.

"Alex, no," I whisper, but I don't move.

His whole body stops for a second as he waits for me to continue, but I don't.

When his hand slides over my waist again, I rush to push it off and I sit bolt upright in bed. My eyes are wide as I stare at the wall ahead of me.

"I'm sorry. I can't," I whisper.

"I know."

I turn to look at him and find him sat with his forearms resting across his knees. The muscles in his shoulders are pulled tight and he has a deep frown line between his brows.

"I know, Erin."

"Know what?"

"That you've been seeing him behind my back," he says calmly.

My mouth drops open and I stare at him. He knows. How can he know?

"My mum saw you out with him yesterday. I didn't believe her so I came back to find out the truth." He pauses and my heart continues to plummet. "And here he was. In the house I live in, with the woman I love, and the boy I think of as my own."

His words gut me, and tears start to pour down my cheeks, yet the words I need to say don't come.

"You've never completely given yourself over to me. I always felt like he'd kept a part of you. It's how I knew you were lying when you said he was dead. If he was, he'd have let you go. I always knew that if he came back for you, I would never be the one you'd choose."

I swipe at my cheeks to clear the tears, but more take their place.

"How long's it been going on for, Erin?"

"Since my car broke down," I whisper. "He was the guy you sent to rescue me."

I don't expect him to laugh, but that's exactly what he does. "So if I'd have come for you that day, this might not have happened?"

I shake my head.

"No, you're right. This was always going to happen. It was just a case of when. Why did you ask me to move in with you?" His voice is so calm and steady. Why isn't he shouting at me? Why isn't he screaming that I betrayed him?

"Because I thought it was the right thing to do."

The bed creaks and I watch as he gets up and starts pulling his clothes on.

"Why did you wait until now to bring this up? Why that?" I ask, pointing down at the mattress.

"Because I wanted you to tell me, Erin. I didn't want to drag it from you." It's the first time he's allowed any emotion into his voice. "Don't you think you owe me the truth?"

I nod at him as I shift around, pulling the duvet around myself and following his movement as he pulls a suitcase from under the bed and begins filling it with his clothes. His hands shake as he tries to fold a t-shirt.

"How many times?" His question confuses me to start with, but as soon as I realise what he's asking, I look away. "How many times, Erin?"

"T-twice."

"When?"

I look away again, not wanting to answer that question but knowing I have no choice.

"The night I dropped his car off." I say it so quietly I'm convinced he hasn't heard.

There's a long pause before he responds.

"The night we went out to celebrate me moving in. Of course," he says with a laugh that's anything but amused. "And?"

"The other night."

"So what were you planning on doing, then? Stringing us both along for as long as you could?" he snaps, his voice getting a little harsher.

"No, Alex, no. I didn't want any of this. I never wanted to hurt you. I thought you could move in and we could get on with our lives. I didn't expect seeing him again would affect me the way it has, and I didn't expect him to want me, to want us."

"But he does."

I nod.

"You're his, Erin. You always have been. I can beg, plead, get angry and shout all I like, but I know it won't make any difference. I've known for a long time this was going to happen, but I'd convinced myself it was all in my head. When Mum's call came, I wasn't surprised one bit. You've been acting weird for weeks so it wasn't hard to figure out what was going on. I just hoped I was wrong," he admits as he zips up the case.

"I'm so sorry, Alex."

"I know you are. I know you, Erin. I know you wouldn't have done this intentionally, but you've done it nonetheless. I may not be shouting at you right now but do not take that to mean I don't care or that it doesn't hurt. It hurts like a motherfucker. I'll be back for the rest of my stuff and to say goodbye to Denny," he says all of a sudden.

And then, he's gone.

I listen to his feet run down the stairs before the front door slams and his car starts.

What the fuck was that? I ask myself as I stay sat cross-legged on the bed.

Have I been so transparent this entire time that he knew deep down I'd never let Jay go? How did he see that when I couldn't even see it myself?

I fall back on the bed and stare up at the ceiling as I run our conversation through my head again and again, trying to figure it all out.

CHAPTER TEN

I don't get a second of sleep. I'm either still dissecting last night's conversation with Alex, or practising what I need to say to Jay.

I texted him in the middle of the night, asking him to come over once Denny's at school, and the longer I sit here waiting for that knock at the door, the more nervous I get.

This is going to be fine, I tell myself. *He's going to understand.*

When the knock comes, I jump to my feet. Nervous energy rushes through my body and gives me the strength I need to get up.

Jay doesn't say anything when I open the door. He just steps forward, forcing me to move out of his way, and looks around. I've no idea what he's looking for until I see his gaze land on the coat hooks and shoe rack.

It's only then I realise there's a lack of male items.

"Please," he begs. "Tell me it's over. Tell me you asked me here because he's gone."

I stare at him, the intensity in his grey eyes holding mine hostage.

"Erin, please. I need to know you're mine, and mine alone."

I can't force any words out so I nod once. But that's enough.

The next thing I know, my back hits the hallway wall and Jay's mouth is on mine. His tongue forces its way in and teases mine until it joins in.

He lifts me from the floor and forces my legs to wrap around his waist. He's rough and his fingers dig into my thighs as his hips pin me to the wall. His kiss continues as his hands start to work their way up my body. He skims over my waist before grabbing onto my breasts. He squeezes and a moan rumbles in my throat.

I hear pinging at the same time cool air hits my stomach. When I look down, I see him staring at my almost naked chest where he ripped my shirt open.

His hands come to my arse and he lifts me high enough so he can pull the cup of my bra down with his teeth. The second my nipple is free he pulls it into his mouth and sucks hard before I feel his teeth press down.

I'm panting as I feel him start to ascend the stairs. By the time we're at the top, I'm desperate for more. My muscles clench as I try to rub myself against him for some friction.

"My girl's so impatient," he says as we both fall down onto the bed.

His lips come back to mine and he continues to rid me of my clothes until I'm naked for him.

I feel his eyes burn a trail over every inch of my body, but in no time, I feel him lean back over me, continuing his torture of my breasts.

"Jay, more," I moan when the teasing of my nipples isn't enough.

He runs kisses down my stomach as he pushes my legs open.

"Fucking perfect," he mutters to himself before I feel a finger run down the length of me.

My hips buck from the bed. "Someone's sensitive. Looks like we're about to have some fun." His tongue is on me almost before he's finished talking.

My hands scratch at his head and over his shoulders as he licks and sucks at me. "Don't come, not yet," he says as he pulls away for a second.

It takes everything I have to follow his instruction, but knowing what's to come makes it so worth it.

"Jay, please," I beg, wanting more.

"You ready for it?" he asks, teasing me with his cocky smile.

"Oh God, yes. Now get naked," I demand. I expect him to start pulling at his jumper or to undo his jeans, but instead he stills. "What's wrong?" I pant, propping myself up on my elbows.

"It's just..." he scrubs his hands over his face.

"What, Jay?"

"I'm not like you remember."

"What are you talking about?" I was so close to coming that my brain's all over the place.

He thinks for a couple more seconds before he lets out a breath and pulls his jumper over his head.

I suck in a breath as his familiar torso comes into view—the one I remember watching every morning as he did his sit-ups. I run my eyes down over his shoulders and pecs, and see black script on the inside of his left arm that wasn't there before.

"Let me see," I say, holding my hand out to him.

His hand slides into mine and he steps forward. I reach my fingers out to run them over the ink.

Everywhere & Nowhere is etched permanently on his upper arm. Underneath, there are Roman numerals.

"What are they for?"

"The day we met."

A giant lump forms in my throat. He never forgot us. My hand comes up to my mouth as I try to keep my emotions in check.

"That wasn't what I was talking about, though."

"Wha—" My question is cut off as he drops his jeans and turns around. My eyes widen and my mouth drops open.

"Oh," I whisper as I run my eyes over the scars across his back and down his legs.

His head's down and his shoulders are slumped in defeat as he waits for my reaction.

I crawl across the bed, get up on my knees and reach out. I gently press my finger to the scar I found the other night, but didn't think anything of. Jay's entire body flinches at my contact. I let my fingers trail across his shoulders and down his spine as I lean forward and place a kiss between his shoulder blades.

It's only then I remember that he kept his clothes on both times we've been together. I didn't think anything of it, but it's so obvious now.

"Jay," I whisper. "None of this matters to me. Of course I love the outside of you, but it's what's on the inside that I really care about."

I feel him hold his breath as I talk, and he slowly lets it out once I've stopped. After a second, he turns back to me and drops his boxers.

We stare at each other and in that second, something passes between us. I don't get time to put any thought into it, because I'm suddenly pushed back on the bed. He pulls my legs apart, and within seconds, he's lined up and at my entrance.

"You're fucking perfect. You know that, right?" he asks as he thrusts forward.

I grunt as he hits as deep as he possibly can before pulling out and repeating it over and over. Sweat starts to run down his brow as he loses control.

I watch as the muscles in his neck and chest tense with his impending release.

"Come, Erin," he demands as he presses his thumb to my clit. I was so lost watching him I hadn't registered that I'm right there. He grinds his hips into me and I fall over the edge on a scream.

His weight lands on top of me and I wrap my arms around him. He stills when my hands touch his scarred skin, but he soon relaxes into the embrace.

WHEN I WAKE, I stretch my arm out to find him, but only cold sheets greet me.

Pulling my arm back, I allow myself a couple of seconds to reflect on everything that happened last night with Alex, and this morning with Jay.

A sudden panic has me jumping from the bed, but I breathe a sigh of relief when I see it's only just after lunch. I would have never forgiven myself if I fell asleep and missed picking Denny up.

My muscles pull as I make my way to the shower. Of course I'm desperate to find out if Jay's still here, but I'm happy to put off the words I need to say to him. I wash myself quickly as I rehearse my speech in my head. I know he's not going to be happy, but I just hope he understands my reasons.

I throw on a pair of jeans and a t-shirt before heading downstairs to see if he's still here. Everything's silent as I descend the stairs and I start to think he's left. Relief floods me as I think about putting off this conversation for a little while longer.

A figure slumped at the dining room table startles me when I walk into the kitchen. He obviously didn't hear me coming, but my presence makes him look up at the last minute. When his eyes meet mine, they're dark and haunted.

I stare back at him, unable to form words to ask what's wrong.

Dread fills me that he's regretting this. That I've just thrown everything I had with Alex away for him. My concerns are soon put to rest when he speaks though.

"No one's ever..." he starts, his voice deep and troubled. "I've not told..."

The pain in his voice has me rushing over to him. He moves back from the table slightly and it allows me space to sit on his lap.

"It's okay," I whisper as I wrap my arms around his shoulders. He freezes when I go to run my hands down his back, but he soon relaxes into my embrace.

"I'm sorry. It just brings it all back. I don't care what you say, you wouldn't have wanted me if I came up to you that day. My legs were fucked, the muscles and ligaments shredded by debris, my burns were slowly healing... but that was only the beginning, because it was my head that caused the biggest problems. I could cope with my body; that would heal. But the constant images in my mind, seeing my guys lying there, dead and dying. Knowing it should have been me. If it wasn't for Johnny, I'd have died that day, and back then I wished I had. Fuck, Erin. You were the only positive thing I had, but I couldn't come to you like that. It wasn't fair."

I pull my head out of his neck so I can look at him. The lone tear I see slowly running down his cheek breaks my heart. I reach out and catch it with my thumb.

"I'm here now, Jay. I'm here," I say softly as I wrap my arms around him tightly once again.

We stay in our embrace at the dining room table for the longest time. When I eventually feel Jay's hold on me loosen a little and I look up at him, I'm pleased to see a bit of his usual sparkle back in his eyes.

"So what's next for us, Skittles?"

My heart drops as I'm reminded of the words I was rehearsing in the shower. This isn't going to go well, and in the aftermath of what he's just told me and what he's been through, I feel like the biggest twat on the planet, but I've got to do it.

I look into his gorgeous grey eyes and take a breath. There's questions in them and his brows draw together. "I need some time, Jay."

"What for?" he asks.

"I need some time for myself, to get my head together and my life back on track. The last few weeks have screwed everything up. I need some time with Denny to attempt to explain what's going on, why Alex has suddenly left his life, and I'm sure he's still confused about where you came from."

I watch as his features harden once again. "What exactly are you saying here?"

"Nothing's going to happen with us yet," I whisper.

"But…" he starts, but I put my fingers up to his lips to halt him.

"I chose you, Jay. It's over with Alex, but I need some time. Just because he's moved out, it doesn't mean I'm moving you straight in."

"But—"

"No buts, Jay. I need this. Denny needs this."

Jay pushes me from his lap and I stumble to keep my footing. He stands and the chair crashes to the floor behind him as he paces across the room.

"You've had five years, Erin. Isn't that long enough? We're a family, we should be together."

"And we will be," I say softly. "I want this, Jay, more than anything, but I will not rush into it."

"This is bullshit," he spits. "How long?"

"I don't know," I answer honestly.

"And what about in the meantime? I go back to the garage and wait? Wait for my life to restart?"

His words threaten to break me, but I need this. I need to think of myself and Denny, do what's right for us.

"Yes," I whisper.

"This is fucking bollocks, Erin."

"I'll come to you, when I'm ready."

"Well you'd better hope I'm fucking there."

The slamming of the front door reverberates through the house. My knees buckle and I fall to the floor.

The last thing I want to do is hurt him. He's been through enough, but I want to do everything right this time.

The rest of the day goes by in a daze. I collect Denny, make his dinner, do all the usual things, but I feel like I'm watching it all happen from outside my own body. It's been like that since Jay left. I can't get his parting words from my head. *"Well you'd better hope I'm fucking there."* He wouldn't leave. Would he? I told him I've chosen him. He's got a family here. Surely he must understand my need for a little time.

My phone pings and hope rushes through me that he's calmed

down and is texting to apologise. My heart drops when I get to my phone because it's not him. It's Alex.

> Alex: I'm coming to collect my stuff in the morning.

There's no asking. It's just a statement. I wonder if his calmness has worn off.

I don't respond. It doesn't sound like he needs one, but instead I text Jay.

I type and retype my message over and over. I don't know how to put into words what it is I really want to say to him. In the end I go with simple.

> Erin: I'm sorry. I'll be there soon, I promise. x

I don't get a response. I'm not all that surprised, but when I see he's read it, my hope rises a little.

I get myself ready for bed. I'm not sure why I really bother; I won't be sleeping. I grab my sketchbook from my workshop, thinking I may be able to make use of my time.

I'm flicking my pen against the page trying to find some inspiration when something catches my eye.

My ring's gone. The one Jay gave me the day he left. The one I haven't taken off since, and the one I told Alex was from my dad so he wouldn't question me wearing it.

Fuck, fuck, fuck.

I jump out of bed and start pulling the covers off, praying that it'll fall out any minute. I must make and remake the bed five times before I give up and drop down on my hands and knees.

I turn the entire house upside down, but come up empty.

"How is this happening?" I sob into my hands as I sit back against the living room wall. It's got to be here somewhere.

By the time the sun starts to rise, the only room that hasn't been searched through is Denny's, because I didn't want to disturb him.

But I'll be straight in there when I get back from dropping him at school.

In my panic, I completely forget about Alex coming over, so when I hear a loud bang downstairs, my heart jumps into my throat. That is, until I hear his voice.

"Hiding upstairs with your new, or should I say old, man? Fucking him on the bed I used to make love to you on, are you?" His angry words confuse me as they register. It might sound like Alex's voice, but I've never heard him so spiteful and cruel.

I'm exhausted, and as I pull myself out from under Denny's bed, all I want to do is cry.

"Too scared to face me now I know the truth?" he continues to shout as I hear things being thrown about.

Taking a calming breath and wiping the tears that have been continually falling since I discovered my missing ring, I start to head downstairs.

I'm stood on the bottom step when Alex appears from the kitchen. His face is hard and angry. It's almost like I'm looking at a different person those first few seconds. Then, as soon as he sees me stood there, his face softens. I watch as his anger leaves him.

I know him well enough to know that he wants to be angry. He wants to shout and mean all those things he just said, but that's not who he is. He's calm, thoughtful and loving. He takes everything in his stride and doesn't let anything get on top of him. Many people admire that about him, and at the beginning of our relationship, I did. He reminded me of myself back before I met Jay. I was that quiet person who rolled with everything. I thought that Alex would be perfect for me. And to a point, I was right. We had a good life together but it wasn't until Jay reappeared that I realised how much I missed the excitement he'd shown me. How sometimes I needed that argument, the passion, to be able to get it all out. I never had that with Alex. If I was angry and accused him of something, he'd calm me down and get me to talk it out when all I wanted was for him to scream back at me.

It's glaringly obvious to me now that what I saw in Alex was the exact opposite to what I had with Jay. He left such a gaping hole in my life when he didn't come back that I couldn't risk being with someone like that again, so I went for safe, easy.

As he looks at me, I see love in his eyes just like every other time he's looked at me. He's trying so hard to hurt me like I have him, but he's just not got it in him.

"I'm—"

"Do not even think about apologising. You've done nothing wrong. This is all on me. I deserve all those things you said and more, Alex."

He puts the stuff in his arms down. "I don't think I have much more here. I never really moved in properly. I guess I knew it was coming," he says sadly.

I think the fact he knew I was going to break his heart hurts me more than if he was shouting at me right now. He knew it was coming yet he stayed here anyway.

I nod at him, unable to speak through the emotion clogging my throat. I sit myself down on the bottom step as Alex wanders in and out of each room, collecting his belongings and putting them into the bags he brought.

"I'm glad to see you at least allowed me to get all this before you moved him in," he says with a tight laugh when he returns with the last of it.

"It's not like that, Alex."

I can tell by the look on his face that he's desperate to ask me more, to find out what's going on, why I look as horrendous as I probably do, because he's just that nice a guy. But thankfully, he doesn't. Not that I have any intention of explaining my issues with Jay to him, anyway.

Alex leaves a couple of minutes later. He looks like he wants to hug me as he says goodbye, but I keep my arms wrapped around my middle and he stands there awkwardly, telling me not to be a stranger. I love his positivity but I don't think we can ever be friends after this. Every time I look at him, I'm sure all the guilt I've been carrying around for the past few weeks would just slam right back into me. I'll never forgive myself for what I've done to him. He didn't deserve any of this.

I drag my exhausted body back upstairs and put Denny's room back together. I continue to tell myself the ring's got to be here somewhere, but I have this horrible feeling in my gut that it's gone. Just another thing in a long line of things I've fucked up.

I settle myself on the sofa with a coffee and put the TV on for some background noise. Loose Women chat away, but I don't hear any of it. I let out a huge sigh as I stare down at my naked finger.

CHAPTER ELEVEN

Jay

The whisky doesn't burn anymore. It's lost its effect of distracting me and easing the pain.

She's had five fucking years. Why the fuck does she feel the need to have more time? She's had plenty.

I bring the bottle back up to my lips. I gave up on using a glass days ago.

I think back to that morning all those weeks ago in the coffee shop. I knew it was her the second she walked through the door. As I watched her from the corner, I felt everything click back into place. I'd been to hell and back in the past five years and I'd got to the point where I thought I could cope knowing I wasn't ever going to see her again.

Returning to Bristol was a huge decision. I'd been down south with Johnny as we both recovered, and I had no intention of returning, until one day I got the phone call I was dreading. It was the hospital calling to tell me Arthur had had a stroke.

I'd promised him years before that when the time came, I'd ensure his business continued. It had been in his family for generations but he never married or had kids. I was the closest thing he had to family, so I always knew I was going to inherit it. I never planned to be the one running it—not for a few years, at least. I'd always thought I'd stay in the army until they kicked me out, and then I'd have the garage to fall back on.

But when the time came, I was hauled up inside Johnny's one bed flat, sleeping on his sofa with no life. I decided maybe it was the wake-up call I needed. I knew I couldn't keep it up, so I packed my stuff and got on the train to Bristol. I was so low, I didn't even own a car.

The garage was running fairly smoothly, Arthur had worked until the second before he had the stroke. Dean had been there since he was sixteen, so the business was going to be fairly easy to run.

It wasn't long before I started to feel more and more like my old self again. Getting back under the bonnet of a car helped massively, and I soon wondered why I hadn't thought of doing it before.

I bought myself a clapped out old Porsche and rebuilt the entire thing. It felt good to be rejoining the world again, but there was no doubt something was missing.

Then I saw her again.

She was even more beautiful than I remembered, and the second I saw her, I immediately wondered if I'd made the wrong decision five years ago. I told myself it was pointless questioning it. It felt right at the time, and what's done is done.

I watched her intently as she was waiting in line and placed her order. I didn't think she was going to notice me, and I was in two minds as to whether that was a good thing or not when she glanced up.

I kept my head down so I couldn't see her reaction, but I felt it. I was just about to stand when she ran. I hoped what I did hadn't changed her.

I thought that was it. My one little glance of heaven, of what could've been, to tease me as I began to rebuild my life. I wasn't expecting fate to jump in once again and force us together.

"BAX, YOU LOOK LIKE SHIT," Arthur says when I walk into the care home lounge the next afternoon.

"Thanks, old man. You're not looking too chipper yourself." It's a joke, and he knows it. He recovered incredibly well from his stroke, but because of some weakness on his left side, he decided to move himself into a home where he would have the support he needed as he got older. It was a sensible thing to do, even if I do hate visiting him in what I always saw as a place people go to die.

"Seriously, Jayden. What's happened?" His use of my full name tells me he's serious. I must really look like shit.

"The girl with the sketchpad?" he asks when I finish telling him what's been going on. "She was so sweet."

"I thought we were getting our second chance," I admit.

"You are. Women can be fragile beings, Jayden," he says with a wink. Arthur may never have married but that doesn't mean he didn't spend all his adult years trying to find the right woman. "Just give her the time she needs. She'll come back to you."

"And what if she doesn't?"

"Have faith. Here, help me with this crossword," he says, changing the subject, and I couldn't be more grateful. His advice sticks with me though. Will it all be okay in the end?

EVERY DAY, I get a message from her, and every day, I don't respond. I don't want her texts. I want her. It's been over a month since I left her house that day. She promised me she would come for me. Well, where the fuck is she?

I know I could go to her, but the stubborn fucker inside is stopping me. I need her to be here because she wants to be, not because I dragged her. It's killing me that I know both her and my son are so close yet so far away.

I told myself after seeing Arthur that I would give it until Christmas, but if she hasn't made up her mind then, I'm leaving. I've just started rebuilding my life. I opened myself up to her again and showed her who I am now. No one, other than the doctors and nurses who treated me, knows what effect that day had on my body, but I showed her. I trusted her with the ugliness I was left with, and she ran.

I shut everything down after getting back to the UK. It was easier to deal with it all if I couldn't feel. Then she walked back into my life and I opened the door I'd bolted all my feelings up behind. I don't want to sit around here waiting for her to possibly give us another chance. Life's too short for that shit. I know that all too well.

"You're gonna fucking leave? Fuck that shit, bro. I only just got you back," Dean says when I tell him my plans to fuck off.

"Why not? I've already been through hell. There's no point sitting here waiting for the inevitable." I know I sound dramatic, but I can't help it.

"I wouldn't know. You haven't fucking told me what you've been through," he snaps.

"Jay, you can't just leave," Frankie says in a slightly softer tone. You'll have her back in no time. She's just got shit going on. Denny's been ill—"

"Denny's ill? What's wrong with him?" I ask in a panic.

"Don't get your knickers in a twist. He's just had a cold." I let out a breath I didn't know I was holding. How can you go from not having any clue someone exists to being totally in love and overprotective in seconds?

"He's okay, though?"

"Yes. He just had a bad cough. But Erin was already having issues with the shop's books after her accountant upped and left. She's just had a lot going on. Plus Christmas, you know?"

I get what she's saying, but I can't help feeling like she's just putting everything off.

"How about we go away for Christmas?" Dean asks, shocking the fuck out of me.

"What?"

"Me and you. Let's fuck off somewhere."

"Me and you?" I repeat.

"Yes. Me," he says pointing at himself before turning his finger on me, "and you. Somewhere hot, with loads of pussy."

I just about manage to contain a laugh at the look Frankie pins Dean with after that comment.

"Charming," she mutters, screwing up her nose.

They're just friends, apparently. I'm not entirely sure how much 'benefiting' is going on, but I'm fairly sure it's quite a bit if the way Dean looks at her is anything to go by. He'd never admit to it, but she has him exactly where she wants him. The only problem is they're both so adamant they're only friends that neither of them can see it. Fucking idiots, the pair of them.

"Why not?" Dean asks, looking back over at me. "It's not like either of us have any family here to worry about." Once again, Frankie gives Dean a look. She looks like someone just stole her puppy at the thought of him going away for Christmas.

"If you want to organise something, go right ahead," I say, knowing the idea of Dean making plans is laughable.

"Ibiza, Majorca... Shagaluf!" he says with a salacious smile that earns a slap to the shoulder.

I get talked at for over an hour about how I shouldn't leave, but neither of them can come up with any real reason for me to stay. Frankie telling me over and over again that Erin will turn up soon gets a little tiresome.

I HAD a text from Dean last night saying he'd booked a last minute surprise trip and to be packed and ready by nine in the morning.

I wasn't convinced by this idea when he mentioned it, but now I'm really regretting it. I'll be the first to admit that my suggestion of leaving was ridiculous. It sounded so good in my head, driving off into the distance with two fingers held up to the world. But in reality, the only place I want to be is here, even if it means I'm still waiting for Erin.

Having no idea what I should pack means I end up with almost everything I own—which isn't a lot—in my duffel bag. I'm just zipping it up when the song on the radio catches my attention. I've no idea why; it's always on in this place as background noise, but the lyrics filter through to me. The words take me right back to the beginning. To that first moment I saw Erin across the club dancing with her friends. I run through our time together, our first night in that shitty hotel where I thought she was going to run at any moment. She definitely didn't come across like a girl who disappears off with a guy she'd only just met, so I didn't for one second believe she'd follow through with it. But she did, and we had the most amazing two weeks together.

Everything seemed to happen so fast. One minute, I thought she was the most beautiful girl I'd ever seen, and the next, I'd fallen in love with her.

I remember the exact moment I realised it was love. It's probably not a story I'll ever repeat to anyone but her, but it was the night we went dancing. The whole experience had driven me crazy, and I was dying to get my hands on her again. The little bits of contact she'd allowed me up until that point were nowhere near enough. Seeing her face as she came on my fingers in the Lake District was a great memory but I needed it again.

Allowing her out of my sight and into her room that night was painful. I tried to do the right thing. I stripped out of my clothes and got into bed like I should. But my entire body was aching for her, and getting myself off only got me so far.

My frustration got too much after a couple of hours, so I snuck out of my room and into hers. I wanted to chastise her for not locking the door but I could only be so angry when it allowed the entry I needed.

I could hardly see her sleeping under the covers but the second I leant over her, I knew she was aware of me.

Her taste was addictive. I could have spent all night making her writhe and moan, but the second I felt her coming on my tongue was the same moment reality hit me.

I'd fallen in love with her.

I panicked. I'd promised her a two-week thing, and there I was head over heels for her.

I left her room as fast as I entered, pulled my clothes on, and got in my car. I had no clue what I was doing or where I was going. All I knew was that I had to get my head together.

Unfortunately, that wasn't a possibility. Erin Roberts was officially under my skin and in my heart. It's been that way ever since. I was able to somewhat put it to the back of my mind, but the second I saw her again, the feelings came back even stronger.

She was made for me, and me alone. She just needs to hurry the fuck up and realise it.

"That was Niall Horan with *'Too Much To Ask'*," the DJ says as the song comes to an end.

Seconds later, I hear the beep of a horn as Dean announces his arrival. I turn the radio off and lock up my makeshift home. I always intended for this place to be a temporary thing, but everything with Erin and Denny kind of distracted me.

Grabbing my bag, I flick all the lights off behind me and pull my keys from my pocket, ready to lock the place up for Christmas. At the last minute I turn back to my bedroom and grab Erin's ring from beside my bed. It's the only piece of her I have, and I want it close.

I let out a breath before pulling the door open. I don't want Dean to see I'm anything but excited about this, so I tell my face to look happy and wrap my hand around the handle.

When I look up, I can't believe what I'm seeing. I feel my mouth drop open and my hands come up to rub at my eyes. I know I haven't been sleeping and consuming way too much whisky, but this can't really be happening.

Dragging my eyes away from the scene in front of me, I look around for who I was expecting to see, but Dean isn't here.

Instead, parked out the front of the garage is a car I never thought I'd see again, with the two most important people in my world leant against it.

"Fuck," I mutter as my hand comes back up to my face, and I stare at them like they're not real.

"Surprise," Erin says sheepishly.

It's only then I notice how unsure of herself she looks, just like that night in the club; totally out of her comfort zone.

"You could say that," I say, but it comes out so quietly I'm not sure she hears me.

"We thought we could go on a Christmas road trip."

"Is that right?" I ask, my brain starting to catch up with what's happening in front of me.

"Yeah. She's had a full service and ready to go on an adventure. What do you say?"

I look from Erin, to Denny, and then finally to Peggy. She looks as perfect as the day we left her in Cambridge.

"You kept her?"

"Of course. I couldn't bear not to. She's been in my garage under tarpaulin all this time."

"What did Al—" I stop myself, not really wanting to say his name.

A cheeky smile appears on Erin's face. "He thought she was my dad's."

"Well, okay then."

"So is that a yes?"

"Of course it's a fucking yes."

"Daddy, bad word," Denny chastises, and I can't help but laugh.

I go to take a step toward them but Erin beats me to it and she launches herself at me. I hold her tightly as I shove my face in her neck and breathe her in. She smells exactly like I remember.

My desire gets to be too much after a few seconds and I pull back so I can find her lips. She's just as desperate and we cling to each other as we both pour everything we have into that one kiss. We only break apart when Denny starts complaining how gross it is behind us.

Our lips part and we both laugh before looking back at our son, who looks like he could puke at any minute.

"Where are we going?" I ask when I've put Erin down and thrown my bag into the boot with theirs.

"Everywhere and nowhere," she answers, and I feel the final piece of my life fall back into place.

———

Keep reading for more of Jay and Erin!

EVERYWHERE
& NOWHERE

CHAPTER ONE

"He's asleep," I say, walking back toward the living room in the cottage I'd booked. The three of us are staying in the Lake District for five days before continuing to Scotland for New Year's.

Jay sits forward, places his beer can on the coffee table, and then looks up at me. That look ensures I stay exactly where I am. Standing, he walks with purpose, eating up the space between us in seconds. With each step he takes, my heart pounds faster and my butterflies increase.

"You'd better be right, because I'm going to make you scream."

My entire body yearns for his touch as he comes to a stop, only inches between us. He continues to stare with hooded eyes before they drop to my body. I'm wearing the jeans and t-shirt I've been in all day, but the way he's looking at me, I may as well be naked.

I start to get concerned when he doesn't do anything more. "You okay?"

When his eyes come back to me, they're filled with hunger and fire. The sight makes my stomach flip in excitement. "Just appreciating what's mine."

My mouth goes dry as he pulls his own t-shirt over his head and drops it to the floor. I let out a sigh as I run my eyes over his sculpted chest and stomach. Just as perfect as the image I have in my dreams each night.

I hate it, but when I look back up to his eyes, I see concern. He's still worried about what I think about his scarred body. I decide there and then that by the end of this night, there will be no more doubt in his mind that I'm in love with not only who he is as a person, but also his body—every freckle, mole and scar.

I go to copy his action and grab the hem of my t-shirt, but his growl stops me. "What are you doing?"

"Uh... getting naked," I say, like it should be obvious.

"*I* get you naked," he states, before stepping up to me and replacing my hands with his own. He pulls the fabric up torturously slowly. It skims my sensitive skin, making me shiver, and it only increases my impatience. I want his hands on me now.

My t-shirt joins his on the floor and his fingertips slowly trace across my collarbone before dropping to run along the edge of my bra. My breasts strain against the lace, begging to be released, and my chest heaves with my panting breaths. Instead, he continues down my stomach and circles my belly button. He drops to his knees and kisses a line across my waistband before popping the button and pulling the denim down my legs. I lean on his shoulders as he pulls them off, and I smile when I notice he doesn't flinch as I touch his back. Maybe he is starting to understand.

Sitting back on his haunches, he looks up at me. I'm wearing a simple black lace underwear set, but you'd think I was in something much sexier from the way he's staring at me.

"I imagined doing this every single day." The sincerity in his eyes ensures I believe every word. "Just to have the chance to hear your voice again. To kiss you," he says, leaning forward and once again pressing his lips to my stomach. It takes a while to register, but I notice he's kissing the faint marks left behind from my pregnancy. "To touch you," he says, running his hands down my sides, tucking his thumbs into the lace and slowly pulling them down my legs. "To taste you," he adds with a quick glance up at me. My mouth goes dry as I watch him lean forward and nudge my legs apart. Our eyes stay connected as he gently licks at me. My hips buck the second he makes contact with my clit, and a whimper falls from my lips.

His restraint snaps.

I'm pushed back against the wall and one of my legs gets thrown over his shoulder as he devours me. I'm panting in seconds, his skilled tongue getting me close to the edge in no time at all.

He continues until I come on his tongue, and the one leg holding me up buckles as the pleasure rushes through me.

He pulls me into his arms and carries me down the hallway, to the bedroom.

"I realised I was in love with you the first time I ate your pussy," he whispers in my ear. His voice is hoarse and full of emotion. A deep ache pulls at my lower stomach.

"Was that meant to be romantic?" I ask with a laugh.

"No. Just the truth."

Together, we fall onto the bed. I expect him to kiss me, but to my surprise he gets up and walks to the other side of the room. Before bending down to his bag, he looks back at me. Vulnerability creeps back into his eyes but he doesn't say anything as he stands and drops his jeans.

My eyes immediately fall to his arse. That was always my favourite part of him. Yes, it's different now with his scars, but it's no less perfect.

He grabs something from his bag and closes his fist around it. When he turns back, he's got a cheeky smirk on his face but his eyes are all serious.

"What are you doing?" I ask, sitting up as he crawls onto the bed next to me.

"I need to do something before I make love to you."

"Okay..."

"I'm going to ask something I've asked you before, but I hope you'll realise I'm serious this time." My heart starts to pound in my chest as I consider what he's saying. No... surely he's not going to...

"Marry me?"

I see his hand come out but I don't take my eyes from his.

"Yes," I whisper.

"Yes?"

"Yes!"

The weight of his body forces me back onto the bed. His lips descend on mine and he kisses me until I'm breathless.

"Thank fuck for that," he pants. "I don't think I could take the rejection again."

I laugh with him as I think about that day in Gretna Green over five years ago until his eyes suddenly turn serious.

"I love you," I say softly as I reach out to touch his cheek.

"Oh shit, wait," he says, totally ruining our moment.

He sits up and holds his hand out. Slowly, he uncurls his fingers to reveal what he's hiding.

"My ring!" I exclaim. "How did you? When did you?" I can't help the tears of relief falling down my cheeks. "Do you know how long I've been looking for this?"

"I have some idea. Can I?" he asks, nodding to my finger.

I hold my hand out for him and he slides my ring back onto its rightful home.

"I took it the day I came over, thinking that was it, that we were together. I was going to propose then. But—"

"But I fucked it up."

"Yeah, pretty much."

"Thank you."

"For what?"

"For coming back. For waiting for me. For everything."

"I love you, Skittles."

Jay falls back on top of me and sets about showing me just how much he really does love me.

I've no idea what the time is once we collapse on the bed, both utterly spent from countless orgasms.

"Jay?" I ask just before I doze off to sleep.

"Yeah?" he whispers.

"Why do you call me Skittles?"

"Because it suits you." I let out a laugh and squeeze him tighter.

"Just so you know, not a day went by where I forgot about us."

"Me either, Skittles. I could never forget you."

I SHOULDN'T BE surprised when I find myself alone in the bed the next morning, but a huge wave of disappointment floods me when I reach out and find him gone. Keeping my eyes shut, I listen for any sign of him, but it's silent. I was hoping he might be down the side of the bed doing his sit-ups, just like our first road trip together.

Tearing my eyes open, I glance around the room in case he's there, but I know he's not. I bring my hand up to my face and something catches my eye. My ring. A smile pulls at my lips as memories from last night play out in my mind. Jay had it all along.

Butterflies flutter in my stomach as I think about his proposal. He wants me to be his wife. My heart pounds inside my chest as I replay the words he said to me last night. *Marry me?* Simple, to the point, yet perfect.

Hearing a noise from another room, I fling back the duvet before grabbing Jay's t-shirt from the floor and pulling it over my head.

I quietly walk toward the living area of the cottage, aware that it's still early and that I'd like a little time with Jay before Denny wakes up and monopolises his attention.

The second he comes into view, I have to stop. He's stood at the kitchen counter, staring down at a newspaper. His hoodie is in a pile next to him and his joggers are hanging low on his hips. The muscles of his back are pulled tight as he concentrates on whatever it is he's reading. It's an incredible sight to wake up to. I smile to myself that he feels confident enough to stand there topless, knowing he could have company at any moment. When he first showed me his scars, I was worried it was something that was going to cause issues, but it seems he was more worried about my reaction than anything else. Of course, it hurts me to see them, knowing he was injured so badly and there was nothing I could do about it, either at the time or in the months that followed. It's always going to haunt me. He should have come back to me. I would have been there for whatever he needed. But I do understand his reasons, and although they've kept us apart for five years, maybe it was how it was meant to be. We've both grown so much in that time. Maybe we needed that to happen before we could be together.

My thoughts of the past get cut short when I see his head turn my way. "Are you just going to stand there staring, or were you planning on coming a little closer?" His voice is deadly serious. It almost feels like a warning. Excitement shoots down my spine and as much as I want to stay put and see what he'll do, I find my legs moving and the space between us disappearing rapidly.

The second I'm in reaching distance, he wraps his fingers around the back of my neck and pulls me to him. His lips touch mine and before I can complain about my morning breath, his tongue is in my mouth. The taste of coffee mixed with Jay explodes on my taste buds, and my concern vanishes.

His fingers tangle in my hair as he presses his body against mine and forces me to step back until I hit the counter.

"How long have we got?" he groans in my ear as his fingers find the bottom of his t-shirt. They tickle up my thighs before he grabs my arse and lifts me onto the counter.

I've no idea what the time is; my only clue is that it's still pretty dark out. "Long enough," I answer on a gasp as his fingers find my nipples and pinch.

"I hope you're right," he says as his hands leave me. I go to complain but when I see his thumbs hook into his waistband and push, I shut my mouth.

Jay's joggers fall to his ankles, exposing his nakedness beneath.

I bite down on my bottom lip as I watch him take himself in his hand. I feel his eyes on me, but I'm too fascinated by his movements to look up.

"Lie back," he demands.

The moment my back hits the counter, he grabs onto my thighs and tugs. My arse hangs off the edge and my legs rest on his arms. He gives me two seconds to adjust before I feel him pressing at my entrance.

"You on birth control?"

"Yeah, I've got it covered, don't worry." My frustration builds at his sudden need for a conversation about this.

"Worry?" he repeats with a strange look in his eyes. "Stop taking it."

"What?" My stomach twists as a bolt of anxiety hits me. He can't be serious.

"Stop taking it. I want to see you pregnant with our child."

My brows draw together at his words and I can't help but pull away from him. "We've just got back together."

"So? We're meant to be, Skittles. I missed out on everything with Denny, and I want it all."

The thought of having another baby right now affects me more than I thought it would. I feel sick even considering the possibility. Images of everything I've wanted to do if I ever got Jay back run through my mind, and not one of them is having another baby again so soon. My temperature increases and I feel anger start to nudge its way in as I consider the repercussions for all of us if I were to agree to this. Pushing Jay to the side, I jump down from the counter and cover myself back up. "No." My voice doesn't come out as strong as I was hoping.

"No?" The look on his face guts me. It's clear he really wants this, but can't he see that it's not the right time? We need to get to know each other again before we can even think about bringing a fourth person into our family. Jay's barely got used to the idea of being a father to Denny; how would he cope with another added into the mix? Then, there's Denny himself. I've already thrown his world into turmoil this year. He needs his life to settle down a little, to get used to the idea that we're now a family. And most importantly, he needs to spend quality time with his dad. They've missed out on five years together. Suddenly having to share Jay with another baby would not be a good idea.

"I'm sorry, Jay. In the future? Yes, I'd love to have more kids with you. But we've got a family. We've got Denny, and he adores you. Don't you want to spend time with him? Make up for what you lost before having another?"

I can see reluctance written all over his face. He really wants this.

Walking back toward him, I wrap my arms around his solid frame and hold tight. "One thing at a time, yeah?"

I feel him press his face into my hair and breathe me in as he nods slowly.

We stand there for the longest time, but eventually, a noise from another room forces us apart and I step away to meet Denny.

"Morning, baby," I sing happily when I see his sleepy body plodding down the hallway.

His eyes light up a little when he sees me, although he still looks a little asleep. He blinks a couple of times before looking around at his surroundings.

I see the moment reality hits him.

"It wasn't a dream. Daddy's here." His smile melts my heart.

"He's in the kitchen." I pull Denny into my arms and hold tight as I walk toward Jay.

"Hey, buddy." The moment Denny's eyes land on his dad, he's fighting to get out of my hold. No sooner have his feet hit the ground than he's up in Jay's arms.

I don't think I'm ever going to get used to seeing them together.

Their similarities are almost as striking as their good looks. I can't take this time away from either of them.

"Why's the newspaper on the floor?" Denny asks when he's put down. I glance over to where he's pointing and my cheeks flush red as I realise why it's there.

"I must have dropped it," Jay says to Denny, but his wink says he knows exactly how it ended up there. "Come here," he whispers as he opens his arms for me.

I breathe in his scent and snuggle into his side. Happiness that I've never experienced before flows through me as we stand together and watch our son.

"Where'd you get the paper?" I ask after a few seconds of silence.

"I went for a run and found a corner shop. You two go and sit down; I'm making you breakfast," Jay announces as he gently pushes me toward the dining table that sits between the kitchen and living area of the open-plan room.

I do as I'm told but I can't help wondering what he's planning on making, seeing as I'd brought the bare minimum, having planned a shopping trip today.

After making me a coffee and pouring Denny a glass of orange juice, I get a front row seat to Jay's cooking skills—or lack thereof.

The first round of bread he puts into the toaster ends up like charcoal and goes straight into the bin, while Denny complains about the smell. It was the toaster's fault, according to Jay. I can't help but laugh at him as he has a second go.

It's a little more successful as he keeps a watchful eye on the toaster instead of leaving it to do its thing.

He brings us over a plate full of freshly toasted bread along with the tub of butter and Marmite I brought with us.

"Don't tell me you two like that stuff?" he asks, nodding toward the jar of Denny's favourite food in the world.

"YES!" Denny says, sounding affronted that Jay could even question it.

"Don't tell us you're a hater."

"Daddy," Denny warns, and I can't help but laugh at the serious look on his little face.

Jay's lips twitch a beat before a wide smile stretches across his face. "Gotcha, I love it," he says as he ruffles up Denny's hair. "Pass it over."

I love watching them together. I'm pretty sure it's something I'm never going to get bored of. The image of Jay holding a newborn slams into my head, his huge arms cradling a helpless baby as he stares down with a level of love and adoration I know he's capable of. I bat it away, feeling ridiculous that his suggestion has me thinking such things. We have the rest of our lives for all that.

Focusing on what's next for us, I turn to Denny. "Guess what?"

"What?" he asks around a mouthful of toast.

"Mummy and Daddy are getting married."

A bright smile lights up his face as he looks between the two of us. Dragging my eyes away from him, I glance over at Jay, who's also looking down at Denny with a wide smile. I can still see the shadows in his eyes from my refusal earlier, but I hope he understands.

"Do I get to wear a suit? And be a pageboy?"

"You sure do, buddy."

"And does that mean you're coming to live with us? Mummies and daddies usually live together."

Jay glances up at me and he once again looks a little unsure of himself.

"Of course, baby. As soon as we get back we'll get all Daddy's stuff."

"Yesssss."

"WHEN WAS the last time you had a proper Christmas dinner?" I ask Jay as we walk into the supermarket later that day.

"Uh..." he grunts sadly as he thinks. "Not since I was a kid. Once my dad left, everything went to hell."

I reach out and wrap my hand around his. "I'm sorry," I whisper. I'm not sure if it's for asking the question in the first place when I knew it would only drag up old memories, or for what his Christmases had been like in the past. "We'll make up for all of them this year," I promise as we make our way down the first aisle.

"It's already a million times better. Thank you." He leans over and places his lips to mine for a quick kiss, but even that sends tingles shooting around my body.

I know we're only staying here for five days before moving on, but knowing I need to make this the best Christmas ever, for both my men, means the trolley is overflowing with food and drink when we eventually make it back to the car.

"Where exactly were you planning on putting all that?" Jay asks with a laugh, looking between the bags and Peggy.

"It'll be fine."

"Are you sure that letter will be okay?" Denny asks from the back seat where he's surrounded by bags of food.

"Santa doesn't need letters, baby. He knows where all the good children are," I say, for the thousandth time, trying to put his concerns about missing out to one side.

"But how does he know?"

I see Jay flick a look over at me from the driver's seat, his face amused.

"He just does. But we left that letter with our address just in case he has any issues."

"What if he can't find us?"

"He will find us, baby."

Jay's smile only gets wider the longer the conversation goes on. "Feel free to help out any time," I whisper with a laugh.

"You're doing just fine on your own."

The amusement on his face is wiped away when his phone starts ringing. "Shit," he mutters. "Sorry, but I need to get this."

"Okay," I say as he indicates and pulls off to the side of the road.

I wasn't expecting him to get out of the car before answering but that's exactly what he does. I decide it's probably something to do with the garage before Denny starts talking about Santa again and distracts me.

"Sorry about that. Ready to get back?" Jay asks when he gets back in. I go to question him about his phone call but he leans over and plants a kiss on my lips and places his palm on my thigh. His contact ensures all thoughts vanish in favour of focusing on him.

The tingles his simple kiss ignited in the car continue throughout our short drive home and the entire time we put the shopping away. It's not helped by the little caresses and kisses he grants me every time he's in touching distance. Glancing over at Denny, who's sat in the middle of the living room watching some Christmas film, I wonder if we'd get away with sneaking off for a few minutes.

My hopes are soon squashed when Denny perks up and tells me he's hungry. Jay winks at me when I look over at him. The cheeky smile on his face tells me he could read my thoughts, and I can't help a blush tinting my cheeks.

"Don't worry, it'll happen the first chance we get," he says with a gentle slap to my arse.

"TIME FOR BED, BABY," I say, trying to drag Denny's attention from the TV.

"But—" he starts to argue but I'm having none of it.

"It's Christmas Eve tomorrow," I remind him. "And you've been such a good boy all year. It would be a shame to spoil it now."

He huffs out a big breath and eventually starts to get himself up, sulking toward an amused Jay to say goodnight.

"But I wanted to go in the hot tub," he tells Jay as he looks longingly over his shoulder and out the window.

"I know, buddy. We'll go in tomorrow." I can see a little trepidation on Jay's face and it makes me wonder what the issue could be. I know he's not scared of water.

"Promise you won't go in without me."

"Promise."

That satisfies Denny enough to say goodnight and head off to bed, albeit with a sad, sulky face.

"Did you mean that promise?" I ask Jay when I rejoin him on the sofa with a fresh glass of wine and a beer for him.

"I wouldn't lie to a five-year-old, Skittles. Why, did you have plans?"

"Uh..." I stutter as thoughts of what I had in mind for the hot tub flush my cheeks. "It's fine. You've promised now, so I'll just forget about it." I plonk myself down and grab the TV guide. "Oh look, Love Actually is on in a bit. It wouldn't be Christmas if we didn't watch it, so I guess it all worked out perfectly."

From the look in Jay's eyes, I expect him to snatch the magazine out of my hands and march me to the bedroom, but he surprises me by relaxing back into the corner and pulling me into him. "I've never seen it."

"You've never seen it?" I repeat, astounded by his admission.

"Nope."

Thoughts of how he must have spent his Christmases over the years dampen my mood a little, but it's soon forgotten when he leans his head down to kiss me.

We have the most incredible night. It's everything I dreamt of after he didn't come back. I'd have given anything for him just to hold me one more time. I'm still trying to wrap my head around how we got here. Everything that's happened with Jay has been such a whirlwind, both back then and the past few weeks. I know I told Jay that I needed time before we could get together, but I mostly spent that time missing him like crazy. In hindsight, I don't think it was worth it. I still feel as guilty as ever whenever I think about Alex and how I treated him, but every time I look at Jay, I can't believe how lucky I am to have a second chance with him.

This really is the thing dreams are made of.

CHAPTER TWO

"It's Christmas Eve," Denny squeals excitedly at some ungodly hour the next morning.

I open my eyes and his blurry smiling face wakes me up instantly. Feeling movement beside me, I glance over my shoulder to find Jay still in bed. It's a weird sight because I don't think I've ever woken up next to him before; he's always been gone.

"Morning," he croaks out as he rolls over onto his side and places a kiss on my shoulder. "Hey, bud." No sooner have the words left his mouth than he's moving again so he's lying on his back. Looking over at him, I want to reassure him that it's fine, that Denny will probably think his scars are cool and make him an even bigger hero, but I keep my mouth shut.

Denny must be able to sense something's up because his face drops when he sees Jay roll away from him and look to the other side of the room.

"Are you hungry?" I ask, trying to distract both of them.

Unsurprisingly, Denny's answer is yes, so I tell him to go out to the kitchen while I get myself sorted.

"Stop worrying, he isn't going to care," I say, rolling over to Jay and forcing him to look at me.

He doesn't say anything but I can see his turmoil in the depths of his eyes.

"Denny loves you. You're his hero, and what you've been through will only make that more evident in his eyes. Talk to him."

I understand how strange this must be for him. He hasn't been eased into parenthood, instead thrust right into the middle of it. I start to wonder if this road trip might not have been the best decision after all. He can't really get away if he needs a break to get his head together.

"I don't even know where to start. He's five; he doesn't need to know about all the ugliness in the world."

"That may be true, but it's a world he's going to have to live in. You don't need to give him all the details. He already knows you were a soldier, he knew you were in another country fighting. Just talk to him—you'll find he has more understanding than you give him credit for."

"It's not that I don't think he'll understand, it's that he'll understand too much."

"You can't wrap him up in cotton wool, Jay. As much as you want to protect him, he needs to know all this stuff. What if he wants to follow in your footsteps—" Jay's eyes go hard and he cuts off what I'm saying instantly.

"No," he argues sternly.

"Jay"—my voice is soft as I reach out to cup his cheek—"he has to make his own decisions, as hard as they may be." In truth, just the thought of Denny following in his dad's footsteps scares the shit out of me, but I would never try to stop him from something he wants to do.

I watch as Jay lets out a long breath and scrubs his hands over his face. "Is parenthood always this fucking scary? Do you ever feel like you know what you're doing?"

"No—never. I make it up as I go along."

"But you're so perfect. You just seem to know how to deal with everything."

Tears fill my eyes and I feel my bottom lip tremble.

"Shit, what's wrong?"

"Nothing, it's just..." I pause as I try to pull myself back together. "No one's ever told me that before. Mum was always the one to support and encourage me, but with her gone... I just... I think I really needed to hear that."

Jay pulls me on top of him and holds me tightly. "Didn't he ever tell you that?" he whispers in my ear.

"It wasn't the same. Hearing it from you means everything to me."

I feel myself starting to well up again so I sit up and wipe my eyes before grabbing my pyjamas so I can go and sort Denny out.

"Erin," Jay says, as I'm about to leave the room.

Stopping and looking back, I see he's sat in the middle of the bed with the covers pooled around his waist. I can't help my eyes dropping to his sculpted chest before they find his. I watch as he swallows and his fingers grasp the duvet. It's a long couple of seconds as we stare at each other before he remembers he was the one who called me back.

"I love you," he eventually says, his voice full of emotion.

"I love you, too, Jay."

"Mummy" being called through the cottage puts an end to our little moment.

I set about making us all breakfast as I hear Jay get up and go straight into the shower. Everything in me wants to stop what I'm doing and join him, but I can't; I've got a hungry child to sort out.

"That smells incredible," Jay says when he appears a while later just as I'm lifting the bacon from the grill pan. "I missed you," he whispers so only I can hear when he comes to stand next to me before kissing the sensitive skin below my ear.

A quiet whimper leaves my lips before Denny once again complains about being hungry.

"Can we go in the hot tub now?" he asks the second he's finished eating.

"It's up to Daddy." I don't miss the panic on Jay's face again, I don't want to force him into anything before he's ready. I already know it's him Denny's going to want to go in with.

"Please, Daddy. You promised." Denny gives him *the look*—the one I'm sure no parent is ever able to say no to.

Jay's eyes flick over to me and I smile encouragingly at him. I know he's making a bigger deal out of this than he needs to, but I understand his concerns.

"Yeah... sure," he says, unconvincingly.

"Yes!" Denny squeals before getting up and running toward his room to get changed.

"Go and help him find his shorts and you can talk to him," I encourage, nodding in Denny's direction.

I can't help but smile when Jay disappears off after Denny. My big strong army man is afraid of a five-year-old.

I desperately want to go and eavesdrop, but I fight it and continue with the washing up. I want Jay to do this alone. I think it's important.

It's only a few minutes later when Denny comes running back through the kitchen dressed in his swim shorts and dragging a towel behind him. He doesn't stop to say anything; he just continues out the door and onto the decking. He stands looking very cold, waiting for Jay to come out and take the lid off so they can get in.

"Everything okay?" I ask when Jay walks into the room a few seconds later.

"Yeah, you were right."

"Of course," I say with a laugh. "What did he say?"

"That scars are cool!" Jay rolls his eyes, and the move reminds me so much of our son.

I resist the urge to say *I told you so.* Instead, I nod my head toward the door. "I think he's waiting for you."

Jay gives me a quick kiss and tells me to hurry up and join them before marching from the room. The sight of his naked back, as always, makes me a little sad. But I'm so proud of him for being open with Denny and for showing him the amazing man he really is.

I stand at the sink in front of the window and watch them for the longest time. Nothing makes me happier than seeing the wide smiles on both their faces while they mess about in the water, splashing each other and making a whirlpool with their bodies. Images of Jay surrounded by our children flash into my mind.

Eventually, my attention catches Jay's eye. His expression brightens even more when he realises I'm watching them before he waves me out to join them. I dry my hands and walk over to the back door.

"Are you getting in, or what?"

"You look like you're having plenty of fun without me." It's not that I don't want to join them—I do, more than anything, but I'm aware that Jay and Denny need to spend some quality time together.

"Get your arse in here," Jay demands.

"Yeah, Mummy!" Denny says with his hands on his hips. I'm a little taken aback by his attitude, but really, what can I expect now he's spending time with Jay?

"I'm going, I'm going," I say with my hands up in defeat, deciding I don't need to tell Denny off when he's enjoying himself so much.

I make quick work of stripping my pyjamas off and slipping into my new bikini. I ordered it specially when I found out we had a hot tub here. Knowing I was going to be sharing it with Jay meant I really didn't want to wear my usual child friendly all-in-one.

Taking one last look in the mirror, I wrap a towel around myself and walk out to join my men.

The second I step into the kitchen, the sound of their laughter hits my ears and my pace increases with the need to join in.

My movement stops Jay in his tracks. His eyes run over my towel-clad body and I watch as they darken with his desire. Butterflies erupt in my stomach under his gaze. I take a big breath before untucking the towel and letting it drop to the ground. Jay bites down on his bottom lip as his eyes dart around my body, not knowing where to look first.

Thankfully, Denny is totally unaware of what's going on; he's too busy playing with the lights.

"Maybe this wasn't such a good idea," Jay mutters as I see him shift about in his seat.

I can't help the wicked smile that creeps onto my lips. I've never been much of a flirt, but seeing Jay obviously struggling brings it out of me.

"Oops," I say before bending over to pick up the towel I dropped.

I hear Jay's growl loud and clear before Denny asks him what's wrong.

I'm still laughing after I've placed the towel over the back of a chair and turn toward them. However, Jay doesn't look so amused. His eyes are still dark, and they're narrowed at me in warning.

His stare doesn't waver as I start moving toward him. His intensity sends electric waves straight to my clit, and the only thing I can focus on is getting to him.

The words, *'hurry up, Mummy'*, somehow breaks through my lust fogged brain and I shake my head to allow reality to seep back in.

"I've forgotten something," I say in a rush before turning and walking back into the cottage, not forgetting to ensure I have a little extra sway to my hips.

I don't need to because I know his eyes are still on me, I can feel them, but when I get to the hallway, I look back over my shoulder. As expected, Jay's stare is glued to my arse. I smile to myself before rushing into our bedroom to grab what I need.

"What's that?" Denny asks the second he sees me with a present in my hands.

"An early Christmas present. Here," I say, handing him a towel. "Dry your hands and you can open it."

He rushes to do as I say before holding out his hands for the box excitedly. I chance a glance over to Jay, who's quietly sat in the corner. I can still see the heat in his eyes, but his curiosity is getting the better of him.

"Ah cool," Denny exclaims as he drops the first of three rubber ducks into the hot tub. The elf duck bobs off happily while he pulls the reindeer and Santa duck from the box. "Thank you, Mummy."

"You're welcome, baby." I smile as I watch the three of them float around.

"Are you getting in now?" Jay asks, sounding bored.

"I am," I say before taking his outstretched hand and stepping into the warm water. "Oooh, that's good," I groan as my body sinks down into the soothing water.

I can feel his eyes on me but I don't dare look over for fear of wanting to do something very inappropriate for our five-year-old to watch. Instead, I reach out and grab the closest duck to me before throwing it at Denny.

Jay clearly isn't amused, because moments later I feel his hand wrap around my waist and he pulls me to his side.

"You're so fucking hot," he whispers in my ear. "And this is fucking torture."

I can't help myself; I run my hand up his thigh before finding exactly what I was expecting, him as hard as steel beneath his shorts.

"Erin," he warns, his shock evident in his voice.

I keep forgetting that Jay still sees me as that shy twenty-year-old he first met, who wouldn't say boo to a goose. I hadn't realised how much I'd changed over the past five years until we reconnected and I saw the shock on his face when I did things like this, that I never would have dreamt of doing back then.

I lean farther into him and whisper in his ear, "I've learnt that it's best to just go for it when you want something. You never know when it might be taken away from you." His head turns to me and his brows draw together in understanding. He stares at me for a second before his hand comes up to my neck and he pulls me toward him. His lips are still against mine for a long time. I can only imagine he's thinking about what we could have lost and how grateful he is that we're here, just like I am.

He smiles at me when he pulls back and it tells me everything I need to know.

WE SPEND way too long in the hot tub. When we eventually get out, we're all like prunes.

After wrapping Denny in a towel, I direct him straight to the bathroom so he can shower. We leave Jay behind; he told us to go on and that he'd put the lid down and tidy up. I know this is true, but I also know the real reason he didn't want to get out in front of Denny. He's still sporting the same issue as he was earlier, thanks to my continued teasing.

I know he's going to get me back for it. I could see the threat in his dark, heated eyes. But I was enjoying torturing him too much to care.

After ensuring Denny's distracted with his lunch and Elf on the TV, I head off to our room to find Jay. I know he's in the shower, as I heard it turn on a few minutes ago. Excitement almost has me running down the hallway.

The door's ajar so I slowly push it open and peer inside. As predicted, he's stood under the spray of the shower. His head's tipped back and the water pours down his neck and over his chest and abs. I stand and stare as I watch the rivers of water cascading over his incredible body.

I don't realise I've stepped forward until I see him move and he grabs my wrist. My chest crashes against his and he stares down at me.

"You think you're funny, don't you?"

He clearly isn't expecting a response because his lips slam down on mine before his tongue sweeps into my mouth. After a few seconds, I feel his hands run down my neck and he starts undoing my top before coming around to play with my naked breasts once it's fallen to the floor.

I moan into his mouth, just as desperate for release as he is.

He's soon moving again and I feel him tug at both sides of my bottoms before the fabric tickles my thighs as it drops to the floor.

His fingers skim my stomach before he thrusts them inside me. "Torturing me turned you on, didn't it?"

"Uh-huh," I moan, unable to form words.

"You're going to regret it," he warns, but I couldn't care less. I'll take whatever it is he's got planned—and probably beg for more.

He shoves me into the shower before the heat of his body burns my back.

"Bend over and put your hands on the tiles."

I immediately follow his instructions, and in seconds, I feel him at my entrance.

A loud moan falls from my mouth, and he covers it with his hand. Realisation hits that this needs to be fast, and it needs to be quiet. I nod against his palm before I feel him slam into me.

I feel the rumble of Jay's groan against my back when he fills me to the hilt. "Fucking heaven," he grunts as he really starts to move. His hands leave my hips and I feel them against my stomach. "As soon as you say the word I'm going to fill you with my seed, Erin," he pants. "You're going to be swollen with my baby before long, and you know it."

The huge rush of desire that floods my body at his words surprises me. I flex my hips and allow him even deeper.

"The idea of me filling you turns you on, doesn't it? You're wet as fuck right now."

The long build up of foreplay in the hot tub means it's over even quicker than I expected, but it only takes the edge off, and I can tell by Jay's expression that he feels exactly the same.

Once he's finished and I've had the pleasure of watching him rub shower gel all over himself, he tells me to take my time and heads out to find Denny.

I stand and let the power of the water jets relax my muscles. If you'd have asked me just six months ago how I would be spending Christmas this year, I never would have thought it would be like this. I expected it to be a repeat of last year with Alex and his family. There were so many signs that we weren't meant to be and how uncomfortable I was around his family was just one of them. I put it down to jealousy. I'd only ever had Mum, and with her gone, I felt so alone. I didn't realise it would only take one look at Jay for that feeling to completely disappear. I wasn't lonely because of my lack of family; I was lonely because the other half of me was out there somewhere, not by my side.

Thoughts of Alex dampens my happiness. I wonder if he's found someone else already but I know the thought is stupid. He was fully immersed in our relationship and our future together. I'm under no illusion that I totally broke his heart. I think it's going to take him a while to trust someone again. I will forever hate what I did to him—he's such a kind and gentle man. But at the end of the day, it helped lead me back to where I'm meant to be, and I'll always be grateful for our time together. He helped me grow and become the person I needed to be when Jay did show up again and turn my world upside down.

Jay must be able to tell something's wrong when I find him and Denny sat watching the TV a while later because the second he sees me, he's up and following me to the kitchen.

"What's wrong?" he whispers in my ear as he wraps his arms around my waist.

"Nothing. I'm fine."

"Skittles," he warns.

"I was just thinking about everything that happened for us to get here. Honestly, it's nothing. I'm fine."

"You'd tell me if you weren't?"

"Of course. This is exactly where I'm meant to be."

"I really never thought this would happen," he admits.

"At least you didn't think I was dead." The expression that falls over his face at the thought is enough to have me apologising for my not so funny joke. "I'm sorry. All that is behind us now. We've got a future to look forward to."

"I can't wait." His lips gently touch my neck as he peppers kisses across my skin. Goosebumps erupt over my whole body, and I begin to ache for him once again.

***

"IS IT TIME YET?"

I glance over at the clock on the mantelpiece before looking back at an excited Denny. Jay glances between the two of us with a bemused look on his face and it reminds me that he has no idea about our Christmas traditions—something we're soon going to rectify.

"Yes, I think so," I say before getting off the sofa and walking out of the room.

When I return, I have two sets of grey eyes watching my every move. Denny scrambles off the sofa as I place the two boxes down on the coffee table, while Jay watches me curiously.

"What are they?"

"Christmas Eve boxes." A line forms between his brows. "Denny gets one every year so he's prepared for Santa, and this year he wanted to get you one too," I explain as Denny grabs the box closest to him and I hand the bottom one over to Jay.

His fingers run over the engraving on the top of the box, but that's not what holds my attention, it's the serious look on his face that captivates me. Anyone would think he'd never been given a gift before.

"You can open it."

"Denny can do his first," he says, dragging his eyes away from the box on his lap and to our excited child.

"Yessss!" he says, flipping the clasp and opening the lid.

He pulls out what he's expecting, but if he's at all disappointed he doesn't show it. The new Thomas the Tank Engine pyjamas are placed on the table ready to be changed into shortly as he turns the DVD case over to see what it's about before diving back in and pulling out the rest of the contents.

"Daddy, it's your turn."

"Okay," he says, but it's laced with apprehension as both Denny and I stare at him, waiting.

Everything inside that box was Denny's idea. I had no input on this part of Jay's present at all.

Jay's smile lights up his face when he pulls out a pair of pyjama bottoms covered in trains; they're not too dissimilar to the pair I bought for Denny. They're followed by a DVD, a book, a sachet of hot chocolate, a bag of mini marshmallows, and a *World's Greatest Daddy* mug.

When he looks up from inspecting everything, I don't expect to see the tears in his eyes. My breath catches and I find myself pulled down onto his lap and wrapped in his arms.

"Thank you," he breathes.

"It was all Denny," I say as I gesture for him to join us.

Denny hops up on to Jay's other knee and snuggles in. Our group hug lasts for the longest time. I don't think I've ever felt so content as I do in those few minutes.

Jay looks to have composed himself when he pulls back. He has the widest smile on his face as he looks between the two of us like we couldn't possibly be real.

"What are you two waiting for? Go and get changed and I'll make the hot chocolate. We've got films to watch."

Denny is off in a split second. Jay takes a little longer, preferring to thank me properly once Denny's out of sight.

We've all settled in front of the TV to watch the DVD I bought for Denny with mugs full of hot chocolate when my phone rings. Reaching over to grab it, I see Frankie's face looking back at me. As much as I want to stay where I am, I'm also desperate to talk to her about everything.

"Hey."

"Hey, bitch. How's the festive fuck fest going?" I feel Jay's stare and when I turn back to him, his eyes are full of amusement. Thankfully, Denny's oblivious, his focus zeroed in on the telly.

"It's a family holiday, Kiki."

"Yeah, with your baby daddy, who you haven't been with in over five years. Don't try to tell me it's all chaste kisses and cuddles over there." My cheeks flush at her statement because that is definitely not the case. My lack of response is all she needs for confirmation. "Point made, I think." The smugness in her voice makes me want to smack her.

Deciding I need to change the subject, I tell her the most important part. "Jay asked me to marry him."

"WHAT!" she squeals at such a volume I have to pull the phone away from my ear.

"He asked me to—"

"Yeah I heard, E. When? How? The ring?" She throws out question after question, making my head spin.

"Our first night here. It was—"

"That was days ago. Why am I only hearing this now?"

I feel awful for not telling her immediately, but I've been so wrapped up with everything that I didn't want to burst the little family bubble we've been living in.

"I'm sorry. It's just—"

"It's fine. I get it. Now, please continue. How did he propose?"

I tell Frankie how it happened and she sighs dreamily on the other end. "I can't believe you're marrying a soldier. That was my dream," she sulks.

"I don't think you're destined to find a soldier, Kiki. Look what happened last time. Anyway," I say, not wanting to drag her down on Christmas Eve with reminders of the past, "what are you up to tonight?"

"Brett's on his way over."

"Brett?"

"Why are you saying it like that?"

"Nothing. I just thought that..." I trail off, not really wanting to voice it.

"You just thought that I'd fallen back into Dean's bed?" she asks, sounding seriously pissed off.

"Well... yeah. I've seen the way you look at each other. I just thought..."

"Then you need to stop thinking," she snaps. "Been there, done that, put the whole disaster behind me."

I know Frankie well enough to know she's not telling me the whole truth. There is way more to her relationship with Dean than she lets on, but I'm not going to poke the beast by continuing to bring it up. I prefer staying on the right side of Frankie.

"Okay. Are you spending tomorrow with your mum and stepdad?"

"Yeah. Sorry, E, but I've got to go. Brett will be here in a bit and I still need to shave my—"

"Okay, okay," I interrupt.

"My legs, Erin. I need to shave my legs. Fucking hell, calm down. If you must know, I went and got my whooha waxed yesterday so she's bare as a baby's bottom, ready and raring to go."

"Frankie," I groan. She knows how much I love her oversharing.

I'm still smiling to myself when I walk back toward the sofa.

"Everything okay?" Jay asks with a smirk when he sees my face.

"Yeah. It was just Frankie... being Frankie."

We have the most incredible evening. It's like something from a Christmas film with the fire burning and the tree twinkling. I can't help but keep looking over at Jay and Denny to remind myself that this is real. We really are spending Christmas together as a family.

CHAPTER THREE

"He's been! He's been!" Denny screams at some ungodly time the next morning as he launches himself at the bed and bounces up and down between the two of us.

"I told you the letter would work," I mutter sleepily as I rub my eyes, desperately trying to get them to focus.

"What time is it?" is groaned from next to me and I can't help but laugh. He's usually so awake, it's odd hearing him fighting his exhaustion.

"Four." I'd told Denny he wasn't allowed out of his room anytime before 4am. Something tells me he's been sat staring at the alarm clock in his room waiting impatiently.

"Come on, it's Christmas," he begs as he tugs at the covers.

I'm not sure who moves faster to grab the duvet as Denny starts to pull it away from us, both attempting to cover up the fact that we're very naked underneath.

"Go and take your stocking into the living room and we'll join you in a few minutes."

Denny is up off the bed and running from the room in seconds.

"Why did you tell him four o'clock was okay?" Jay grumbles as he wraps his arm around my waist and pulls me into his body. His skin burns against mine and his erection digs into my thigh.

"He's not the only one who's excited, I see."

"You're naked. I'm always excited when you're naked." His hips thrust against me and my core tingles.

"We haven't got time for that now."

"I love him more than anything," Jay whispers in my ear. "But he's a right cock-blocker."

I turn over to face him and can't help but laugh at his pouting expression. "It just makes it more of a challenge." I kiss the tip of his nose before getting out of bed and grabbing some clothes.

"Not helping," he groans behind me when I bend over to pull on a pair of knickers.

"Pull yourself together. We've got presents to open and toys to play with."

"Oh, I could play with some toys." His voice is deep and gravelly and it hits me exactly where he intends as I feel a flood of heat between my legs.

I turn to face him with my hands on my hips, trying to look serious. I know the second his eyes land on my naked breasts that I've not achieved anything other than probably turning him on more. "Just get up."

"Oh it's up, Skittles, don't you worry about that."

"Oh my God," I mutter, throwing a pair of joggers at him before turning back around and finishing getting dressed.

When we get to the living room, Denny is sat in front of the Christmas tree, surrounded by presents.

"Two minutes to make coffee, baby, and then it's on."

"Muuuuuummmmy," he complains as I rush toward the kettle.

"I thought you said you didn't bring much?" Jay whispers in my ear as he looks down at Denny who's almost drowning under all the toys and clothes.

I just shrug at him. I thought I'd been good, but looking at it all now, I see that maybe I wasn't very successful.

"Daddy, this one's for you," Denny announces, pulling a box out from the back of the tree.

"Oh, okay." He looks at me sceptically. I'd told him we weren't doing presents so he wouldn't feel bad about not getting us anything. This trip was a surprise for him, so I didn't expect him to have gone shopping after the way I left everything between us.

"It's nothing expensive," I say, and it's true. What he's holding is priceless.

Jay looks between Denny and me for a few seconds before looking down to the box and pulling the paper away from it.

Inside is an envelope. His confused eyes come back to me for a beat and I nod at him to continue.

He lifts the flap and pulls out the card Denny made for him.

"Aw thanks, buddy," Jay says when he reads the front.

"Open it," Denny encourages.

I say the words that are written inside the card to myself as I watch Jay's eyes move over them.

Let's make it official...
I want to be a Baxter.
Merry Christmas, Daddy.

Jay's brows draw together and he looks over at me like he's missing the point to this present.

"Open that." I point to the piece of paper that fell out the card and onto his lap when he opened it.

"It's an appointment for the registry office?" He still looks completely baffled by the whole thing and I take pity on him.

"It's so we can add you to Denny's birth certificate, and get his name changed."

Jay's mouth drops open as understanding dawns.

"That's if you want to."

He looks between the two of us once again. Water fills his eyes. "Of course that's what I want. Come here." His voice cracks as he pulls me to him and encourages Denny up from the floor so we can all have a group hug.

"YOU'RE INCREDIBLE, YOU KNOW THAT?" Jay whispers in my ear later that afternoon while I'm stood at the oven, getting our dinner ready. I don't get to answer because his lips brush against my skin and all I can do is feel. A moan vibrates up my throat as he starts to lick up toward my ear.

"We need to get a wedding booked. You need my surname. Erin Baxter... It has a good ring to it, don't you think?"

"Uh-huh," I agree as he continues to tease me with his tongue.

"How long's dinner?"

"Ah... about thirty minutes."

"Good. Come with me. Denny, we'll just be a few minutes. You okay, bud?"

"Yeah," he calls, but doesn't once look up from what he's playing with.

"Jay, we can't have sex, he'll hear us."

"You've got a one-track mind, Erin Baxter." The use of that name again sends warmth throughout my body. "Come and sit with me."

He gives my arm a tug and I fall down on the edge of the bed next to him. "What—" I begin to ask, but stop when he pulls his phone out of his pocket and hands it over.

I look up at him, confused, but I don't miss the apprehension written all over his face.

"Open it."

I do as I'm told, and when it unlocks, it's open on a webpage. When I look closer, I see that I'm looking at a house.

A house that's for sale.

"Jay... what? Why are you—"

"Do you like it?"

His question makes me look at it a little more, and I realise it's incredible. It looks like the house every kid imagines when they're asked to draw their dream home. There's a big driveway, a perfect and colourful front garden, then the most stunning, symmetrical looking house sitting behind it. Jay hits the picture and it makes it bigger before he begins scrolling through photos of each room. Each is more beautiful than the last.

I stare at it with my mouth hanging open.

"So... what do you think?"

"I-it's stunning. But wh—"

"It's ours."

"It's what?" I move away and stare at him, totally bemused by this whole conversation. "Jay?"

"It's your Christmas present."

"Most guys just buy jewellery and perfume."

He wraps his hand around the back of my neck and pulls me toward him. His cheek brushes against mine before he whispers, "I'm not most guys."

"You don't say." I can't help but laugh. This is a joke. Right? "Are you serious?"

"Deadly. My offer's been accepted and it's been taken off the market."

"When did you... How did you..."

"I've been looking since I found you again. But I saw this one the other day and I knew it was the one."

"Have you viewed it?"

"No. I wouldn't view it without you."

"You bought it without me!"

"Something told me you'd be okay with it."

I'm silent for a few minutes as I allow everything to settle into my brain.

"Can I see it again, please?"

He hands his phone over and I take everything in.

"It's not in Bristol."

"Technically, it is. It's got a Bristol postcode." I raise an eyebrow at him. "Okay, no, it's not really in Bristol. But it's an amazing area, and it's in the catchment for outstanding schools for Denny." My heart melts that he's gone to the effort of finding out about the schools and the area. "And look," he takes the phone from me and scrolls through a couple of pictures, "this is the converted loft room. I thought it would be a perfect studio for you. It's got four bedrooms on the floor below so we'd have plenty of room. Denny could have either of these, and then this one is right next to the master, so it would be a perfect nursery—"

"Nursery?" I interrupt. He really isn't letting this go.

"Yeah," he says, dropping the phone to his lap and taking my face in his hands. "I meant what I said the other day. I want everything with you, Erin. We've already lost so much time and I've missed out on so much with Denny. You're my family. My world."

I feel my first tear fall and Jay catches it with his thumb before placing his lips against mine.

"You bought us a house?" I ask, just to confirm I didn't dream the last few minutes.

"I've put an offer in on a house. If you don't like it or don't want it, we can pull out."

"What about my house?"

"I know you've got connections to that house with your mum and everything, but I felt like it was time for us to make a fresh start. This place would be ours. Our family home. You can keep your house if you want—rent it out, whatever. We don't need the money from it for this place."

"Wow," I breathe. This is all a bit much.

I get a funny look off Denny when we reappear. I tried to cover up that I'd been crying but I obviously didn't do a very good job.

We agreed not to tell him anything about the new house until we see it ourselves, just in case it isn't as amazing in real life as it is in the photos.

"THANK YOU," Jay says as I curl into his side when we get into bed.

"What for?"

"The best Christmas I've ever had."

"I didn't do anything."

"You were here. That's all I need."

I smile at him, trying not to let thoughts of what his past Christmases were like sadden my mood. It really has been the best day.

I look away from him and down to the tattoo just below my head. I run my finger over the text. "When did you get this?"

"It was the first thing I did when I was able to get out and about. I never wanted to forget you, or what we had."

"Not possible," I whisper, because if he feels even half of what I do for him, forgetting about any of that will never happen.

"Never," he whispers back as he leans toward me and places a gentle kiss against my temple.

"I want one."

"One of what?"

"I want this tattoo. I want it on me forever, too."

"Yeah?" he asks, a smile lighting up his face.

"I don't know where, though."

"Hmmm... I think I should explore and find the perfect place for it." He pulls his arm from beneath me before diving under the covers.

"Jay," I say with a laugh as he tickles my sides. That giggle soon turns into a gasp when I feel his tongue against my sensitive skin.

CHAPTER FOUR

It was sad to leave the place we spent Christmas, but I was excited to see Scotland once again. I've no idea how I managed to fit everything in the car to get up here, because it's now a seriously tight squeeze.

"Okay, I think that's everything."

"Thank God for that. I thought we were going to have to strap Denny to the roof."

Denny gives Jay a dirty look from the back of the car as he starts reversing off the driveway.

I tried to book us into the same places Jay and I stayed the first time we were up here, but as it was so last minute, I struggled.

"Are you going to tell me where we're going?"

I've just about kept the plans to myself so far, but as we drive away from the cottage, it's time to confess.

"Gretna Green."

"We getting married?"

"No, I wasn't that organised!"

"Stick it in the satnav then."

"How long are we driving for?" Denny asks from the back. He still hasn't got over the long drive to get up here in the first place, so he's less than impressed by another journey, even if he has his new tablet to play with.

"Not long," I say, hoping it'll pacify him until he gets distracted.

"Oh, I love this song," I say, leaning forward and turning the volume up. Rita Ora's voice fills the car and I continue before I start singing along. I see Jay glance over at me while I sing my heart out to her part of *For You* before I go quiet when Liam Payne takes over. I don't expect him to, but suddenly Jay's voice makes the music fade into the background as he sings lyrics that hit me deep. Everything about this song reminds me of him and what we've been through. A lump forms in my throat and tears sting my eyes. I just about pull myself together enough to continue our little rendition.

When the song comes to an end, Jay returns my stare. His eyes are dark and I know it hit him just as hard as it did me. '*I love you*', he mouths to me before turning his attention back to the road.

"OTHER THAN THE OBVIOUS ADDITION, it feels like it was yesterday that we were here before," Jay says as we come to a stop where we sat all those years ago, watching the newly married couple having their photographs taken.

"Did you really mean it when you asked me to marry you that day?"

"Yes. I knew the moment I saw you that you were different. That for whatever reason we were meant to meet, and that you were going to change my life," he admits.

"You hardly knew me, yet you'd have committed yourself to me?" I'm not sure why I'm asking him to explain, because I felt exactly the same.

"I'd have dragged you in and said *I do* there and then. I wished so many times over the past few years that we could have. Things would have turned out so much differently if you were my wife."

I stay silent as I think about what he just said. If I were his wife, I'd have been his next of kin. I'd have been the first to know he'd been injured, and I could have been there. We wouldn't have lost those five years.

Jay suddenly tugging at my finger pulls me from my thoughts. "What are you—" I start to ask, but once he has what he wants, I watch as he lowers himself to the ground.

"Erin, will you do me the greatest honour of being my wife?"

It doesn't matter that he's already asked and that I've already said yes, because my heart pounds in my chest and butterflies go crazy in my stomach, like it's the first time.

"Of course I will," I laugh. He smiles his heart-stopping smile and slides my ring back into place on my finger.

I glance over to Denny, who's stood beside us with a bemused look on his face. I'd love to know what he thinks about all of this. I did my best to explain everything that happened with Alex, how his dad was suddenly in his life and that we were a family, but I'm not convinced how well his five-year-old brain computed it all. I'm sure as the years go on he'll have plenty of questions. When he notices my attention, a smile breaks across his face.

"Come on," Jay says, tugging my arm.

"Where are we going?"

"To get married."

"We can't—"

"I know, you said last time. We need paperwork and stuff. We can totally book it though. What do you say?"

I stop dead on the spot. The second he realises I'm not following, he turns back to look at me. It looks like he's about to plead his case, but I lose the fight to keep a straight face. "It's perfect."

He turns back and begins marching toward the building where all the couples seem to disappear into. He moves so fast that both

Denny and I are practically running to keep up with him. Anyone would think he's desperate to marry me.

Half an hour later, we have a date booked for me to become Mrs. Jayden Baxter. I swear I have a constant smile on my face for the next three days. It seems we both have similar ideas for our upcoming nuptials, and I couldn't be happier that Jay also wants something small—*small* might be the wrong word; I think *tiny* would be better. None of them know it yet but Frankie, Dean, and Arthur will be spending the anniversary of our first meeting up here in Gretna Green, watching us get married. I couldn't think of anything more perfect than sharing it with them. We can only hope Frankie and Dean have got their shit together by then, otherwise it could be a little awkward, because with only three guests, they can't exactly not turn up.

WE STAY in a hotel just outside Gretna Green for three days before we once again pack the car to continue to our last stop before heading back down south. I'd love to have longer on the road, but we need to make sure we're home for Denny to start back at school in the new year.

"I think I know the answer to this question, but where are we spending New Year's?" Jay asks as he buckles himself in and starts the engine.

"Where do you think?"

"I think we're heading toward the home of the mother of all New Year's celebrations, or should I say Hogmanay?"

"We could well be. I couldn't get us tickets for any of the good stuff, but I thought just being able to see the fireworks over the castle would be worth it."

"Definitely. Let's do this then. We've got a new year and a new start to celebrate."

Goosebumps cover my skin as I think about everything we have to celebrate and the future we have ahead of us as a couple—as a family.

The hotel is a little farther out of the city than I'd have liked, but it was the best I could do at such late notice. Edinburgh is buzzing with excitement of the impending celebrations, and I'm instantly reminded of why I loved it here so much the first time.

We drag Denny around the city, showing him things we enjoyed before, along with a couple of sights we didn't manage to fit in. He looks about as unimpressed as every other child getting pulled from sight to sight. I remember it well from my childhood and I know for a fact it's something he'll look back fondly on in years to come, so I don't feel too bad about it when he starts complaining his feet hurt after we realise we're lost. Again.

New Year's Eve, we planned to have a quiet day, mostly chilling out in our hotel room in the hope Denny would make it to midnight, as we'd have to head out if we wanted a decent view of the fireworks. He managed to have a short nap while we all watched TV, but it wasn't enough for him not to be fighting his exhaustion before 10pm.

"Come on, let's go. Hopefully the cold will wake us all up a bit."

As we make our way out of the hotel, we find people dressed up to celebrate everywhere we look. I couldn't think of a better way to spend tonight than stood out on a bitterly cold Scottish street with the most important people in my life.

"How much farther?" Denny complains.

"It's only ten minutes until the fireworks, baby."

He gave up walking quite a while ago and Jay's been carrying him since. His arm must be killing him by now, but he hasn't complained once as we make our way closer to the action. The streets are packed with people waiting for the countdown to start.

I'm pretty sure I've never been as excited to see a new year in as I am right now. I've got so much to look forward to and I can't wait for it to start.

I can almost taste the excitement as the time approaches. The second the first person shouts *ten*, chills run down my spine and goosebumps prick my skin.

"Nine... eight... seven..."

I look over to Jay to find him staring back at me. The love and admiration I can see in his eyes brings a lump to my throat.

I'm so grateful for our second chance. I don't think I'll ever get over the emotion that engulfs me as I think about being able to spend my life with him after thinking it had been ripped away from me five years ago.

"Three... two..."

I drag my eyes away from his and up to the sky.

"One."

The first loud crack reverberates through us, and I see Denny lift his head from Jay's shoulder just as the sky lights up with a million colours and the crowd cheer and clap as they welcome in the new year.

I watch two more fireworks light up the sky before I feel Jay's attention on me. Turning to look at him, my breath catches at the expression on his face.

His spare hand comes up and his fingers thread through my hair as he pulls me to him. My entire body ignites when our lips collide. It starts off sweet, but his tongue soon sweeps into my mouth and I press my body up against his side. People are still cheering and hollering around us and the fireworks bang and crack, but it all fades into the background as Jay kisses me.

The man who changed my life.

The man who made my life.

The man who is my life.

"COME ON, I've got a surprise for you."

"For me?"

"Yep."

I watch as Jay grabs our coats before throwing them over to us. We eventually got back to our room sometime after 1am this morning, so we had a lie in, ordered room service, and stayed in bed. I wasn't aware we had any plans, but it looks like we're going out.

The first of January in Edinburgh is bitterly cold as we make our way down a cobbled street we've not been on before.

"Where are we going?" I ask for the millionth time. Most places are shut for the day; everyone's probably still sleeping off their hangovers.

"We're here," Jay announces as he comes to a stop outside a dark shop.

I take two steps to see where we are, and my stomach turns over as nerves race through me. I know I said I wanted this, but now I'm stood here, I'm more scared than I expected.

I breathe a sigh of relief when I see the sign on the door. "It's closed," I say over my shoulder to Jay, hoping I don't sound too relieved.

"No, it's not. I organised this. They're just not open to the public. Knock," he encourages.

I do as he suggests and seconds after my knuckles hit the glass, a guy with a beard, piercings all over his face, and tattoos covering every bit of skin I can see unlocks the door.

"You must be Erin? I'm Carl."

"U-uh..." I stutter.

"Yes, that's her. I think she's a little nervous," Jay says behind me with a laugh.

"Come on in then. Hey, little man, do you want to take a seat over on that sofa?"

I watch as Denny walks off, but panic that I'm about to leave him in the reception of a tattoo parlour.

"Don't worry, my wife's just out the back making him a hot chocolate. She'll keep a close eye on him." Right on cue, a gorgeous blonde woman appears with two mugs piled high with marshmallows. She has almost as many piercings and tattoos as her husband.

Carl ushers me into a back room and I sheepishly follow behind him.

"It'll be okay," Jay whispers in my ear. The feeling of his breath on my neck calms me down slightly.

I get myself on the chair as Carl wheels himself over on a little stool.

"So then, you're boyfri—"

"Fiancé," Jay interrupts.

"Sorry, your fiancé here tells me you want a tattoo."

"I... uh..." I blow out a breath and try to ground myself a little, because I do want this. I want a reminder of us and everything we've been through permanently on my body. "Yes," I say with much more determination. "I would like exactly what Jay has on his upper arm but on the top of my foot. Is that okay?"

Carl waits while Jay removes his hoodie and pulls up his sleeve. "Looks good to me. Show me where you want it and I'll get it sorted."

I pull my boot off and point.

"Okay. It'll be sore there, mind you. You ready for that?"

"Yes." I try to sound confident about my ability to cope, but I'm not sure my pain threshold is all that high really.

I shut my eyes and rest my head back when Carl's ready to start. Jay comes to stand next to me and I grab onto his hand as I prepare for the pain to start.

"Okay, all done. What do you think?"

"Oh, is that it?"

"Yeah, look," Carl says with a laugh, nodding down to my newly tattooed foot.

I smile as I look down at my new ink and let out a big sigh. That wasn't half as bad as I imagined, and totally worth it.

Now not only is Jay a permanent fixture in my heart and my life, but a part of who we are is marked on my skin.

Everywhere & Nowhere.

EPILOGUE

I've no idea how he did it, but five weeks after he put an offer down on our house, we have the keys and we're about to put them into the lock for the first time.

We're not officially moving in for a few weeks as we want to decorate and make it ours. But today is our first day owning our first home together.

We walk in and out of each room, me with a notebook, pen and paint chart, and him with a tape measure. I make note of the window sizes in each room and we debate what furniture we want where, what we can make use of from my house, and what we can buy new.

After a lot of thought, I eventually put my house on the market. It holds so many memories of my parents and my younger years, but I can't imagine renting it out and having others live there, and there's no point in it sitting empty. We might not need the money for this place, but I don't want it to do nothing for us. I'd rather invest it somehow, maybe buy another place to rent out that I have no attachment to.

The last room to measure up is the smallest of the bedrooms, the one Jay mentioned could be our nursery when he first told me about this place when we were away at Christmas.

"Shall we just leave this room as it is for now?" Jay asks as he looks at the fairly fresh walls.

"Yeah, I guess. We can then decorate it the right colour once we've had a scan."

"Yeah that's wha... Wait, what?"

I put everything in my hands down on the windowsill and walk over to him. I stare up into his eyes as I thread my fingers through his. He doesn't breathe the whole time.

"In about sixteen weeks we should be able to find out if we'll paint it blue or pink." I can't help my smile as I say it.

"You're... you're pregnant?"

"I am. I did a test first thing this morning but I've been suspicious for about a week."

"Oh my God," he gasps. The shock is clear on his face. I'm worried for all of two seconds because his lips twitch into a stunning smile before he grabs me and starts spinning me around the room.

"You're pregnant!" he shouts as he puts me down. "How? When?"

"I've no idea. I was on the pill, but..." I trail off with a shrug.

Jay stares down at me with a look I've never seen before. It's so serious and intense, yet full of emotions but after a few seconds a smug smile starts to play on his lips. Neither of us says anything as we stare at each other. Then he snaps, and he steps toward me and backs me up against the wall.

"I think it's time to christen our new house, Skittles."

"I can't wait," I whisper.

The End
(It really is this time!)

Keep reading for a sneak peek at the Falling Series with Falling for Ryan: Part 1

SNEAK PEEK
FALLING FOR RYAN: PART ONE

FALLING FOR RYAN: PART ONE
PROLOGUE

Molly

Eight years ago...

"Mum, I'm going to Becky's sixteenth birthday party tonight, then sleeping at Hannah's," I remind her as I walk into the kitchen where she's sat with her head in an interior design magazine, waving her hands around—presumably trying to dry her nail varnish. I pull out a can of Coke from the fridge before continuing. "I've taken the litre bottle of vodka from the drinks cabinet, and I've got a pack of condoms...you know, just in case." I lean back against the counter and watch for a reaction. *Any* reaction.

"Uh huh."

"I'm pretty sure some of the boys are bringing ecstasy."

"Hmm..." She hums as she turns a page and studies the room pictured.

"Didn't you only have a manicure yesterday? Why are you painting your nails already?"

Now, that gets her attention. Her head snaps up the moment the words 'nails' and 'manicure' leave my mouth. Surprise, surprise; my mother cares more about that than about alcohol, drugs, sex...and me.

"Yes, I did, but I just couldn't find a thing to wear tonight."

I doubt that's actually true, seeing as she's recently turned my eldest brother's old room into her personal wardrobe after already filling her own walk-in. "So, I went to that little boutique in town this morning and found the most perfect dress. Your dad will love it, but it didn't match the colour I chose for my nails yesterday."

"Wow, what a disaster," I mutter as I leave the room. "I'll be going out in about an hour. *Not that you really care.*" I say the last bit quieter, but I'm not sure why; when I look back, Mum is once again too engrossed in her magazine to acknowledge me.

I let out a huge breath and head back up to my room to finish packing for the party. I'm getting ready with my best friend Hannah and her twin Emma, who live next door. We've all been friends for as long as I can remember. Being twins, Hannah and Emma are really close, but Hannah and I are not far behind. The three of us do almost everything together; their parents have often joked that they have triplets, really.

I always laugh along.

Even though they know what my life is like, I don't think any of them really appreciate how much I wish that were true.

I'm just shoving my fourth outfit choice for the night into my bag when I hear my brother downstairs, greeting Mum. She instantly responds to him, which makes me laugh to myself, although it's anything but funny. One of her golden boys has come to visit. I bet if he needed something, she'd ruin that new nail varnish in an instant. God, I can't wait to get out of this hellhole I call home.

"Is Molly still here?" Daniel asks.

Her reply sounds suspiciously like, "I have no idea."

Walking to the other side of the room, I rest my hands on the windowsill and blow out a long breath as I gaze out over the countryside, trying to calm myself down. I keep telling myself not to get worked up by their actions, but sometimes it's easier said than done.

"Hey sis, I'm glad you're still here," Daniel says as he enters my room a few minutes later. My brothers are a lot older than me; I was an unplanned accident fifteen and a half years ago. Daniel is my youngest older brother and, at thirty years old, he's crazy protective of me. Steven is, too, but he now has a serious girlfriend so I'm seeing less of him these days. Daniel is my idol—always has been. He doesn't take life too seriously, does exactly as he pleases, works bloody hard, but always has fun. That's exactly what I want my life to be like, and I plan on making it so—once I get out on my own.

"Hey." I only manage one word because, as soon as I see him, I burst into tears. He pulls me into a tight hug. I hate that Mum and Dad can do this to me. Can make me feel so worthless. It makes me angry every time a tear falls for their actions. I wish I could be stronger.

"What have they done now?" Daniel asks. Both he and Steven know how our parents treat me. Hell, I couldn't count the number of arguments I've overheard about it on both hands and feet, but nothing ever changes. I'm just grateful that I have two amazing older brothers to turn to if I need to. Plus, I have my adopted family next door, who I'm pretty sure would do just about anything for me if I needed it.

"Nothing. I'm fine," I say, pulling away from him and wiping my eyes. I look at him and see the questions in his. "No, really; I'm just being a silly, hormonal teenager."

"Hmm...whatever you say, Molls. You still going to that party tonight?" I don't believe for a second that he buys my lie, but he knows it's easier for me not to discuss it. Nothing he can say is going to make any of it better, anyway.

"Of course, why?"

"I got you something." I watch as he reaches into his coat pocket and pulls out a small bottle of vodka before handing it to me.

"What's this for?" He looks at me and quirks an eyebrow. "I know it's to drink, you fool, but why are you giving it to me?"

"Because I remember what it was like being your age, and I didn't think anyone else would be buying you some. You deserve to act your age, Molly. Let your hair down. You work too damn hard trying to get your grades. But please be sensible. I don't want to be visiting you in the hospital or be an uncle yet. Actually..." He pauses as he reaches into his back pocket and pulls out his wallet.

My eyes widen in embarrassment. "No, no, no...I'm good, you don't need to worry about that."

I hate to admit it, but Daniel is the only one who knows what I've been up to. He let himself into my room one day while I was in my ensuite to find an open box of condoms on the bed and, being the protective brother that he is, counted them and realised two were missing. I'm hoping he doesn't want more of an explanation than that, because I really don't want to sit here and explain to my adult brother that I took myself off to the doctors a while ago and got myself on the pill—you know, just in case. Wouldn't that make Mummy and Daddy proud, to be grandparents while their daughter was still a teenager? Imagine the embarrassment.

"Okay, well, have a good time tonight, and ring me if you have any problems, yeah?"

"I promise."

I know I mentioned drugs and alcohol to my mum downstairs, but my group of friends isn't really into all that. I only said it as a way to provoke her in the hopes of getting some kind of reaction. Yes, there are plenty of kids at school who are at it every weekend, but my group actually cares about getting good grades and good jobs. The bottle of vodka Daniel just handed me will probably be it for us tonight.

"See you later then, kid," he says before kissing my forehead and leaving my room.

"That was awesome," Hannah squeals as the three of us stumble into the twins' bedroom sometime in the early hours of Sunday morning. Emma heads straight over to her side of the room and immediately starts replacing her party clothes with her pyjamas, while Hannah and I sit on her bed and reflect on the evening.

"So...come on, spill it...where did you go with Callum?" Hannah pleads.

"Just for a walk in the garden. I told you earlier!"

"I didn't believe you then, and I still don't now. I saw you two getting off with each other in the corner before you disappeared."

Callum is the boy at school that every girl dreams of. He's sporty, clever, funny and, of course, seriously hot, which is exactly why no one expected him to show his face tonight. But he did, and let's just say that I got to know him a little better than I did before. I'm yet to decide if that's a good thing or not.

"Will you two keep it down? I want to get up early tomorrow to do some coursework before we go to Grandma's," Emma complains from her bed.

Okay, so I said before that we work hard to get good grades, but Emma takes it to the extreme. I was actually surprised she gave herself tonight off. She's doing A-level maths already and does Spanish lessons after school to get herself an extra GCSE. I think she's putting too much pressure on herself, but she can't seem to stop in her quest to be the best accountant Oxford has ever seen.

"Sorry," we whisper simultaneously.

"So...come on, Molly, tell me," Hannah says, keeping her voice low.

I let out a frustrated breath and go for it. "Okay, so we went outside and found a quiet corner in the garden behind a bush. He pulled me down to the ground and we kissed for a while and let our hands...roam a little." I look up at Hannah and can see her excitement about what might come next.

"Oh my God, did you have sex with him?" she asks, but says the word *sex* much quieter. I don't know why; it's only Emma who could be listening.

"No, I didn't. I sorta thought we were going to, but by the time I got into his boxers, he was so worked up that he went off like a firework!" I can't help it, I burst out laughing at the memory, earning me another grumble from Emma.

"But I thought Callum's slept with loads of girls?" Hannah asks, confused.

"That's what the rumour mill says…I would be inclined to say that this was his first experience and the rumours are just that: rumours." We fall about giggling like the schoolgirls we are; I guess that vodka hasn't totally worn off yet.

"So, you *were* going to have sex with him, then?"

"Yeah, I guess," I say, shrugging my shoulders.

"But don't you want to wait until you're in love?" she asks innocently.

The only thing I have never told my best friend is that I lost my virginity last year at a party. Hannah has a different outlook on life thanks to her normal, loving family, and I don't want to have to explain my reasons for doing what I did that night—and a few times since. I totally understand her desire to wait until she's in love, and I admire her for it, but what I needed that night—what I *still* need—is to feel wanted by someone. And that first night? That was exactly how I felt.

DOWNLOAD NOW to continue reading Falling For Ryan: Part One.

ABOUT THE AUTHOR

Tracy Lorraine is a *USA Today* and *Wall Street Journal* bestselling new adult and contemporary romance author. Tracy has recently turned thirty and lives in a cute Cotswold village in England with her husband, baby girl and lovable but slightly crazy dog. Having always been a bookaholic with her head stuck in her Kindle, Tracy decided to try her hand at a story idea she dreamt up and hasn't looked back since.

Be the first to find out about new releases and offers. Sign up to my newsletter here.

If you want to know what I'm up to and see teasers and snippets of what I'm working on, then you need to be in my Facebook group. Join Tracy's Angels here.

Keep up to date with Tracy's books at
www.tracylorraine.com

ALSO BY TRACY LORRAINE

Falling Series

Forbidden Series

Rebel Ink Series

<u>Defy You</u> #3

<u>Play You</u> #4

<u>Inked</u> (A Rebel Ink/Driven Crossover)

<u>Rosewood High Series</u>

<u>Thorn</u> #1

<u>Paine</u> #2

<u>Savage</u> #3

<u>Fierce</u> #4

<u>Hunter</u> #5

Faze (#6 Prequel)

<u>Fury</u> #6

<u>Legend</u> #7

<u>Maddison Kings University Series</u>

<u>TMYM: Prequel</u>

<u>TRYS</u> #1

<u>TDYW</u> #2

<u>TBYS</u> #3

<u>TVYC</u> #4

<u>TDYD</u> #5

<u>TDYR</u> #6

<u>TRYD</u> #7

<u>Knight's Ridge Empire Series</u>

<u>Wicked Summer Knight</u>: Prequel (Stella & Seb)

<u>Wicked Knight</u> #1 (Stella & Seb)

<u>Wicked Princess</u> #2 (Stella & Seb)

Wicked Empire #3 (Stella & Seb)

Deviant Knight #4 (Emmie & Theo)
Deviant Princess #5 (Emmie & Theo

Deviant Reign #6 (Emmie & Theo)

One Reckless Knight (Jodie & Toby)
Reckless Knight #7 (Jodie & Toby)
Reckless Princess #8 (Jodie & Toby)
Reckless Dynasty #9 (Jodie & Toby)

Dark Halloween Knight (Calli & Batman)
Dark Knight #10 (Calli & Batman)
Dark Princess #11 (Calli & Batman)
Dark Legacy #12 (Calli & Batman)

Corrupt Valentine Knight (Nico & Siren)
Corrupt Knight #13 (Nico & Siren)
Corrupt Princess #14 (Nico & Siren)
Corrupt Union #15 (Nico & Siren)

Sinful Wild Knight (Alex & Vixen)
Sinful Stolen Knight: Prequel (Alex & Vixen)
Sinful Knight #16 (Alex & Vixen)
Sinful Princess #17 (Alex & Vixen)
Sinful Kingdom #18 (Alex & Vixen)

Knight's Ridge Destiny: Epilogue

Ruined Series

<u>Ruined Plans</u> #1

<u>Ruined by Lies</u> #2

<u>Ruined Promises</u> #3

<u>Never Forget Series</u>

<u>Never Forget Him</u> #1

<u>Never Forget Us</u> #2

<u>Everywhere & Nowhere</u> #3

<u>Chasing Series</u>

<u>Chasing Logan</u>

<u>The Cocktail Girls</u>

<u>His Manhattan</u>

<u>Her Kensington</u>